PRAISE FOR UNITL PROVEN

"ALL FAMILIES HAVE SECRETS. Some Southern families seem to have more than most or keep them closer, tighter, longer. Nora Gaskin writes of times and situations that hold you fast to your chair, pull you to places and into people's lives that linger long after the last page. Move over John Grisham, here's a story with legal complications, that has heart. Gaskin writes a graceful prose that spills magic like the silver in mercury. She knows this world, of court rooms, clients, wrongful charges, and the wrecks of mistakes."

Ruth Moose, poet and short story writer,
including *Neighbors and Other Strangers*

"TWO MURDERS A GENERATION APART entangle two families: one white and entrenched in the leadership class of the North Carolina city in which both live, the other African American and closely involved in the civil rights struggles of their time and place. Nora Gaskin's *Until Proven* is a page-turner of a double mystery, and much of that is due to the characters and relationships Gaskin brings to life. Attorney Colin Phillips, retired domestic employee Marie Minton, and their two complex families are closely and believably drawn. Both families are deeply embroiled in events that leave none of their members unchanged. They will remain in my memory. Gaskin has a fine sense of the time, the place, and the people, and as a reader, I was thoroughly involved. I know others who like substance in a mystery will be, too."

Joyce Allen, author of *Hannah's House*
and *Those Who Hold the Threads*

UNTIL PROVEN

~

NORA GASKIN

Nora Gaskin (signature)

LYSTRA BOOKS
& Literary Services

Until Proven
©2012 Nora Gaskin Esthimer
Published by Lystra Books and Literary Services
391 Lystra Estates Dr.
Chapel Hill, NC 27517
lystrabooks@gmail.com

Nora Gaskin Esthimer 1951-

ISBN 978-0-9884164-0-6 paperbound
ISBN 978-0-9884164-1-3 eBook

1. North Carolina – Fiction

Second Printing 2013

Book design by Kelly Prelipp Lojk
Author's photograph by Steven W. Esthimer, used with permission

Printed in the United States

~

To Steve, with deep gratitude and love,
and in memory of my parents,
James R. Gaskin and Nora J. Gaskin

~

Until Proven

PART 1

MAY 9, 1963

Rhetta Phillips unwrapped the package from the butcher's shop. She put the two steaks on a broiler pan and sprinkled them with salt and pepper.

All the windows in the sunroom behind her were open to the soft evening air and the peepers sang in the garden. They eased her anxiety about the news she had to tell Colin.

She checked her watch. He had said he'd be home by eight o'clock and he was always prompt. It was ten till so she put a bottle of bourbon, two glasses, and an ice bucket on the long work table in the middle of the kitchen. She took a tray of ice out of the freezer and cracked it into the bucket just as she heard the crunch of gravel in the driveway and saw lights sweep across the windows. Perfect, she thought.

Colin came in the side door. His tie was loose and he carried his suit jacket over the elbow of one arm. He was her height, five feet nine inches, not heavy but solid in a way that made her feel safe. She saw the spark that lit up his brown eyes when he saw her and remembered, he loved her.

"Sweetheart," he said and she moved to him so they could hug.

"Long day," she said. His hair was clipped short and tidy, but she combed it with her fingers anyway.

"Better now." He hugged her again. "Are the girls in bed already?"

"Wren is. She played with Susie all day and went out like a light. Eden's in her room, reading I'm sure."

"I'll run up and say goodnight." He trotted up the back stairs, just off the kitchen. From the sounds of his feet above her head, Rhetta knew he went first to Wren's room, then to Eden's where he stayed a few minutes.

Then his feet were on the stairs again, coming back to her.

"Do you want a drink?" he asked.

"Please."

He put a lot of ice in one of the glasses and a small pour of bourbon. "Do you know what Eden's reading?"

"What?"

"*To Kill a Mockingbird.*"

"That's not a child's book, is it?" She accepted the glass and added water from the tap.

"It's about children. In a way." He poured a measure of two fingers of whiskey over three cubes of ice. "Never mind, it's fine for her to read it."

"Look what I'm making for you." Rhetta held up the pan of steaks.

"Wow. I expected leftovers of whatever you fed the girls."

"Fish sticks? I can do that if you'd rather."

"No ma'am."

She leaned back on the counter next to the stove and he leaned against the work table, five feet away. She looked into his eyes. "Laurence called from London this morning."

"Is everything okay?"

"He wants to come back to Piedmont, to stay."

"Great. I know that makes you happy." He sipped his drink. "But remember, Laurence is Laurence." Meaning, she knew, her twin brother was given to changing his mind without warning.

"There was something in his voice that made me believe him this time." She peeped into the oven, judged the broiler to be hot and slid the pan under the glowing coils.

"Not static on the phone line?" Colin asked. She heard his concern for her.

"I think he's figured out there really is no place like home."

"'And when you go there, they have to take you in.'" He sipped again.

"He wants to live in the cottage."

"The cottage here? In the back yard?"

"The property belongs to him as much as it does me." She couldn't keep her voice from getting tight, or the blood rising in her face.

He stepped across to her and put his hands on her waist. "I know he has a right to be here. I'm just surprised he doesn't want a little more privacy."

"I need to turn the steaks."

He stepped back to give her room. "If I'm annoyed with Laurence it's because he's come and gone all these years, without a thought for you or the girls. Or his responsibilities. If he comes back and takes over your father's estate, I'll be very happy."

"And living here? In our back yard?" She faced him again and saw that his focus was less intense. "You won't mind?"

"I bet we see less of him than we would if he lived across town."

She reached out to touch his face. "Now go sit down and I'll serve the plates." Then before she let him go, she said, "Thank you."

He took her glass from her, refreshed both drinks and took them to the table. She put steaks, wedges of lettuce with Thousand Island dressing, and scoops of potato salad on plates and carried them down the two steps to the sunroom. Colin had turned on the outside lights that illuminated the rose garden. The peepers hushed as if also on a switch.

"It's so peaceful," Colin said. "You did a great job with this room. You said you wanted to feel as if the garden comes right into the house, and that's what you've done." He lifted his glass to toast her. "All I ever want is right here. You and the girls."

"Me, too," she said, thinking, and soon Laurence.

There had been a time when her brother and her husband were good friends, but neither of them had taken care of that friendship and she wasn't sure how it would wear now.

They began to eat and Colin nodded to indicate his steak was just the way he liked it, very rare. Then he looked up and caught her still watching his face.

UNTIL PROVEN ✍ PART 1 [5]

"What was this last minute meeting about?" she asked.

He put down his fork. "Clyde asked me to meet with him and Reverend Abraham Jones."

"I don't know Reverend Jones. What's his church?"

"Church of the Living Lord. It's in Sweet Side."

"I should have known it would take a colored preacher to get Clyde into church." She took a bite of her potato salad.

"The Reverend is an organizer. He's got a sizeable group ready to push for full integration in Piedmont."

"But we are integrated. I see colored ladies in the stores downtown all the time now. And if they can't go to one grocery store because of somebody's ignorance, they can go to the other two." She knew this argument exasperated him, but it seemed common sensical to her.

"It's not about the A&P. It's about civil rights." He chewed on a piece of meat as if it had turned into leather.

"All right," she said. "I agree, and you know I'm glad we've come so far. But people need to be patient."

He put another bite in his mouth. She speared a cube of potato and a slice of celery.

"How do you fit into this?" she asked. "What has Clyde dragged you into?"

He swallowed. "I've agreed to help him defend anyone who gets arrested while carrying out civil disobedience. It'll be pro bono."

She closed her eyes, exasperated. How often had they argued because he wanted to support the family on what he earned, rather than spend her inherited money? And now he was going to work without getting paid?

She composed herself and looked at him again. He seldom did anything he knew would make her unhappy. When he decided something like this—knowing she wouldn't like it—he was unmovable. She'd accept it, and they just wouldn't talk about it.

MAY 12, 1963

The first ring of the bedside telephone inserted itself into Colin's dream; the second dragged him upward, but the best he could do was interrupt the third.

"Phillips," he whispered. His back to Rhetta, he felt the rustle and shift of bedding and bed as she sat up. He listened a moment, then said, "Give me half an hour."

Rhetta turned on the lamp. He stood and looked at her. She wore a white nightgown with pale blue stripes. The loose braid of her thick auburn hair fell over her shoulder and lay along her collar bone. She slid it back and gave him a sleepy smile.

"What time is it?"

"Sorry," he said, still whispering. "It's 1:30.

"Who called?"

"Clyde. A number of people got arrested."

He reached for his wallet and watch.

"Please tell Clyde to tell those people they'll just have to exercise their civil rights during office hours from now on."

"Lie down and I'll tuck you in." He walked around to her side of the bed, smoothed her hair, breathed in her scent, and kissed her on the forehead. "Thank you for understanding why I'm doing this."

"Did I say that?" She put her hands around his neck and kissed his mouth. "I love you. See you in the morning. In the daylight, I mean."

As he went down the hall toward the stairs, he paused to listen at his daughters' doors, inhaling the warmth of their silence.

The front staircase led to the wide entry hall. The room known as the library was Colin's study. He kept clothes in a cabinet there so he could change to go out in the middle of the night without disturbing Rhetta more than necessary.

He slid back the heavy pocket door. Its sound was like a raspy breath. Old George Vance, Rhetta's father, had died in the library. Colin had only known Mr. Vance in the last year of his life, the last year of a decade of small strokes, a heart attack, the loss of his wife who was twenty years his junior—and yet everyone who had known the man was surprised that he'd died, that he'd finally let go and rested.

Colin had lived in the man's house for more than thirteen years now. As he changed into tropical weight wool trousers and a white dress shirt, as he tied his tie and put on a sports jacket, he was well aware of how old George would disapprove of the mission that took him out into the night.

"Colin, my man," Clyde Raeburn greeted him.

Clyde's gray cotton suit looked slept in, for more than one night. Abraham Jones wore a black suit and his clerical collar. It gleamed like a star in the dim lighting of the magistrate's office at the back of the courthouse. Colin shook hands with both of them.

"Gentlemen, good morning. Where are we?"

A door separated the office from the narrow steel staircase that went up to the jail on the third floor. As Colin spoke, the door opened and Magistrate Roy Epps stepped in, followed by a young black man.

"He's all yours," Epps said. "What did they drag you down here for, Colin?"

"I'll tell you when they tell me, Roy."

Even Reverend Jones chuckled. "We'll leave you in peace, Mr. Magistrate." He nodded at the man and led the others outside into the alleyway behind the building.

Clyde made the introduction. "Mr. Colin Phillips, this is Dex Long. He's a leader in the Reverend's little army. Let's not stand out here in the dark. Let's go to my office."

His office was in one of the small frame buildings along the alley, occupied by lawyers, mostly. They had easy access to the courthouse but didn't have to pay the higher rents along Court Street.

As they walked toward it, Colin was aware that another figure—a male—emerged from the shadows and fell in step with Dex.

Clyde went in first and turned on lights. The front room should have been a reception area but it was a maze of mismatched chairs and stacks of books. Clyde's office proper wasn't much better. With some clearing and shifting of chairs, all five men could sit.

Now Colin saw the man who'd joined them. "Jabel, how are you?"

Jabel Clark sat in a place where lamp light happened to fall on his high cheekbones and show the striking green of his eyes: a family trait. "Fine, Mr. Colin."

He was eighteen, but looked younger with a smooth-planed face.

"I didn't know you'd be involved tonight," Colin said.

Jabel looked from him to Reverend Jones to Dex, and then to the floor. "We heard Dex got picked up and Granny let me come down and see about him. When I saw the Reverend and Mr. Raeburn go in and then you came along, I knew it'd be all right."

"So things went according to plan?" Colin turned to Reverend Jones.

"They did. About midnight, Dex and the others set up camp in front the theater. Bedrolls, folding chairs, a portable radio. A nice camp."

"Crackers and cheese and a cooler with Coca Colas, too," Dex said. "And I made sure there wasn't any liquor, just like you said, Reverend. When the police showed up, we said we just wanted to be first in line when the theater opens in the afternoon. They said we were on private property and I explained we weren't, that we were on a public sidewalk. Then they said we were blocking access and I showed them how we weren't. So then they said we just needed to leave or get arrested. Everybody but me was already sitting down, so I sat right where I was and in no time, more police showed up and they hauled us up and dragged us down the street." He spoke with pride.

Colin reached over and put a hand on Dex's arm. "And nobody got hurt? Good job."

"I don't know." Dex lost his bravado. "It's kind of a letdown. The magistrate fined me for interfering with a policeman. He just let the others go."

"It was just the beginning," Clyde said. "Just the groundwork."

The telephone on his desk rang and he picked up the receiver. "Raeburn here. Yes sir, he's here. Reverend Jones paid the fine and we're just talking things over. All right, I'll tell him."

When he hung up, he gestured to Dex. "That was your father. He's at your Aunt Marie's house and he's coming to pick y'all up."

"We can start walking that way," Jabel said.

"No son," Clyde said. "You don't need to be on the street right now."

Abraham Jones locked his fingers and stretched his arms. He stifled a yawn. Then he turned to Colin as if he hoped to stay awake by making conversation. "I take it you know Marie Minton?"

"Oh yes. She worked for my wife's family for a long time."

"I see."

Colin was uncomfortable in the silence. It was Jabel who lessened it. "I work for Mr. Colin some now."

"My wife and her brother own properties around town," Colin said. "They employ Jabel."

"But you're the one who pays me," Jabel said and smiled.

That was true. Jabel reported to Colin's office with his work records and Colin paid him with money from George Vance's trust.

"So what's next, Reverend? Dex?" Colin asked.

"The theater has a matinee at two o'clock today," Abraham Jones said. "After my services end, a number of my flock will go line up at the box office."

"As the downtown churches are letting out," Colin said.

"We hope some of those good folk will join in with us."

Dex's face lit up. "When those doors open, we're going straight in. Heading for the front row downstairs."

"What's playing?" Colin asked and they all laughed.

Two hours after he'd left home, Colin was back. He planned to bed down in the library, where Rhetta had replaced her father's old chair with a long couch. This time, the sliding door was silent and the air in the room was still. He changed back into his pajamas and stretched out, pulling an afghan from the back of the couch over himself. He thought over what had happened.

He and Clyde had been friends since they were undergraduates at the local college, Mangum. Clyde was a hardheaded man from the mountains of North Carolina who went to college on the GI Bill after World War II. He was eight years older than Colin. Colin was a scholarship student from a nearby mill town, Black Haw. The scholarship was paid from an endowment that Rhetta's maternal grandfather had established after making his personal wealth from stock in the mill company, banks, and railroads.

Clyde had never cared much about appearance. At Mangum, he didn't care that people poked fun at his clothes, his mountain twang or dialect. Even then, when war memories were fresh, he didn't talk about his experiences, but there was a worldliness about him that Colin envied.

And I'm still trailing along, picking up crumbs of conscience, Colin thought. He shifted and rolled to his side, punched the throw pillow under his head into shape, and fell asleep.

It was morning. He heard soft footsteps outside the heavy pocket door, then somewhat heavier steps and a whisper. Wren would have sneaked out of Rhetta's sight to try and get in to him; Eden, a diligent big sister, would have come to corral her.

His watch told him it was 7:30. Rhetta would take the girls to Sunday School and go to the early service herself. He could sleep another hour and when they got home, he'd be in the kitchen drinking coffee, with a bowl of pancake batter ready for the griddle.

JUNE 1963

In the three weeks before Laurence arrived, Rhetta had the cottage painted inside and out, moved a wall to allow for a small kitchen suitable for a bachelor, and furnished the living room and bedroom. The girls helped—Eden by making the bed and arranging some books on shelves; Wren by bouncing on the furniture and then, when reprimanded, redeeming herself by fluffing up the throw pillows.

The actual arrival fell on a day Colin had to be in court and Eden's class was on its year-end fieldtrip to the state history museum.

"Is Wren going with you?" Colin asked Rhetta. They were together in their bedroom, dressing for the day.

"She doesn't know it yet, but I'm going to take her to the Lyles' for the day."

"She loves to play with Susie." He buttoned up his white shirt and tucked the tail into his trousers.

"Today, she may fuss. She's crazy to see her uncle." She was in her slip, sitting at the dressing table, doing her face.

"This way, you get some time with him first." He reached for his belt. "That's good."

"I need to look him in the eye and see if he means it this time." She put down her powder puff and turned toward him.

"He'd better, after all the work you've done." He let the belt fall and held out both hands to her. She took them and stood.

"You're the most patient man. I may forget to tell you, but I appreciate it more than you can know."

He loved her smile when she was within herself, not flying off on the wings of an emotion where he couldn't follow. When she stood still and smiled at him, she was the girl he'd first met.

She patted his cheek. "I'd better check on the girls. Lord knows what Wren will be wearing."

She padded barefooted down the hall. He hoped that however Wren was dressed, it wouldn't spoil the mood. Their little girl insisted on dressing herself and topping every dress with layers of pop beads she then spent the rest of the day shedding all over the house. Sometimes Eden tried to intervene but that never went well.

As he often did, he planned to walk the two miles to his office, so he carried his jacket. His tie and the gold tie clip Rhetta had given him were in his pocket. He stepped into the hall just as Eden came out of her room.

"Hi, Daddy."

"Hi." He kissed the top of her head. She had inherited Rhetta's rusty curls. He knew she hated them, but he of course loved them. "How're things going in there?"

He nodded toward Wren's door.

"Pink dress. Green knee socks. White shoes. All the beads." She shrugged. "I'm staying out of it."

"Smart girl. I'm sorry I can't loiter to see the outcome."

"You're lucky. I wish I could go with you."

He laughed and kissed her again. "Have a good time at the museum."

All day, he was aware of time and what Rhetta would be doing: taking Eden to school, then leaving Wren at the Lyles' house, probably taking time for a cup of coffee with Janet Lyle, then going to the depot to meet Laurence's train. Brother and sister embracing, going back to their childhood home, she talking, he listening, adding the occasional observation, but letting her fill him in on the girls, on Colin's career, and everyone they knew in Piedmont.

Laurence had last visited for two weeks at Christmas—was it 1960 or '61? Colin didn't remember. He'd been cheery, easy to have around, yet distant, as if he'd left part of himself in London or New York or Paris. One of those places where he collected material for a book. Colin did remember that Rhetta asked more than once, "I think he's happy. Don't you?" He always agreed with her and always accepted the book explanation without letting an eyebrow twitch to show any doubt.

And now the prodigal brother was coming home. To live in the housekeeper's cottage.

The judge adjourned court at four o'clock. Even though he'd promised to be home as soon as he could, Colin decided to go by Clyde's office.

Clyde wasn't there, but Colin made an educated guess and went into a small shop that also opened off of the alley behind the courthouse. It was the Court Street Jeweler's repair shop, where Fred Franklin worked. Clyde liked to have somebody to talk to and Fred was a captive audience.

Sure enough, Clyde was there, sitting on a ladder back chair tipped so that he could rest his feet on an old trunk.

"Afternoon, Mr. Phillips." Fred had been leaning on his counter but he straightened up when Colin opened the door. He was one of the few black men who worked in the white public up town. Besides his starched and pressed dress shirts, he was known for the habitual nod of his head and his skills with watches, eye glasses, and jewelry repairs.

"Hello, Fred," Colin said. "I thought I'd find you here, Clyde. I'm hearing a rumor about the movie theater integrating."

"They've surrendered without a shot being fired," Clyde said. "Fred's going to take his little girl this weekend, right Fred?"

"Yes I am. It'll be her first moving picture ever."

"Congratulations," Colin said.

"Abe Jones says the stores on lower Court are next," Clyde said. "Can you imagine, if it's Fred's little girl's birthday, he can't

he saw that Laurence was still standing, staring out toward the garden and the cottage. He was over six feet tall and slender, the male version of Rhetta's frame, but now Colin saw that he was a bit too thin and his face at rest looked aged beyond his thirty-four years. He'd let his straight brown hair grow long and tucked it behind his ears. He wore a black shirt, a pair of fitted tan trousers that came just to the ankle so his soft-looking boots showed.

Colin had a flash of intuition that clothing and hair were the reflections of unseen changes. This wasn't the brother Rhetta longed for.

"He's been telling me about his book," Rhetta said as she took her drink in hand. "I'm so glad I put Grandfather's desk in the cottage for him."

"I'm glad to do my part to clear out the attic," Laurence said. He shifted his body and his gaze to rejoin them.

"Stop it," Rhetta said. "That attic's a treasure trove. And our heritage."

They bantered, an old back-and-forth that sounded natural enough. Colin sipped his drink and tried to be reassured.

∽

Jabel graduated second in his class. He stood on the stage as salutatorian to welcome the six hundred family and friends who had come to celebrate the accomplishments of the Sweet Side children. His own invited guests were Granny; her brother, Marcus, who lived in New Jersey; Dex; and Dex's parents, Raymond and Dee. They sat in the fourth row, right in the center. Their faces glowed with expectation. Behind him on the podium, he felt the gazes of Reverend Jones and the principal and the white school superintendent.

"It is my honor to welcome all of you here today, on behalf of the Class of 1963." He had a speech that should take him three minutes to deliver. Then he would introduce the valedictorian.

Everybody there knew him and it seemed to him that they shared one thought: why isn't this boy going straight on to college? Why isn't he doing us proud?

He didn't have a good answer, only the truth. He didn't want to admit he had no idea what college meant, even though he'd been told all his life that he could and would go. What he said instead was, he wanted to work for a year and save up some money. He also said he was worried about leaving Granny on her own.

"You don't have to worry about Marie," Dee and Raymond told him back. "You think you're the only one that loves her?"

He gave some thought to joining Dex to fight for the cause. The Reverend had said that he ought to finish school first. "And then, take time to think about what you really want. We need people, but we need people who are clear and committed and understand the risks."

Suddenly Jabel was saying, "And now, I want to introduce to you the pride of Lincoln High, our valedictorian, Annie Blaylock." He was done. There was a chair for him on the stage, just behind the Reverend.

The next day was Monday and he was up at the same time he'd always gotten up to go to school. Granny had his breakfast ready, as usual.

"It seems like nothing's changed," he said as he sat down at the kitchen table.

"You'll learn different," Granny said. She put down a plate with scrambled eggs and two strips of bacon. "Biscuits are nearly done."

He'd worked at Mr. Dave Shipman's Chrysler dealership the previous summer. Now it would be fulltime, year-round. His job would be to have the new cars shiny as could be for the shoppers and buyers. If people brought in a car for service, the car would be clean as if new when they came back to pick it up. Besides an hourly wage, he expected to do okay with tips. And he'd still be able to do odd jobs on weekends.

For sure, nobody would be able to say he was lazy.

"Butter them while they're hot." Granny slid four of her thin, crisp biscuits from the baking pan to his plate.

Jabel caught a ride with a neighbor that morning and got to the Chrysler dealership a good fifteen minutes early. The garage wasn't even open yet, but he knew Dave Shipman would be in his office. He went in the back door of the building and knocked on the boss's door.

"I'm ready to go to work, Mr. Dave."

"All right, Jabel. I knew I could count on you." Mr. Shipman motioned for him to come in. "I have a big job for you. You know the Vances? Well, Mr. Laurence Vance called me on Friday and said he'd be in this morning to buy a car. I got two I figure he'll like. They need to get a little extra polish before he gets here."

"I thought Mr. Laurence lived somewhere foreign," Jabel said.

"He did, but he's come back."

He says that like it's a big deal, Jabel thought. But if I just stay, nobody's going to make a big deal out of that. What's the difference?

Jabel spent the morning washing and waxing two Newports, a midnight blue convertible and a black hardtop. When he was done, one of the salesmen would drive them into the showroom and focus the lights on them. He was still checking for streaks on the chrome, though, when he heard Mr. Dave's voice. Then the boss and a tall thin man came around the corner of the building.

"I tell you, Laurence, another five minutes and we'd have them inside where you can see them proper," Dave Shipman said.

"It's all right, Dave. I can see them very well here, I'm sure."

This is Laurence Vance, Jabel thought and backed away from the cars, pulling the hose with him. Mr. Laurence had his hands in his pockets and a sly sort of smile, like he knew he wasn't acting the way Mr. Dave wanted him to, and he didn't care.

When Jabel was little and first came to live with Granny in the cottage, Mr. Laurence played catch with him sometimes, and gave him gum. Granny told stories about the years when she worked for the Vances and it seemed to Jabel she had a soft spot for Mr. Laurence more so than Miss Rhetta.

The two men walked all around the cars and Laurence listened while his boss pointed out the details of each.

"I'll have to go with the black one, Dave," Laurence Vance said.

"Let me get the keys and a tag and get you out for a test drive." Dave Shipman used the back door to get to his office.

"Mr. Laurence," Jabel said. "I doubt you remember me."

Laurence turned fast, as if he had not seen Jabel until he spoke.

"I'm Jabel Clark. Marie Minton's my grandmother."

"Oh my God, Jabel. You were about so high the last time I saw you." He reached down and motioned at knee height. "You resemble Marie, especially those eyes." He smiled.

"Yes sir." Suddenly he felt he'd made a mistake. "I just wanted to say hey. I better get back to work." He began to coil the hose.

"Are you the one who cleaned the cars for me to see?" He took a wallet out of the inside pocket of his light jacket.

Jabel saw his boss heading back toward them, within earshot now.

"That's all right, Mr. Laurence. Mr. Dave pays me."

"It's okay, Jabel. Just so long as you didn't ask for it or suggest it." Mr. Dave looked to Mr. Laurence to see the answer.

"Not at all," Mr. Laurence said and held out a ten-dollar bill.

Jabel was used to fifty cents or a dollar from the customers. The bill felt too thick and new to be real. It didn't seem right to fold it or to put it in his pants pocket, his pants damp from the hose spray and sweat. He rolled it and tucked it into his shirt pocket instead. "Thank you, Mr. Laurence."

⌒

Marie Minton swept her front stoop, then leaned on the broom and lifted her face to feel the sun.

I need to move from here, she thought. She'd already boiled a chicken to get her cooking done before the house got hot and she wanted to make chicken salad to take a neighbor whose husband was ill. But it would wait a minute more, because the last bit of cool in the morning air felt good. She'd begun to feel she had earned a bit of ease like this.

She heard a car coming down the unpaved street. She gave the brick step another lick with the broom so whoever drove by wouldn't see her lazing. Then she raised her hand to greet whoever it was, bound to be somebody she knew.

The car was new and shiny black. It stopped in front of her house and she felt a little surge in her heart when the driver got out.

"Good lord. Laurence Vance, you rascal."

He waved and then crossed her yard in a few long-legged steps. She put down the broom and let him grab her into a bear hug.

"Rascal," she said again. "You don't send me a word beyond happy birthday and Merry Christmas for all these years and now you come to catch me in my house dress." She squeezed him back and then they both let go.

"I was afraid to call first," he said. "I was afraid you'd tell me you don't ever want to see me again."

She took a moment to study his face. Still good looking, maybe more so. Hair too long for her. Made him look like he was way beyond Piedmont. Eyes blue as ever but shadowed. Sadness, that was it. And women could be fools for that, as she knew.

"When did you get home?" she asked.

"About two weeks ago. I meant to come see you sooner, but I didn't have a car till this morning." He pointed. "I saw Jabel at Shipman's and I decided … well, here I am. Taking my chances."

"Come on in. You know I'm not ever going to turn you away." She held the screened door open and shooed him through. "I guess Rhetta's mighty happy."

"She is." He laughed. "You used to call her my little mama. That hasn't changed, at least not when I'm under her nose."

"She's still out of sorts with me." She motioned for him to sit and he took the sofa in front of the window. She had her chair opposite him, nearest the kitchen door.

"I got that idea," he said. "I'm sorry. She was wrong to think you owed her anything."

When Rhetta got married, she'd wanted Marie back and Marie'd said no. When the first baby was born, she'd wanted Marie back and this time when Marie said no, Rhetta'd said hard words about the lack of gratitude.

"She may not say it, but she knows she was wrong." Laurence leaned forward, his elbows on his knees. "If there's any owing, it's what we owe you."

She didn't doubt he meant it, but it felt like another weight on her shoulders. And she had loved the boy he'd been. Did he still want somebody to love him like that? At his age? She hoped not.

"You saw my Jabel?" She changed the subject. "I have to say, he makes me proud."

"How old is he now?"

"Eighteen. Just graduated from high school. Second in his class, too."

He had a way of looking at her so she knew he was listening close. "What about you? Are you still working?"

"Can you see me not working?" She laughed. "I'm still at the elementary school cafeteria. Still feeding children. I do look forward to my summers, just like a child does."

"Do you think about retiring?" He looked as if there was something behind the question.

"I need to build up my pension a little more. And I still have my hopes that Jabel will go to college."

"If he does, I'd like to help pay for it."

So that's it, she thought. Money to make everything right. She pulled a frown and shook her head. "I gave your mother and father what they were paying me for, and more. I kept my part of that bargain. I walked away to raise my grandson and I never looked back. We're fine."

She pressed her shoulders into the chair cushion and raised herself high, her arms crossed. He was quiet, looking at her and for a moment she thought he would sink into an old familiar pout, the one he had worn when he couldn't get around her. Instead, he sat up straighter, too.

"I'm not trying to buy you, Marie. Just do what's right." He sighed. "If I can't have that, may I take you to lunch?"

AUGUST 1963

"This is Sheila," Laurence said. "We were married this morning."

Colin stood with an arm around Rhetta's shoulders and felt the shock that ran through her bones.

"Well," he said when she didn't speak. "What a surprise. Sheila, best wishes. Laurence, congratulations."

He would have offered to kiss the bride and shake his brother-in-law's hand, if he was sure that Rhetta wouldn't collapse. "Sweetheart, isn't this good news?"

"Where are the girls?" Laurence asked.

"They're at Susie Lyle's birthday party," Rhetta said.

"Oh, too bad. I want Sheila to meet them."

Laurence had chosen to bring his bride to the front door. He had rung the bell and waited until Colin, who had been in his study reading, answered and Rhetta had come from the kitchen. The four of them, and their tension, filled the wide foyer.

"Your home is beautiful, Rhetta," Sheila said. "I came once before, on the Christmas house tour."

Her voice was soft. Sincere, Colin thought. She looked soft herself, strawberry blond, blue-eyed, and she smiled at him as if she already felt kinship with the other person who'd married a Vance.

He decided he liked her, but he imagined when he told Rhetta that, she'd say something about how simpleminded men are.

You use up all the complexity I can muster, he'd tell her. Besides, for Laurence to fall in love enough to marry, there had to be more to Sheila than the obvious. Not that there was anything unlovable about the obvious.

"Our father built the house long before we were born," Rhetta said. "We grew up here."

"I know. Laurence has told me a lot about all of you and the family history."

"Really?" Rhetta said.

Colin jumped in before she could say more, something like, he's told us nothing about you. "We should drink a toast. We don't have Champagne but I can make Old Fashioneds." It wasn't yet 3:30 but it was the best idea he could come up with, and under the circumstances, seemed none too soon.

"I'll help you," Laurence said. "Rhetta, will you show Sheila around?"

"Of course," Rhetta said in the voice she used for the house tours. "We'll meet you in the sunroom."

Colin and Laurence went back into the hall and followed it through to the butler's pantry between the dining room and kitchen.

"A pitcher, do you think?" Colin asked. He took a new fifth of bourbon out of a cabinet.

"At least." Laurence laughed. "That went better than I feared."

"You didn't think of mentioning it at breakfast this morning?"

"Sure I thought of it, but in my experience, Rhetta rallies faster when you take her unawares."

"Easy for you to say. You'll go off on your honeymoon and I'll have to deal with what's left in your wake." He put glasses, a jar of Maraschino cherries and a bottle of bitters on a tray. "Bring that."

"You're a great man, Colin."

"That's the nicest thing you've ever said to me. Give me ten minutes and I'm sure I'll return the sentiment."

In the kitchen, Colin took ice trays out of the freezer and pulled the lever to empty cubes into a bucket. His hands shook. He'd made jokes, but his lungs were filling and emptying in fast shallow waves of anger. The summer had been good. Now he thought, too good. Colin and Rhetta and the girls had gone to the beach for two weeks. Eden had gone to her first sleep away camp for two weeks. Colin had won a case and lost a case. He'd been called out on three Saturday nights to meet Reverend Jones and Clyde at the magistrate's office when demonstrators were arrested.

And all the time, Laurence had been there. In the cottage. In the sunroom. In the rose garden. He worked at his writing—or so he said. He ate meals with the family. Affectionate brother. Playful uncle. Still more at home in the house than Colin himself.

And now he shows up with a wife?

"Damn right I'm mad," Colin muttered.

"Sorry?" Laurence asked.

"Nothing. Let's sit down." He carried the pitcher the two steps down into the sunroom and let his brother-in-law bring the tray of glasses.

When he faced Laurence again, he was shocked to see his eyes were glossy.

"Hey, isn't it the bride who's supposed to cry? Here, if you're in this kind of state, we'd better not wait for the girls." Colin poured two drinks, and let go of the anger, at least for the moment. "Here's to your happiness."

"Thanks. I hope we can come close to you and Rhetta in that regard. You set a high standard, you know."

"Here we are," Rhetta said as she and Sheila came in. "You two aren't drunk already, I hope."

"Only on love," Laurence said. He took Sheila's arm and pulled her close. "You can be happy for us, Rhetta. Really, really happy."

"I remember this from the tour," Sheila said. "How the kitchen and the sunroom connect."

"It was Rhetta's idea," Laurence said. "She added the sunroom where an old utility porch used to be."

"Everybody seems to like it," Rhetta said.

"The roses are gorgeous," Sheila said. "They weren't blooming at the house tour."

"Mother planted them all," Laurence said. "She loved them more than anything."

"And when we acted up, more than anybody," Rhetta laughed.

"Right," Laurence said. "Anytime we caused trouble, you'd find her out there snapping the heads off of something."

"It's Rhetta's garden now," Colin said. "Heart and soul." He was glad she and her brother had fallen into their patter, their practiced back and forth. Later he could tell her that would never change; Sheila or no Sheila, she'd never lose Laurence.

"And that's my hovel, at the far side of the garden." Laurence pointed to the white frame cottage. "Rhetta and Colin will be glad to have me off the premises I'm sure."

"You know that's not true." Rhetta sipped her drink. "We love having you live there. The girls will be heartbroken if you leave."

"I have a little house a couple of blocks from the University," Sheila said. "It's modest, but it's what I could afford with some money my grandmother left me."

Colin saw her blush and wished Rhetta would make her feel at home, and not like the poor relation.

"Sheila is a librarian at Mangum University," Rhetta told Colin. "That's how she and Laurence met. She helped him with his research."

Laurence put his hand on Sheila's knee. "We gazed at each other over an ancient tome and I was a goner."

The front door of the house slammed and Colin heard his daughters' voices and he relaxed. It always happened and always surprised him—when they weren't home, anxiety crept into his blood, unnoticed until it eased.

"The grownup party's over," Rhetta said to Sheila. "We're back here, girls." She set her glass down and went to the front hall to meet them.

Laurence made his usual fuss over the girls and introduced Sheila.

"Want to see my room?" Wren asked.

"I'd love to. Do you mind, Rhetta?" Sheila had barely touched her cocktail, Colin noticed, but her face was flushed.

"Just please don't notice the chaos." Rhetta sat back down and took up her glass again. Wren led her Uncle Laurence and new aunt out, with Eden following.

Colin looked at Rhetta, studied her frown, and waited for her to say whatever she was going to say. She was angry with Laurence but it never lasted. The only question was how long it would take her to forgive him.

"She's lucky Empire waists are in style." Her silence was over.

"What do you mean?"

"That dress? With the high waist?" Rhetta held her hands just under her breasts. "She's pregnant, Colin."

"Sweetheart, they'll hear you."

"I don't care."

"Yes you do, or you will when you've had time to get used to the idea."

"She's taking him away from us, Colin. To live in whatever house she can afford on her salary."

"I'm sure that's temporary, until they find something else." Then he was sorry he'd said it. It reminded Rhetta that her brother was a wealthy man, and that would reinforce the notion of Sheila as fortune-hunting husband-trapper.

"Rhetta." He waited until she looked at him, then leaned toward her, his elbows on his knees, and held her gaze. "Give her a chance. Give him credit."

She pressed her lips together and closed her eyes tight. "You're right. I know you are, but … I don't understand how this happened."

Colin thought of their two weeks away. And he remembered that at least twice he knew of, Laurence had eased his car out of the driveway, headlights out, when the house was dark. The first time, Colin had been working late. When he quit for the night, he'd turned out the study lamps and walked down the hall to the kitchen. He didn't need a light on to get a drink of water. Had he not heard the tires on the gravel, he wouldn't have looked to see the black car creep by the windows.

He'd chosen not to say anything to either Rhetta or Laurence but had been alert. Sure enough, it happened again a few nights later. It reminded him that even in college, Laurence had been secretive about his personal life. Clyde had brought a rolling cast of girlfriends into their group, but Laurence, never. So that hadn't changed.

Wren clumped down the steps, ran into the room and threw herself at her mother. Colin stood up when Laurence and Sheila followed. They were both smiling. He saw Sheila falter a little as if she sensed something in the air.

"We should go, Laurence," she said. "I don't want to wear out my welcome first thing." She turned to Rhetta. "You've both been really nice, considering this wasn't exactly on your plan for the day. Thank you."

OCTOBER 1963

As Sheila's belly grew, Laurence began to understand what it was to be responsible for another person's health and contentment.

"Stop fussing," she said, laughing at the way he jumped every time she sighed or groaned. "I'm fine. The doctor says I'm doing just fine."

"If anything happened to you, I'd lose my mind." He held her face and studied it for signs, of what he didn't know. "And that goes for you, too." He put his hands on her stomach and addressed the baby.

"You take such good care of us, nothing can possibly happen." She ran her fingers through his hair to massage his scalp. "Are you happy, Laurence?"

"Beyond belief." He liked being depended on, giving care rather than receiving it.

He fretted every day that she dressed and packed her lunch and went to work. "The library can get along without you better than I can," he said.

"I don't want to sit around getting fatter and fatter. It's good for me, and I've got all the rest of our lives to be home."

"But the next few months are the only ones we'll have together, just the two of us."

"I love every minute with you, but I've worked for so long, I'm just not ready to give it up yet."

"We don't need the money." He knew that she didn't like to hear that, but somehow he thought that if he said it again, she'd get it. And he didn't know what else to offer her.

"I've got to go," she said. "I don't want to argue with you. Not about anything, and especially this."

"No arguments, I promise." He kissed her. "We agreed on a color for the baby's room, right? I'll call a painter today."

Laurence opened the door early on Saturday morning. "Jabel, thanks for coming."

Jabel grinned. "I appreciate the job."

Sheila came from the kitchen.

"This is my wife," Laurence said. "Sheila, this is Jabel Clark."

"Hello, Jabel. We're so glad you're here."

"Thank you, ma'am."

"Come on down the hall," Sheila said, "I'll show you the nursery. We've bought the paint and brushes and rollers and tape. I've got drop cloths and a ladder from when I first moved in, but anything you need, we'll get."

"Sounds good, ma'am."

Laurence didn't go with them, but he listened to their conversation, listened to Sheila put the young man at ease by talking about her own painting experiences when she first bought the house. He needed the minutes to calm his own breathing and pounding heart. He'd seen Jabel at the car dealership but somehow the vivid green eyes and the smoothness of his cheeks had not registered as they did now. The boy was beautiful. He should never have called him for this job.

He heard Sheila say, "You've got it under control, Jabel, so I'm going to ask my husband to take me shopping and to lunch. You don't need us underfoot."

They stayed away from the house for several hours, as long as Sheila wanted. When they returned home, Jabel was gone.

"Let's see how much he got done." Sheila went straight to the nursery. Laurence followed her, suddenly apprehensive that Jabel wouldn't meet her expectations.

"He washed the walls. He spackled. Look how he layered the drop cloths and taped them down." She stood in the middle of the room and turned to take it all in.

"Is that good?" Laurence asked.

"Have you honestly never lifted a paint brush?" She took his arm and gave it a little shake. "He'll do a better job than I ever could. And he's a sweet boy."

"I'm glad you like him."

"He doesn't have a car. He told me that this morning so it made me think." She held his hand. "You've wanted to get me a better car. What if I let you do that and we give Jabel the one I'm driving. It can be part of his pay."

"That's a sensible girl." He leaned over and kissed her forehead. "Why don't you ask him next time he comes?"

⤳

The next Wednesday evening, Laurence paced in the living room. Finally, at half past six, he heard a car stop outside. He stepped out on the porch and saw Jabel Clark wave at him from the passenger's window.

The driver came in with Jabel and was introduced as his cousin, Dexter. Dexter was older than Jabel, in his mid-twenties, Laurence guessed, and it occurred to him that the cousin was there as a sort of chaperone. No. He shook that off. Nothing had happened to make Jabel feel that need.

"We met before, Mr. Vance," Dexter said. "When I was a kid. Marie Minton's my great-aunt and I used to come see her when she worked for y'all."

Laurence smiled. "I should have recognized you."

"It's been a long time." Dexter drew his lips together. Laurence felt himself blush. Identity was tricky. To mistake one black man for another or to fail to recognize an acquaintance was a double insult: they all look alike and white people are all blind.

"Where's Miss Sheila?" Jabel asked.

"She had to work late. Somebody called in sick. But she's already signed over the title and had it notarized."

"I need to thank her."

"You'll see her when you come back to finish the job." Laurence went to the desk and opened a drawer. "Here's the title. And the key."

The three men walked out. Sheila's car, a ten-year-old Dodge, its once-white paint grayed, was in the driveway. Its windows were dark and soft, as if there were no glass in them.

"Cool." Dexter tapped Jabel on the shoulder. "I got to go, man. You all set?"

Dexter whistled as he walked down the street to his own car.

Jabel got in and fumbled to adjust the seat. Up close, the windows reflected Laurence's face back at him. Then Jabel rolled the glass down and they were close. "I sure do thank you."

"It'll need some work." Laurence stepped back.

"Mr. Shipman's going to let me use the garage weekends and one of the mechanics said he'll help." Jabel turned the key and the engine sputtered before it started, proving the point.

They both laughed. Jabel's surprising eyes sparked. That's when Laurence realized his hand was moving on its own, moving to stroke Jabel's cheek. He mastered it just in time and pounded the roof of the car instead. He was relieved that the young man didn't seem to notice.

"It's yours now. If it breaks down half way home, good luck to you." They laughed again.

When Jabel was gone, Laurence's knees went weak and he staggered back to the house. He went to the bedroom and fell across the bed, pressing Sheila's pillow to his face, smothering the hope, the idea, the idiocy that she could save him. She and the baby, dear as they were to him, were supposed to be the final bricks in the wall he'd come back to Piedmont to build.

Sheila came home tired and hungry and achy from her long day. He ran her a bath and scrambled eggs for their supper, then massaged her feet until she fell asleep. He tried to match his feelings for her to his actions, but all he could manage that night was pity for both of them.

Laurence was surprised when Jabel showed up on Friday morning. "We didn't expect you until tomorrow."

"I hope it's all right. I was due a day off from the car dealership, so I decided I'd take it and work here."

They walked down the hall into the baby's room.

"It's going to look like my granny's lemon pie," Jabel said. He'd gotten one coat of creamy yellow paint on the walls.

"And the trim will be the meringue." Laurence laughed. "Sheila didn't want pink or blue, says it would guarantee that the baby is the opposite, and then it'll be traumatized."

Jabel looked up and wrinkled his forehead. It gave his face a quirk of personality that made Laurence smile.

"A pregnant woman seems to have an infinite capacity for worry," Laurence said. "Do you have a girlfriend?"

The young man pried the lid off a can. "I did in high school, but she left to go to New York and I can't seem to get around to finding another one."

"Broken heart?"

Jabel shrugged. "My cousin Dex, he says you can't live with them and can't live without them."

"Oh, I don't know. Until Sheila, I was a man who could live without them." Laurence watched while Jabel poured paint into a tray and eased the clean roller into it, giving no sign of having heard him. He had planned to work at home—he had notes he needed to type up, a new idea for a book—but an old, familiar restlessness came over him.

"I've got to go out. There's food in the refrigerator. Help

yourself when you get hungry."

He stayed away until after five o'clock and felt relief when he saw that Jabel's car was gone. But when he walked in the front door, he heard Sheila talking to someone in the baby's room and it was Jabel who answered her.

"Hello." Laurence went to his wife's side and she took his arm.

"Isn't it lovely?" she said. "Jabel's doing a great job."

"I thought you must have finished for the day," Laurence said. "I didn't see your car."

"No sir. When I went home to lunch, I left it for my auntie to use." He stepped closer to the window frame and studied his work. "I was just saying, it's hard painting over this old oil paint. I want to do it right for y'all so if you don't mind, I'll come back and do a third coat."

"You are a dream come true," Sheila said. "Now, how are you getting home?" She shifted her weight so that Laurence felt her belly against his side. It came naturally to her to share the physicality of the baby's presence and usually he welcomed it, but it made him uneasy with Jabel there.

"Walking."

"All that way? Laurence can drive you."

"I used to walk farther than that all the time, ma'am."

"Laurence doesn't mind, do you, sweetheart?"

"Of course not." Laurence said. "There's really no point in either of us arguing with her, Jabel."

"I want a nap," Sheila said. "So take your time."

"Miss Sheila is a real nice lady," Jabel said as Laurence backed his car out of the driveway. "I told Granny about how nice she is and she said she's glad. She used to worry you'd never get married."

"Marie always worried about me. She stood up for me, too, when my sister bossed me around."

"Yeah, she frets about me, too. That's her way."

"Fret's a good word. Of course, my mother and sister fretted over me, too. Come to think of it, I think my wife's the only woman in my life who doesn't. I appreciate that."

"Yes sir."

Laurence knew Jabel was ending the conversation before it became any more personal. He wondered if somebody explained these things to young black children or if they grew to know instinctively how to redirect white people to safer ground. They rode without speaking for a few minutes. Jabel began to tap his fingers on his knees and Laurence almost groaned. He had to say something.

"Jabel, I've known you most of your life and Marie has known me all of mine. We can be comfortable with each other, I hope."

"Yes sir. I hope so, too." He stopped fidgeting all of a sudden, like a child who's caught a note of disapproval in a parent's voice.

The car passed under a streetlight and Laurence glanced at Jabel. His face was set, less still than tense, wary, as if he was ready to jump.

"I'm glad you see how good a person Sheila is." Laurence hoped it was safe ground. "Sometimes I worry that I've set Sheila up for a lot of unhappiness."

"She seems happy to me." The words came out slowly.

Laurence turned onto Court Street, heading away from the center of town. "Do you think a person can live an honest life and still keep secrets?"

"I guess I never thought much about it."

"But you do it, too, don't you?"

"What do you mean, Mr. Vance?"

"When a young man like you interacts with someone like me, does he show himself in full? His real self?"

"Are you saying you think I'm lying about something?"

"No. Not at all." Laurence tried to laugh. "I must be going through the husband's version of pregnancy. It turns out to be rather lonely. I have no one to talk to these days."

Jabel stared straight ahead through the windshield.

"You're thinking I have my wife to talk to," Laurence said.

"Seems like it."

"My greatest fear is that I'll hurt her. Sometimes I think she'd be better off if we'd never met."

"Mr. Vance, I got to say, I don't feel like I'm the one you ought to be saying this to."

Laurence heard Jabel's discomfort but his own thoughts and words ran ahead. "It's just that she doesn't deserve the pain she would feel if she knew ..."

"Turn here."

"What? Oh, sorry." He turned onto the street that went into Sweet Side. They didn't speak again until Jabel pointed out Marie's house on the corner.

"Give Marie my best," Laurence said as the boy jumped out and almost ran across the yard.

Sheila had said not to hurry, so Laurence drove out from Piedmont into the country. Beyond the street lights, he chastised himself. How stupid to talk to Jabel that way; was he losing his mind? He pounded the steering wheel, accidently blowing the horn. There was no one to react. In another mile, he saw a dog on the side of the road, just barely in range of his headlights. The rearview mirror showed it cross and trot toward a small house. Going home. Laurence turned around and did the same.

When Laurence got there, he found Sheila in the kitchen peeling potatoes. He kissed her. "I thought you'd be resting."

"I did, for a few minutes, but the phone rang." It was unusual for her not to return his kiss but she kept working with the peeler, her eyes on her hands.

"Who was it?"

"A man. For you. He said his name is Adam. No, that's not right. He said it in a strange way. 'Tell Laurence his first man called. Adam.' And he laughed and said, 'Does he call you Eve?'" She began to cut the potatoes into wedges and drop them in a pot of water.

Laurence sat down, feeling dizzy.

"Who is he?" Sheila sounded irritated. "I didn't like him."

"An old acquaintance. I don't like him either."

She turned to look at him, frowning.

He got up, his legs heavy. He took the pot from her and put it on the stove. "Why don't you finish your nap? I'll do that. What else are you planning?"

"The leftover chicken. A salad." He reached out to put an arm around her shoulders and she stepped back. "I'm beyond tired. That's probably why this Adam struck me so wrong."

When she left, Laurence leaned against the counter, braced with his arms. He'd gone for months without thinking about Adam or any of the things he represented. It had only been in the days with Jabel around that he'd found himself backsliding. He wondered if it was possible for him to have somehow signaled Adam—sent out some sort of psychic energy. It was too coincidental.

He and Sheila went to bed early and he lay curled around her, breathing with her while she slept. His mind wouldn't rest, though, and in the small hours his thoughts settled on how to protect her, thereby protecting himself.

NOVEMBER 1963

Colin assumed Rhetta saw Laurence from time to time during the fall, but she seldom mentioned him and never Sheila. Yet somehow it was known that she'd been right about the pregnancy. Rhetta went to Garden Club meetings, had lunch with her friends, volunteered at church and at Eden's school, and worked in the rose garden—the things she always did.

In early November, she began planning for the holidays.

"They'll be here for Thanksgiving," she said and he knew she meant Laurence and Sheila.

"I'm glad," he said.

And then it was Friday, November 22, 1963, and the President was killed.

School was cancelled for the holiday week and Colin closed his office. He and Rhetta and Eden sat and watched JFK's life replayed on television, repeated accounts of the Kennedy family tragedies, then saw another murder take place in a vast, dim garage. They watched a riderless horse, a flag-covered coffin on a caisson, a widow in a veil, brothers with ravaged faces, a little boy's salute. Rhetta and Eden cried and Wren clung, not understanding, but sensing that the world was suddenly unsteady, suddenly out of orbit.

"We don't have to do the big dinner," Colin said to Rhetta. "Laurence and Sheila will understand."

"We do have to do it." She polished silver, scrubbing with a tooth brush. "We need tradition." She looked up at him. "For the girls, if not for us."

So, for four adults and two girls, Rhetta made consommé, turkey, dressing, sweet potatoes, green beans, tomato aspic, dinner rolls, and both pumpkin and pecan pies.

Sheila and Laurence arrived, came in holding hands, letting go only to shed coats and to be made welcome. Eden took her turn being hugged and kissed. Then Colin saw her, his watchful child, take a place on the sidelines. He wondered if it was Sheila's shape that made her reluctant. Sheila was full and round, bigger than Rhetta had been at the same stage of pregnancy.

Laurence didn't offer Wren the usual piggy-back ride. Instead, he made sure his wife was settled on a loveseat in the sunroom and then went off to find her a footstool. While he was gone, Wren climbed up by her aunt.

"Wrenny, come sit with me. Don't crowd Aunt Sheila." Colin sank into a big overstuffed chair.

"She's fine," Sheila said, "let her stay." Wren gazed up at her and then reached to touch Sheila's face. Sheila grabbed the girl's hand and kissed it, laughing. Colin looked around and saw that Eden had come closer. He gestured to her and she sat with him in his big chair. He glanced back to see what his wife was doing. She stood at the long work table watching them. Laurence came up behind her and draped an arm across her shoulders. She smiled. The tears Colin had held back since the assassination stung his eyes and sinuses. Rhetta had been right about Thanksgiving. Family and ritual were the only comforts.

DECEMBER 17, 1963

With her usual efficiency, Rhetta had long-since stuffed their bedroom closet with Santa Claus presents but when Laurence suggested she go to Raleigh with him to shop, she was excited.

"I don't have anything for Sheila," she told Colin, "or the baby. Laurence can tell me what they need."

Colin doubted it; he didn't think his brother-in-law would be any better than he'd been himself when it came to knowing what an unborn baby needed, but he agreed to a day of work at his home so he could watch the girls, happy to see Rhetta happy.

The telephone call came at 3:30 in the afternoon and later Colin was glad he'd been the one to answer. Rhetta, near hysteria, insisted that he come to Laurence and Sheila's house right away, but wouldn't say why beyond, "something horrible has happened."

Colin's hands shook so he could hardly dial a phone number. He called their friends, the Lyles, and dropped the girls off there. He'd never been to Laurence and Sheila's house but he knew the streets around the university well enough to find it. And there were three police cars in front of it. He pulled up beside one and identified himself to the young officer who stood beside it.

"Yes sir. We knew you were coming," the officer said.

Laurence sat in a porch chair, his face in his hands, shoulders shaking. Rhetta knelt beside him, her arms across his knees, and was talking, talking, talking. Colin knew how it was when she spoke that way, close and intense and uninterruptible. When he leaned over them, Rhetta said to her brother, "Do you understand? Do you?"

Then she turned to Colin. Her face was colorless, her lips taut. "Sheila's been murdered."

She stood and Colin held her. Laurence rose, seemed to totter, and then reached for Colin's shoulder. The three of them embraced and hung together for a measureless span of time. Finally, Colin became aware of the police chief, Lewis Bland, in the doorway to the bungalow, watching them.

"They told me you're here, Mr. Phillips." The chief's face was pale and his voice was weary.

Laurence stepped away first, then Rhetta, but she kept hold of Colin's hand.

"This isn't a good place for these folks to be," the chief said, "but I don't judge either of them in condition to drive."

"I don't want to go," Laurence said. "I want to be with my wife."

"I'm sorry, Laurence," Bland said, "I'm not going to be able to let you in here tonight."

"Come home with us." Rhetta said to Laurence. "Colin will take us."

She looked at the chief. "Can't we just get some of his things?"

"No ma'am. Nothing can be moved or touched till the state crime scene folks get here and do their work."

"You've already called them?" Colin asked, thinking, that was fast.

"You know it. We don't see much of this kind of thing in Piedmont and we need help processing this scene." Bland made a small gesture toward Laurence. "We're going to do this right, Mr. Vance. We're going to find out who did this."

Colin felt Rhetta stiffen.

"There's the coroner now," Chief Bland said.

Colin turned and saw a black Cadillac make its way down the street. The driver had to go by the house to find a place to park.

"Chief, may I speak with you?" Colin asked. He let go of Rhetta's hand and moved to the far end of the porch.

When Chief Bland joined him, he said, "With due respect, the elected coroner is an undertaker. I don't think the family will be satisfied with his services."

"Yeah," Bland said. "All the bigger counties where they get more murders, they're going to real medical examiners. Guess it's a little late for us."

"Someone at the Mangum medical school can do a proper autopsy."

"You haven't seen her, Mr. Phillips. She's got a gash on the back of her head and a lamp cord tied around her neck. That's a pretty good autopsy right there."

"Nevertheless. I'll make the arrangements. When can she be moved?"

"You speaking as a family member here, or as a lawyer?"

"A lawyer." We got here fast, Colin thought.

"I'm just wondering who's going to officially ask for an autopsy. It's a stretch for my budget if I do it."

"Laurence is making the request. And he'll pay for it, if necessary."

Colin felt a twinge of nausea, having to talk about autopsies and legalities. He pressed his fist against his lips and looked back toward Rhetta and Laurence. This time she sat in the rocker and he stood beside her, staring off into the night.

"I need to get them home, but I want to stay. Will you get somebody to call a taxi?"

The chief nodded. "I'll do better than that. I'll get one of my men to drive them. You bring them in tomorrow to give their statements."

It crossed Colin's mind that the brother and sister ought to have been separated as soon as the police arrived and that statements should have been taken in the first hour. The state investigators weren't going to be happy.

Or maybe he'd been wrong about where the chief's thoughts were going.

He was the observer for the next eight hours, staying out of the way but taking in everything. Sheila's body was not visible from the doorway so he persuaded the state forensic team that as the family's attorney, he should be allowed to see her before they began to do their job. They gave him one minute to stand, touching nothing, and look. He tried to be objective and failed. Most of the minute he spent in the deepest grief he'd ever felt.

It was after midnight when Colin got home. He found Rhetta alone in the living room, in the dark except for the lights on the Christmas tree.

"Where's Laurence?" he asked.

"He went to the cottage." She made room on the settee for Colin and took his hand.

"Did you tell the girls?"

With her free hand, she dabbed at her eyes. "Laurence did. He was so sweet, so gentle with them. He explained that they won't have a baby cousin to love. You must be starving. Let me fix you some eggs."

"That would be nice, thanks." But neither of them moved. "Rhetta?"

"Yes?"

"It's only just starting."

"I know. I've got to be strong for Laurence. I've got to make him strong."

"I'm not sure you understood me."

She didn't answer.

"It's likely that Laurence will be a suspect," Colin said.

"He was with me all day," she whispered.

"A loving sister isn't the best alibi." He lifted her hand and held it against his chest. "The investigation will be pretty agonizing."

"But you'll defend him and everything will be all right."

"I'm too close to be objective. And I've never handled a murder case. I'll find somebody, the best, for him."

She shifted so that they were eye to eye. "But you have to do it. If you abandon him, you abandon me."

Her voice was strident but he saw what it was supposed to obscure: she was terrified. He put his free hand on her cheek and said, "Never."

DECEMBER 18, 1963

"Why can't they just take my statement?" Rhetta asked. "Why put a man who just lost his wife and child through this?"

The three of them—Colin, Rhetta, and Laurence—were in the car, Colin driving, on their way to the courthouse.

"I'm sure Chief Bland will be as considerate as possible," Colin said.

"It's inhumane." Rhetta reached over the seat toward her brother.

"Nothing can hurt me now," Laurence said. "All I care about is that the police do everything possible to find him."

"Him?" Colin asked. "Who do you mean?"

"Whoever did this horrible crime." Rhetta answered before her brother. Her voice conveyed shock at the question.

"Now listen, both of you," Colin said. "You've got be calm. You've got to be forthcoming. You've got to understand that this is necessary."

Colin had been to the police department hundreds of times, but never like this. A uniformed sergeant served as receptionist and without speaking to them, picked up a phone to call the chief and muttered, "Vances are here."

Chief Bland appeared from an inner office. "I'm sure sorry, folks, but we have a procedure we've got to go by." Then two officers took Rhetta and Laurence into separate rooms. When they were gone, Bland turned to Colin.

"How're y'all doing? Is anybody bothering you?"

"Bothering us?" Colin didn't understand.

"You know, this is the kind of crime that can't happen here. Not in Piedmont. People can get ugly when they're scared."

"And you think people will assume the worst."

"I already got calls from it seems like every newspaper in the state. And the mayor and every preacher in town and the President of the University and I don't know who-all. My own secretary's a single lady who lives alone and she asked me this morning if she ought to get a gun, if there's some homicidal maniac out there." Bland shook his head. "You want to wait in my office?"

"No. I'm fine here."

Colin sat on a bench and waited, as he had many times waited for clients. Laurence came out first and Colin stood up to meet him. "Are you okay?"

Laurence's eyes were red-rimmed. "I have to go to the funeral home."

"Rhetta will want to go with you." Colin glanced toward the door of the interview room she was in.

"I can just about deal with myself and the decisions I have to make. I don't have the energy for Rhetta." Laurence stuffed his hands in his jacket pockets and walked away, alone.

Rhetta said little until they got home, then the words came out as if she could no longer withhold them. "He shouldn't have to do this by himself. You should have stopped him." She covered her nose and mouth with her hands so that Colin saw only her eyes and the dark circles under them.

"It's his choice, sweetheart. It's how he wants to be right now." Colin put his arms around her.

"You don't know how he feels. You don't understand him the way I do."

"That's true. You know him best."

"And you're patronizing me." She broke away.

"Rhetta, I'm not. Look ..." He reached for her again. "We're together, you and I. And the girls. Laurence needs us to hang together."

But whatever it was in the Vance character that made Laurence want to be alone was in Rhetta, too, and she stayed just out of reach.

"I've got to get the girls ready to go to church," she said. "They have to be there early."

"Church? Why?"

"It's the Christmas pageant. Have you forgotten?"

He felt like a kid at the end of a crack-the-whip game, not knowing which way he'd be pulled next. "Do you think the girls will want to do this? No one would expect it, under the circumstances."

"We keep our commitments." She was half way up the back stairs, calling her daughters as she went.

Not even Eden's voice reading the passage about shepherds guarding their flocks by night held Colin's attention. As happened every year, the younger children, including Wren who was dressed as a lamb, stumbled and rambled about the stage before they knelt by the manger.

Colin shifted in his seat and glanced at Rhetta. Her gaze was on the front of the church and anyone else who saw her would think she was spellbound by the ancient story being reenacted. She didn't even flinch when a wise man kicked Wren and she shoved back.

Her mind is with Laurence, Colin thought, a million miles away. He found himself thinking about Sheila as he had last seen her—lying on her living room floor, her face turned away from him, her pink pajamas wrenched in disorder, a flannel robe half-stripped off but draped over her pregnant belly, and her bare foot waxy white.

The congregation rose to sing the last hymn, "O Come All Ye Faithful," but Colin stayed in his place for a moment, riveted by the memory of Sheila's foot. His eyes filled, and he realized that

Rhetta hadn't stood, either. He turned to her and she looked back, her own eyes dry and distant.

The pageant was over. Colin held out Rhetta's coat but instead of sliding her arms through the sleeves, she took it from him.

"We need to go to the party," she said.

The church's multi-purpose room was overheated and all its surfaces were hard, so even subdued voices echoed and its tan walls tended to close in. The ladies of the church had set up a table with cookies and cakes and punch and it was swarmed by children. As soon as Colin and Rhetta walked in, Rhetta was enveloped by friends offering their sympathies for the family's losses and asking questions.

Colin eased away. He made his way to the back of the room where other husbands and fathers gathered. Dave Shipman stepped out of the group and greeted Colin. "Sorry to hear about Laurence's wife." Dave then took his arm and drew him aside. "There's something I need to tell you, Colin."

The two men had never been buddies, just friendly as fathers of children in the same grade, and because Dave was never unfriendly to anyone who had bought or might buy a car from him.

He led Colin to a corner so his back was to the room, to the crowd, to anyone who might look their way. Even before he could ask "what's up?" Dave started talking.

"It's about Jabel Clark. You know he works for me?"

"No." He wondered why Dave thought that, or why it mattered.

"Well, he does. And he trusts me, I guess. Anyway, something's been bothering him and he just told me about it."

Colin was mystified by what Dave was getting at, and at his obvious nervousness.

"Here's the thing." Dave lowered his voice even more. "Jabel says Laurence wanted his wife dead and he said he'd pay somebody to do it."

Colin's knees buckled and his vision pulled to a pinpoint.

"Hey, don't faint, man. People will notice." Dave grabbed his arm.

Colin drew a deep breath and held it until he was sure he'd stay upright. "Okay. Tell me again."

"Jabel came to my office this afternoon. It took him a good twenty minutes to say it. I thought he'd been drinking or something, the way he bobbed and weaved all over the place and finally he came out with it. Said he did some painting for Laurence and his wife a couple of months ago and that's when Laurence asked him."

Colin held his hand up. He didn't want to hear that part again. "What did you tell him?"

"I told him he had to go to the law. And I tried to call the D.A. myself."

"He's out of town for Christmas."

"I found that out. As soon as he's back, Jabel's going to talk to him."

"Do you think Jabel's told anybody else?"

"He says not. He only told me because it's been eating him alive." Dave waved at somebody over Colin's shoulder. "Your wife's coming this way."

⌒

"Mommy." Wren kicked the back of the car seat. "Is Uncle Laurence as sad as Jackie Kennedy?"

"Honey, don't kick," Rhetta said. "Yes, he's as sad as Jackie."

They were in the car, on the way home from the pageant.

"Maybe sadder," Wren said. "She's got Caroline and John-John like you and Daddy have us."

"Uncle Laurence has you girls and Daddy and me. We love him, don't we?"

Colin looked in the rearview mirror to see his daughters. Eden wiped away a tear and leaned her cheek against the car window. The cold glass was probably soothing. He was exhausted, haunted by the deaths of people close and distant, overburdened now by what Dave Shipman had told him.

"Can I ride up there with you?" Wren asked. Colin slowed so she could scramble over the seat and snuggle with her mother. Soon her even breathing let him know she'd fallen asleep.

"Eden? Are you okay?" Colin asked. She didn't answer.

"I think she's asleep, too," Rhetta whispered. Colin doubted it, but he hoped so.

Colin propped himself up in bed and stared at the page of a book. He had forced himself to stay awake because he felt he had to tell her what Jabel said about Laurence.

Rhetta came out of the bathroom in her nightgown. She had brushed out her long, wavy hair. It wasn't stylish, he realized; all of the women at the church seemed to wear theirs in some version of Jackie Kennedy's shorter, puffier hairdo. But he loved it.

"I'm so tired, I don't know if I can sleep." She sat on the edge of the bed.

"Do you want me to braid your hair for you?" He got to his knees and knelt behind her, a little unbalanced on the mattress. Instead of gathering up her hair, he slipped his hands under the flannel gown and massaged her shoulders. She sighed and leaned back against him. He knew this was the moment to tell her about Jabel but his throat constricted.

"Is it terrible of me?" She twisted to face him and kissed him. "I want to make love."

She took the initiative, drawing his hands to her body and he let himself take the coward's way out.

CHRISTMAS EVE 1963

"Young cousin."

Jabel trudged along, bare hands deep in his jacket pockets.

"Young cousin."

It wasn't until the man who called to him leaned on the car horn that Jabel snapped out of the fog of his breath and thoughts.

He turned and looked into the headlights. "Dex? That you?"

"You going home? Get in."

Jabel got in and held his hands to the heat vent.

"My nip bottle's here if you need a little anti-freeze."

"Granny'll get on me." Jabel noticed Dex was chewing gum and grinned. "She won't be fooled by that Doublemint, either."

Dex turned from West Court Street onto Southwest Sugar Street, the entry to Sweet Side.

"Why're you walking?" Dex asked. "Where's that car Mr. Vance let you have?"

"Gas costs money, man. I can walk a couple of miles."

"You are one careful cat, when it comes to your money." Dex shook his head. "You work today?"

"Yeah. Mr. Shipman always has a little Santa Claus for everybody on Christmas Eve."

The pavement ended and Dex slowed down. "I hope Santa was good to you."

"Extra good. That's what I thought when I looked in the envelope. But then after everybody else left, the son of a bitch said he's real sorry but he can't use me anymore. Said Kennedy getting shot slowed business down." He patted the pocket with the envelope that held ten twenty-dollar bills. He knew he'd been fired because of what he had to say about Laurence Vance. This was guilt money.

But even before his boss had finished his phony little speech,

Jabel's mind had run ahead. If Dave Shipman wasn't vouching for him, was he likely to still get those extra jobs painting, window-washing, hauling, driving for folks?

"Damn," Dex said. "That's rough."

"I reckon you want to say, serves me right for trusting a white man."

"No, I don't want to say that." Dex leaned forward as if his car lights weren't enough to navigate the street where Marie Minton lived. Like all the gravel streets in Sweet Side, it was narrow, with no streetlights, lined with small neat houses, bungalows, and shotguns, all decorated with colored lights hanging from the eaves and tinsel draped over bare tree limbs in front yards.

Cars were parked up and down on both sides of the street so Dex had to drive past the house and around a corner to find space. He and Jabel trotted across the side yard and up the steps. The door opened for them and they were pulled in by the greetings of their aunts, Dex's mother, girl cousins, and the small children.

"Merry Christmas, where you boys been?"

"Give me that coat, you need something to eat?"

"Jabel, will you play with me?"

"Dex, you bring your guitar?"

"Where's Granny?" Jabel said. He made sure he held onto the envelope when his coat was pulled off.

"Kitchen. Where else? And she won't let anybody but Marcus in there."

"Uncle Marcus is here?" Despite the warning, Jabel eased through the kitchen door.

Marcus greeted Jabel with a nod of his head and a grin. "Hey there, young fellow." He had both hands in a bowl of dough.

"Hey, Uncle." Jabel patted his back. "When did you get here?"

"In time to make himself useful." Granny turned off the heat under a pot and wiped her hands on the towel pinned to her apron. "If he's here, nobody else bothers me."

"I drive straight through from New Jersey and the woman puts me right to work." Marcus turned the dough out on a floured board and worked it with a light touch.

Jabel smiled and nodded. If there was anybody who came close to the spot he himself held in Granny's heart, it was her brother, Marcus.

"I won't get in the way," Jabel said. "I got something for your kitty, Granny."

Their unspoken agreement was that he gave her half of what he earned and he'd meant to count out five of the twenties for the lard bucket she kept her money in. Instead, on impulse, he stuffed the whole envelope in and kissed her on the cheek before he left the steamy, fat-scented kitchen.

He worked his way through the living room, around the dense cedar tree the kids had hung paper chains and glass balls on, to the back bedroom that was his. This is where he found the grown men: Dex, Dex's father Raymond, other cousins and in-laws, a dozen in all. They sat on the bed, on chairs they'd brought in from the dining room, and on the floor. When the door opened, they froze mid-sentence, the whiskey bottle suspended in air until they knew they were safe from a female invasion. It was understood, as long as they kept it out of sight and nobody got rowdy, Marie would overlook their cheer this once a year.

"Y'all might have saved me a spot," Jabel said.

"We're organizing a boycott," Raymond said. "Be buying Fords and Chevys next year."

"You told them, Dex?" Jabel closed the door and leaned against it.

Fred Franklin, married to Cousin Louise, reached for the bottle that had stopped with Raymond. "There's a story going around the courthouse."

Everybody paid attention when Fred told his rumors. His repair shop was a portal to what the white folks were talking about.

"What're you hearing, Fred?" somebody prompted.

"That white lady who got killed? Married to the Vance man? The story is, there's a black boy saying he did it, the husband did it."

There was a long inhale, then silence. Jabel reached behind his back with both hands and gripped the doorknob. He knew without raising his head that all the men looked at him.

"Anybody who'd tell that, especially when it's against a Vance, things could go bad for him," Fred said.

"He ought to have come to us before he ever opened his mouth," Raymond said.

Jabel sighed. It was scary, how word traveled. He'd been wrong to trust Mr. Dave at all.

"I'm the one who's got to live with it, knowing it," he said. "And I thought about it. Y'all would be surprised, how hard I thought about it." His neck straightened with a jolt of anger. "Let me ask you this, if not but two people know, me and Mr. Laurence Vance, how is that good for me?"

Somebody tapped on the door and he jumped. A bossy little girl's voice said, "Granny says y'all come on. The Reverend just got here."

Jabel stood aside and the men went past him until only Dex remained. Dex gripped his biceps and whispered, "You'll be all right. We got you."

Reverend Archibald Jones said grace and then took up a station where he could bless everybody as they came around with a loaded plate in one hand and a glass of tea in the other. Dex and Jabel were the last of the men and Dex stepped in close to whisper.

"Arch," he said. "We still meeting tonight?"

It surprised Jabel to hear the Reverend called by a nickname and it surprised him that Dex was interested in a church meeting.

The preacher nodded and Dex said, "I'm bringing this one with me." He meant Jabel.

"Jabel, you come sit with me." Cousin Louise called to him while he stood in the middle of the room, pondering what Dex had in mind for him. She led the way to a bench just long enough for both of them to fit side by side.

"Marie says you're doing fine, working hard," she said. "But what I want to know is, when are you going to get yourself back to school?"

"I'm still thinking about it, Louise."

"You know the family would help you," Louise said. "And we'd take good care of Marie if you went someplace like Morehouse or Howard."

He had to laugh. "Even if … it's not going to be someplace like that."

"Don't you sell yourself short." She took up one of Marcus's biscuits and used it to push butterbeans onto her fork. "You'd be an example to the younger ones, like my Janelle."

Jabel ate his ham, sweet potatoes, green beans, baked apples, scalloped tomatoes, while she talked about her little girl.

Then he made his escape. "I think I'll look for some seconds, Louise. Can I bring you something?"

He took his refilled plate and went to join the younger boy cousins where they sat together on the floor in a corner. They were a little in awe of him, he knew, and wanted to take turns trying to impress him. All he had to do to make them happy was laugh and shake his head at the bragging and ribbing. It was a relief.

The table was cleared to make room for pies and cakes and cookies. Then somebody started singing "Silent Night, Holy Night" and everybody joined in. They went on to every Christmas carol anybody knew, until Dex stood and started, "We shall not be moved …" He sang a verse alone, then another voice took up, "Jesus is my savior, I shall not be moved." Then there was silence. Marie didn't like politics in her house and this song was where politics bumped up against church, where people who wanted everything to stay the same bumped up against those who wanted everything to change and fast.

Somebody noticed it was ten o'clock, time for mothers to take their babies home, time for wives to corral their husbands, time for young people to slip out.

Granny caught Dex and Jabel. "You boys make yourselves useful. Move these chairs back where they came from."

They moved the chairs and took the leaves out of the table and gathered up the glasses that somehow got left on the windowsill behind the drapes. Three women in the kitchen washed dishes and laughed at Marcus's jokes.

"Are we done now, Aunt Marie?" Dex kissed her. "There's a meeting at the church."

"And you think you're taking my baby with you?" She poked Dex in the chest with her forefinger.

"The Reverend's expecting us. And don't worry about Jabel. We don't pressure anybody into anything. If he doesn't want to be there, all he's got to do is leave."

"You want me to believe that?" She looked into Jabel's eyes. "Don't let anybody or anything push you, honey."

"It'll be all right, Granny." Jabel hugged her. Then he put on his coat and followed Dex out.

They walked to Dex's car and Dex stopped him. "I'll drive. You walk."

"Man, it's cold out here."

"It's not but two blocks. You don't want to get there with me, in case somebody's watching. Just go in the front door of the church like a man needing to pray. Take a seat and Arch'll come get you in a few minutes."

Jabel walked fast, wishing he'd picked up gloves and a cap. Why was he going with Dex anyway? Whatever Dex and Reverend Jones had in mind, it wasn't half as scary as telling Granny what he had to tell her when he got home tonight.

Jabel knew Granny heard him come in the back door but she didn't change her posture. She sat at her kitchen table, sewing in the circle of light cast by the bulb over her head.

"Come talk with me a few minutes." She put down the fabric and folded her hands on top of it, almost as in prayer.

"Yes, ma'am." He sat. She looked at him with the glinting green eyes he knew he had inherited. He waited, but she waited longer and he began to speak.

He told her how kind Miss Sheila had been, how it seemed like she loved Mr. Laurence a lot, and then he told her what he'd told Dave Shipman.

Marie drew a deep breath and exhaled long and slow. Jabel looked at her and she closed her eyes. "Laurence gave you that car. And I looked in the envelope you brought home tonight," she said. "Two hundred dollars."

"That was from Mr. Dave." And he went on to tell her about being fired. "I guess I should have known, a white man's not going to side with me against another white man."

She clutched her elbows, curled her shoulders inward and bowed her head. "What a grief, what a grief."

She'd as good as raised Laurence and Rhetta. "I had to neglect my own to take care of them many a time," was how she remembered it and Jabel knew she thought of her own daughter, his mother, who had turned out wild and bitter and then dead.

"You're sure, now?" She looked up at him. "You didn't mistake what he said?" Then she lowered her head again. It had to hurt her to think any child she'd put herself into could be a killer.

Marie so seldom needed comfort, Jabel was unsure how to give it. Finally, he moved off his chair and knelt beside her, put his arms around her and whispered how sorry he was.

She raised her head and looked him in the eye. "You're doing right, Jabel. You've got to tell the truth and stick to it. Even if it's Laurence you're speaking against."

Somehow, as they sat together and mourned, one thing became clear to him: he had to do the right thing. About Laurence. And about the world. He would join Dex and Archibald Jones and the others who protested, sat in, and boycotted. He'd do it for the little cousins. And he would come out of both things being the man he was supposed to be. Sitting there while the clock struck midnight, he could not begin to imagine who that man was.

DECEMBER 27, 1963

District Attorney Boyd Sparks was due back in his office so Colin left home early, wanting to catch him before he got busy. But as he opened the door of the courthouse, two people came out of the elevator—Marie Minton and Jabel Clark.

Colin held the door for them to file out. Marie gave him a hard look and a brief nod when he said good morning. Jabel stood aside and insisted that Colin enter. He looked Colin in the eye and murmured, "Happy New Year, Mr. Colin."

Boyd greeted Colin as if he'd expected him. "I'm sure sorry for your family's loss, Colin. Two losses, I should say."

The D.A. was older than Colin by fifteen or twenty years. Colin respected him for the straightforward way he went about his business, even as he knew he'd seize any advantage he could.

"Do you know what Jabel Clark came here to tell me this morning?" Boyd looked weary.

"I've heard something about it," Colin said. "Word gets around."

"And you're here on Laurence's behalf."

"I don't think it'll be complicated," Colin said. "Laurence and Rhetta were together all day on the seventeenth, shopping in Raleigh, and there are people who'll be able to confirm it."

Boyd sat up straighter. "What would you have said if you'd gotten here before Jabel Clark did this morning?"

There was no point in avoiding the obvious. "It'll be Jabel's word against Laurence's. And my wife's."

"It goes beyond alibis for the time of the murder." Boyd looked at him, unblinking, his eyes narrow. "You need to ask your client what else Jabel might have to say, besides this business about murder for pay."

Then he reached into a desk drawer and pulled out a manila folder. "Have you seen the statements Rhetta and Laurence gave the police?"

"No." Colin leaned forward. Boyd took two sets of paper-clipped pages out of the folder and laid them side by side, turned so that Colin could read them.

Laurence's statement began, "My wife did not feel well that morning, so I left her with breakfast in bed. I took my coffee out to the front porch to wait for my sister. We had only one car at the time and I wanted to leave mine for Sheila ..." Colin scanned the rest of the page, then began reading again. "After we left the jewelry store, I asked to borrow my sister's car, telling her that I needed to drive some distance to finish my shopping. We agreed we would meet for lunch at 12:30. I drove to a city park and found a bench where I could sit and rest. It was a cold day, few people out, and I needed to be alone for a while. I may even have fallen asleep. Suddenly I realized I was going to be late. I drove back to Peterson's and bought an opal necklace I had seen earlier, as a gift for my sister. Then I went to the restaurant. I think I got there at about 12:45."

Colin was puzzled. Rhetta had told him they were together all day. He reached for her statement. It began, "Left home, 8:30 a.m. Reached Laurence's house, 8:50 a.m. Did not go in. We drove to Raleigh. Reached Peterson's Fine Jewelry as the door opened, 10:00 a.m. Stayed there until 11:00 a.m. Purchased necklace, ring, china tea set. Laurence purchased diamond earrings." Colin scanned the rest and saw that every minute was accounted for, stores they had been to, people they had spoken to, where they had lunch—all there. Then, "3:15 p.m., returned to Laurence's house. He invited me in. Front door was ajar. Laurence pushed it open and we saw Sheila lying on the living room floor. Laurence ran to her and I went into the kitchen to call the police."

Colin's ears rang. Rhetta had lied. To the police, to him.

Boyd was watching his face and he tried to control it.

"It's pretty obvious who's telling the truth and who isn't. I'll give her a chance to correct it," Boyd said. "And, Colin, Laurence needs to know, given the race problems around here, I can't just take his word. I've got to go wherever this thing leads."

Colin left Boyd's office and started to walk home. He ought to have gone to the office but seeing Rhetta couldn't wait. Normally, the two-mile walk was his buffer between work and family, but that morning, it only gave him time for confusion and puzzlement to build to anger.

Rhetta and Laurence sat at the kitchen work table with coffee cups.

"Colin, I thought you'd be at the office all day," she said.

"What the hell were you thinking?" Colin threw the copies of their statements down between them. Rhetta looked up at him, bewildered, and it made him madder. "You know what I mean," he said. "Or didn't Laurence go along with your plan?"

It was Laurence who gathered up the pages. "I didn't, no."

"What?" Rhetta asked. "What are you two talking about?"

"I told the truth in my statement," Laurence said. "I wrote that we were separated that day."

"But we had it all worked out …" She stopped and put a hand over her mouth for a moment. "It doesn't matter, does it? You can explain …"

"Rhetta. It matters." Colin slammed his hand on the table. "You perjured yourself. Be glad he had the good sense to tell the truth or your little plot could have gotten me disbarred. And now, your lie along with Jabel's story …" He stopped, aware that they didn't know Jabel's story yet. He saw the question on Rhetta's lips and answered it. "Jabel is telling people that Laurence wanted Sheila dead."

Rhetta turned to look at her brother, who closed his eyes and shook his head. Colin read pain in his face.

"You both need to understand," Colin said. "With Jabel's statement and no alibi, it pretty well guarantees that Laurence is going to be charged with murder."

"That can't be," Rhetta said. "That's impossible. Let me get you a cup of coffee and we'll talk about this." The effort it took her to stay calm showed in her wobbly voice and the way she held to the chair back before she moved toward the counter.

"Is she going to be in trouble?" Laurence asked, as if Rhetta had left the room.

"Boyd's allowing her to correct the statement, but he'll be able to use it at trial."

"She did it for me. I should have told her not to, but I wasn't able to think clearly. Nothing was making sense ... It still doesn't."

Rhetta set a cup of coffee on the table for Colin. He sat and pulled it toward him, though he didn't want it. The anger was settling in like the first stages of the flu.

"A man's twin sister isn't the best alibi witness to begin with, and you sat on a park bench for almost two hours? How the hell is that going to sound to a jury?"

"It's still Laurence's word against some black boy's." Rhetta's voice showed she was recovering. She stood so that Colin had to look up at her. "Who's going to believe him?" She loaded the word with contempt, as if it were a curse.

"Don't." Laurence reached for her wrist.

She jerked away and said to Colin, "That is how you'll defend Laurence, isn't it? You'll make Jabel look like a worthless liar. You'll get a jury of rednecks from out in the county who'll want to lynch him." She stalked out of the kitchen and went upstairs.

The two men sat quiet. Colin's head ached and he hated the truth Rhetta had told.

"When are they going to arrest me?" Laurence's voice was an embarrassed whisper.

Colin nodded. "I'm guessing it will take Boyd a few days to get his ducks in a row. He'll give you a chance to come in voluntarily." He paused, then went on. "Boyd hinted that Jabel told him something else. Some second accusation. Do you know what he meant?"

His brother-in-law looked at him almost the same way Boyd had, as if trying to read something in Colin that Colin himself was ignorant of.

Then Laurence closed his eyes and let his shoulders collapse. "Have you ever advised a client to kill himself?"

"Laurence …"

"I won't. I don't see why I shouldn't, but I won't." He folded forward and rested his head on the table. "God help me, I just want to live a real life."

DECEMBER 30, 1963

Colin had spent only a few hours in his office since Sheila's death, so even with the holiday lull, mail and telephone messages had stacked up. He had begun to sort out his desk and pull his thoughts back into order when his secretary knocked.

"Mr. Laurence Vance is here to see you," she said.

Colin sighed and wondered if it was too late to convince Rhetta that her brother should have other counsel.

"So sorry, Colin," Laurence said. "I know you've given a lot of time to my circumstances already."

"It's all right." He nodded toward the client's chair and Laurence sat.

"I'm trying to be honest. Trying." He swallowed audibly. "When you asked me what else Jabel could say about me, I should have answered your question differently. But I didn't want to hurt Rhetta more."

Colin snapped the top on his fountain pen and let Laurence wait a moment. "If you're worried about what I tell her, don't be. I'll keep your confidences as I would any client's."

"I know that. Has she mentioned Sheila's car?"

"No. What about it?"

"We gave it to Jabel Clark."

Colin sat up straight. "Did you?"

"It was Sheila's idea. Her car was old and I wanted to get her another one anyway. She didn't want me to. It was her independent streak, but when she found out Jabel didn't have a car, she said she'd let him have it as payment for painting the baby's room. Two birds, one stone." He held out his hands, palms up, balanced.

"I'm glad you told me," Colin said. "I'll be ready, if it comes up."

"I know it seems like an excessive payment for a small painting job but it seemed he was going to have to put some money into the car, so …"

"It's okay. I can make sense of it." He leaned back. "Rhetta knew?" If so, then this wasn't what Laurence had hidden from her.

"I mentioned it that morning on the way to Raleigh. She's forgotten, I'm sure."

Colin thought of all the whispered conversations and hours the brother and sister had spent together. He doubted Rhetta had forgotten anything.

"But there is something she doesn't know. Has never known." Laurence rubbed his forehead and temples hard with his fingertips. "Colin, you're a wonderful husband. And father. I wanted nothing more than to be as good, half as good, as you. I loved Sheila. I wanted our child more than I've ever wanted anything." He took out a handkerchief and blew his nose. "Do you find that human beings are frail vessels? You must know that more than most, you lawyers."

"I suspend judgment, if that's what you mean."

"You asked me if there was another accusation Jabel could have made. The answer is, yes, there is. I've always had a certain … tendency."

A tendency. Colin heard the mental click as something snapped into place. "Go on."

Laurence looked up and swallowed, but met Colin's eyes. "Jabel can say that I approached him."

"He can say you're a purple giraffe." It was a weak joke and Laurence didn't seem to hear it.

"Here's the truth, Colin. I did not harm Sheila."

Colin leaned across the desk and put his hands on Laurence's forearms. "I believe that." There was no mistaking the gratitude in his brother-in-law's eyes. "You've told me what I need to know. From now on, don't talk to Boyd or the police unless I'm there."

"Do you think Jabel has already told them?"

"Probably." He sat back. "It's no different from the other accusation. It comes down to believability. Next question—is there anyone else who might come forward and say something like that?"

Laurence laughed a single harsh burst. "Ha. Who would? Nobody would put himself in that position. So to speak."

DECEMBER 31, 1963

Colin didn't like the rose garden in winter. Its dormancy had a sinister quality and the sound of his feet on the gravel paths was harsh.

He found Laurence in the cottage waiting for him. His brother-in-law's well-tailored suit hung loose, and he realized that he hadn't looked at Laurence, really looked at him, in days.

"You have your ring on," Colin said. "There's a chance they'll keep you overnight, and they won't let you keep it."

"But I don't want to take it off." He put his right hand over his left as if to protect the wedding ring.

Colin sighed. "I won't be the one to deprive you of it then, but you've been warned." He managed a smile.

They reached Colin's car, parked in front of the house, and found Rhetta there. She and Colin had argued, she wanting to go with them, he insisting she shouldn't. He thought he'd won. She'd been contrite in deed if not word after they fought about the lies in her statement.

"Rhetta." Laurence stepped forward. "Please don't. I don't want you to see me in these circumstances."

"Unless one of you is prepared to tie me to a tree, I'm going." She pushed by and got into the front passenger's seat.

They rode without speaking until they reached the town limits. Then Rhetta asked, "We'll be able to bring him home, won't we?"

"Boyd Sparks promised to try and have a judge available to bond him out, but it is New Year's Eve." They came to the intersection with Court Street and Colin turned right, then had to brake. Two parked police cars blocked the way. Beyond the cars, several hundred people filled the street and part of the square. They were sitting down, right up to the base of the courthouse's granite steps, where a dozen or more policemen stood shoulder to shoulder.

"A sit-in?" Laurence asked.

"For God's sake." Rhetta sounded disgusted. "What a stupid thing to do."

It pained Colin to know his wife was one of the mystified white people who couldn't see that a black alderman and a black school board member were insufficient to maintain Piedmont's moral superiority.

He made a U-turn, parked on the side street and led his charges around to approach the courthouse from the back, to a dingy little door used by lawyers and judges and janitors. That morning, a police officer sat in a folding chair in front of it. He stood up as they approached.

"Officer" Colin said. "What's going on?"

"Morning, Mr. Phillips. You didn't hear? We had to arrest a couple dozen people last night. They still want Little Dixie integrated before this old year runs out and they pulled another sit-in there."

"How bad did it get?"

"Some of the ones we arrested are still at the hospital. Could have been a hell of a lot worse. Excuse my language, ma'am." He nodded to Rhetta. "Now, how can I help you folks?"

"Mr. Sparks is expecting us," Colin said.

"You can come in, Mr. Phillips, but I got orders to keep civilians out today."

"This is my brother-in-law, Laurence Vance, and my wife. It's Mr. Vance who Mr. Sparks needs to see."

The officer sputtered an apology, said he'd been up most of the night, and opened the door for them.

As they went into the narrow hallway, Laurence said, "As a wife-murderer, I expected a warmer welcome."

"No." Colin turned on him and jabbed at him with a forefinger. "No more of that. No irony. No sarcasm. No self-pity. It'll all be taken as an admission. A spontaneous utterance showing consciousness of guilt." He wished again that he hadn't agreed to do this.

Laurence took a step back and nodded. "What would I do without you, Colin?"

"Ask your sister."

The long narrow hallway ended behind a door that opened into the spacious two-story lobby with its brass chandeliers and marble floor. The high arched windows looked out over the square where the demonstrators sat. They were dressed for warmth, some sitting in lawn chairs, some on blankets or rugs on the ground. There were a few white people scattered through the crowd, but most of the faces were young and black. Colin had heard the rumors that janitors and housepainters and nursing home workers were afraid they'd be fired if they took part in any demonstrations. Whether the younger people were braver or felt they had less to lose, he didn't know. Then he saw one person who surprised him. Marie Minton sat right up front, staring up at the higher floors of the building.

"What is this supposed to accomplish?" Rhetta turned away, apparently without seeing Marie.

"I admire them," Laurence said. "I wish I could join them."

Rhetta had the elevator door opened for them. When they got to the third floor, Boyd Sparks and Chief Bland stood in the hallway, outside the D.A.'s office, talking. Boyd saw them first.

"You're here," he said. "Come on in."

There were no smiles, no greetings, and once they were in the office, Rhetta stood between Laurence and Colin and held their hands. The chief went through the formalities of telling Laurence what he was charged with. "I'm going to take you upstairs for processing. Mrs. Phillips, you'll be a lot more comfortable here. All right with you, Boyd, if the lady waits in your office?"

It was clear the chief didn't want her and she didn't argue.

"Boyd, the judge?" Colin asked.

"It's been wild around here today." Boyd grabbed his suit coat off the back of his chair. "You go with your client and I'll go find the judge. I'll be up as soon as I can get there."

On any day, the police department's reception area, if it deserved that designation of graciousness, was crowded and noisy. Telephones and radios blared at full volume and voices spiraled upward, competing to be heard.

Colin saw right away that this was not just any day. The crowd and the noise were twice normal and beside him, Laurence hesitated at stepping into the chaos. The chief walked in ahead of them and the din stopped for a moment as if everybody had drawn a breath at the same time. Then they let it out and resumed their din.

Chief Bland yelled at people to get out of his way and gestured for Laurence to go into the room where he would be fingerprinted and photographed.

Clyde Raeburn pushed through to Colin's side and put an arm around his shoulder. "I've been trying to call you but nobody's answering your phone."

"Laurence is being arraigned today."

"No kidding? God, I hadn't heard."

"You're slipping, Clyde."

"There's more to life than the Vance family. I've been here since midnight, trying to get these folks out of jail."

Someone opened the steel door that separated the cellblock from this public room. In the seconds that the door gaped open, Colin saw that the cells were packed and that men sat on the floor outside of them, their wrists handcuffed to the bars. One of them looked familiar but before he could get a good look, the door closed again.

Chief Bland came back, alone.

"You've got men in there who ought to be in the hospital," Clyde said to him.

"You know they were treated and released to custody."

"What galls me is, the ones who ought to be locked up are the white trash from Little Dixie. Klan, every one of them," Clyde said.

"Don't use that word in here, Clyde. I won't have race-baiting on either side."

The steel door opened again and Colin took a deliberate look for as long as he could. Yes, he recognized one of the young black men.

Just then, Laurence reappeared, jacketless, in handcuffs and with an officer on each arm. Boyd Sparks shoehorned himself into the room and handed a piece of paper to Chief Bland.

"Here you go. Mr. Vance is released on his attorney's recognizance."

"Right." The chief showed no surprise. He unlocked the handcuffs himself and Laurence had the presence of mind to ask where his suit coat was.

"God damn it," Clyde exploded. "We're told no hearings till day after tomorrow for this pissant misdemeanor trespass and the Vances waltz in and waltz out on murder."

Bland's face turned red and his lips looked as if they might not be up to the task of containing words. Then he turned and stalked off.

"Clyde, you're not helping yourself," Boyd Sparks said. "I've got to get back to the office."

Clyde turned to Colin again. "You know I'm counting on you. Help me out."

"I'm sorry. I can't." It hurt Colin to let Clyde think him a son of a bitch, but he had no choice. The person he'd recognized in lock-up was Jabel Clark, and it wasn't the time to explain the conflict of interest.

Jabel's hips hurt. His shoulders and back felt like somebody had pumped cement down his spine.

"A baby in his mama's belly has more room to move than this," Dex said. They were wedged side-by-side on the floor of the jail, their right hands shackled to the bars of the cell doors. The men who'd been arrested with them filled the cells and the aisles between them, jammed together so it took a dance of sorts to allow a few at a time to stretch their legs.

For a while, once the jailers got them packed in, they'd been rowdy, singing, yelling, still het up from the violence and fear and ugliness of the night. Then their lawyer, Clyde Raeburn, had come in. "Please, y'all take it easy. I'm doing my best and I need you to help me out. If y'all quiet down, I think Chief Bland will uncuff you and let me get some food and clothes in here."

"How long?" somebody yelled. That was Jabel's question too: how long were they going to be held?

"First hearing on Thursday. I hope."

Nobody had a watch and there were no windows. We won't know when daylight comes, Jabel thought. He stretched his neck and tried to loosen it.

"You sorry you got into this mess?" Dex asked.

"You don't hear me complaining, do you? I'm just thinking, time doesn't matter a bit in here."

"What does matter?" Dex sounded amused. Jabel knew his cousin and the other men in the jail were way ahead of him in thinking all this through.

"Getting out so we can go do it again and come right back here," Jabel said.

Dex laughed and called out, "Y'all hear my young cousin? He thinks he's riding a merry-go-round."

"Amen," somebody yelled.

"And the white man's still driving it." Another voice.

The door opened again and Chief Bland came in, flanked by two deputies. Behind them, Reverend Archibald Jones. The men on the floor pulled their legs in tight to make room. The place got as quiet as church when the last notes of the organ fade away.

"Here's the deal," the chief said. "We're going to let you move around as long you're quiet and orderly. Where's Dex Long?"

"Here."

"On the Reverend's say-so, I'm making you the leader of this group. That means, if we have to come in here, you're the one we're coming for. All right?"

"Suits me, Chief."

One of the deputies unlocked the handcuff around Dex's wrist and he stood up, slow.

Reverend Jones spoke. "The chief has agreed to let the ladies of the church send up food and everybody's family can put together a bag of clothes. And I want to remind all of y'all, our mission is to work for change through peace and non-violence."

All the men were freed from their cuffs and the cell doors opened, but nobody moved until the reverend and the chief and the deputies were gone, the steel door locked behind them. Then Dex took over and made sure the ones who most needed a cot had one, that everybody was cool and knew to stay that way.

Jabel stood up and almost fell because his legs were rubbery from hours on the floor. For a moment, the pins and needles pain of blood flowing back into them was unbearable. He wasn't alone. Men around him yelped, even those who'd been silent under the blows of broom handles and bar stools. He guessed the next few days and nights were going to be tedious and uncomfortable but not as fearful as the evening he'd just come through.

He had not been told much, just to drive his car, the one the Vances had given him, to the church at six o'clock. Then three other men, two of them white, got in and he fell into a procession of five other cars going he knew not where. It turned out the two white men were both professors at Mangum University and the third man, a black man Jabel knew by sight but not otherwise, talked to them about their families and Christmas like they were just old friends catching up on the news. All Jabel could do was perspire and follow the tail lights of the car in front of him.

The procession headed south out of town and Jabel looked at his odometer. They drove four miles and he figured he knew where they were headed. Sure enough, the lead car turned off the road into a parking lot and the others followed. They were at Little Dixie.

"You want to park where it's dark," a passenger told Jabel.

But it's all dark, Jabel thought. The parking lot wasn't lit but he could see a few cars clumped together at the far end of the building. He wondered, shouldn't he park close to the door so they could get away fast? Then he remembered the point was to get arrested. He just followed the drivers ahead of him. It did mean that of all the cars, his was the one nearest the long, low building with neon beer signs.

"Here." The black man handed Jabel a jar of Vaseline. "Smear this on your face and your eyelids and up your nose. Last time we were here, they dumped ammonia on us. You don't want it in your eyes. You don't want to breathe it. You got a handkerchief? Tie it over your nose if you can."

While he waited for the jar to come to him, Jabel held tight to the steering wheel. He'd driven by Little Dixie often enough on Sunday drives. When he was a boy, someone had told him that the Klan lived there and if they saw a little black child's face, they'd never forget it and they'd come for him and cook him in a stew.

Now he knew it was just half a country grocery store with gas pumps and half a road house with pool tables where rednecks spent weekend nights drinking and fighting. As for the Klan, that part was probably true, he thought.

When he had smeared his face, he got out of the car and joined the group that gathered around the lead car, the one Dex had driven. Somebody offered up a prayer and then the twenty-four of them walked in a rough line of twos and threes to the front door. Everybody else seemed serene and immune to the stomach cramps that made Jabel hope to God he didn't lose his bowels.

Somebody spoke to Jabel and jolted him back into the moment, into the jail. "Man, I'm sorry about your car." It was the black man who'd ridden with him.

"I didn't see it. How bad was it?" Jabel asked him.

"I'd say when that cracker saw he wasn't going to get to kill him a nigger, he decided to kill your car instead."

"I was going to sell it anyway," Jabel said. It was true. He'd come to hate the car.

"Yeah? Well, it'll be for scrap now." The man began to make his way to the back again and Jabel heard somebody starting to snore.

His thoughts went back to Little Dixie. There had been fewer people in the bar than Jabel had expected, maybe half as many of them as there were demonstrators. He remembered seeing a couple of women in a booth. Men played pool. A man came out from behind the bar, cursing them and Dex spoke to him. "We hope you'll serve us tonight, Mr. Shinn."

"You know goddamn well I won't. You stupid coons ..." A string of curses followed and the man grabbed hold of Dex and punched him in the stomach. That was the signal for two things to happen: all the demonstrators sat down right where they were and hugged their knees to their chests; the white men and women all stood over them, screaming and yelling the foulest words Jabel had ever heard. Jabel ducked his head as low as he could, his heart coming out of his chest. The first kick to his lower back made him gasp and the second one knocked him over.

It seemed to go on for a long time but had probably been only minutes, and then over the din he heard sirens. The rescue for the demonstrators was arrest, but they made the cops work. They went limp and got half-dragged, half-carried out of the building. The mob followed them out, one of the women shrieking in Jabel's ear. He felt a wet glob hit his forehead. He looked up and the deputy who held him by the shoulders looked at him with such hatred, he couldn't be sure who it was who'd spit on him.

Now, at the jail, Jabel began to figure things out. Few of the demonstrators had known in advance where they were going or even when. Like him, they'd gotten word just a couple of hours ahead of time. Yet it had been well planned, right down to when the police would be notified so that they would be there before the worst could happen. Or so it was hoped. Jabel was sure there were guns in Little Dixie and in the cars and trucks outside. Maybe, he thought, those white people didn't actually mean to kill. Or maybe their hatred was so strong they'd rather do it with their hands and feet, as close and personal as possible.

NEW YEAR'S DAY 1964

Laurence woke early, unpacked another box of books, sorted out the shirts that Rhetta had stuffed into a suitcase when she packed up his things, and tried to create a sense of order in the living room of the cottage, working as long as he could until the need for coffee began to pound in his temple.

He had gone to Maryland for Sheila's burial. He stayed with her family a few days. They seemed to regard him as an alien being, but grief held them together that long. Then he had gone to New York where he saw no one he knew, and could breathe more freely until Christmas came and went. After that, home to be arrested and released.

He walked through the garden and into the sunroom. Wren was there alone, poking at a bowl of cereal with her spoon, her hair unbrushed, her face still creased from her pillow. He kissed the top of her head and went to the kitchen.

Rhetta, being Rhetta, already had the day's cooking underway. It would be hopping John, greens, and a pork roast. A dozen people would come for dinner, as usual, and neither Laurence nor Colin could talk her out of it.

She was rubbing the roast with seasonings. "I'll make fresh coffee as soon as I get this in the oven," she said.

He picked up the percolator and shook it. "This will do. It's still hot."

She left the roast where it was and crossed to the sink. "Can't you wait a few minutes?"

"Sister, this will do. I don't care."

"I care." She soaped then rinsed her hands, dried them on a dishtowel, and took the pot from him. "And you should, too. You can't let this drag you down."

He didn't answer, didn't want to argue. The collards began

to boil, their earthy, bitter smell taking over the air in the room. Folding money, he remembered Marie Minton used to say when she occupied the kitchen. Eat your greens for folding money.

Laurence let Rhetta make fresh coffee but insisted he didn't want anything to eat. As soon as he could, he slipped out and went to his car.

The street where he and Sheila had lived was quiet. Christmas lights someone had forgotten to turn off outlined the eaves of one house, wan in the daylight. Santa and his reindeer listed and verged on collapse in the neighbor's yard. Laurence had not been there since the seventeenth of December, since he had opened the door on Sheila where she lay. He parked in front of the house and took deep breaths. Sheila was a person others were drawn to because of her nature, sweet and quiet. In fact, he had not quite realized how pretty she was until he'd known her for months because he was so drawn to that quiet core. And as they'd grown closer, they'd discovered each other's well of loneliness. They'd both expected to live singly and it wasn't until she was stricken with morning sickness that either of them realized they could share what other people called love and maybe, just maybe, happiness.

And people thought he killed her.

He owed it to her to see to her house, so there he was, on the front porch, key in the lock, and then inside. With his things gone, the place was Sheila's again. She'd never have tolerated the disarray left by police and the coroner and whomever else had invaded.

He would sell the house and send the proceeds to her parents. He intended to send them something more than that, to take care of them in some way because it seemed to be what Sheila would want.

The furnace rumbled. There had been no one to turn it off. He hung his coat on the front closet doorknob and began to tidy. The afghan knitted by Sheila's mother, the one she liked to wrap

up in, was crumpled on the floor. He lifted it and folded it over
the back of the couch. Something caught his eye and he stooped
to see. A newspaper, rolled and held with a rubber band, was
between the couch and the end table. He pulled it out, loosened
it, glanced at the date and stopped, stunned by a recollection.

The paper was from December seventeenth. He'd waited for
Rhetta outside that morning because Sheila wanted to sleep.
He'd had a cup of coffee while he waited and had left the cup
and the newspaper propped against the porch wall.

He looked around—throw pillows out of place, a dead house-
plant, desk chair turned upside down on top of the desk, no cup.
He went to the kitchen and there it was, in the dish drainer.

No one but Sheila would have washed it and left it there.

"Where've you been?" Rhetta asked, "You and Colin need to
put the leaves in the table."

"Where is Colin? I need to talk to him."

"In his study. Why?"

Laurence tapped on the closed study door.

"Come in," Colin said.

"It's me."

"Thank goodness. Rhetta's on a bit of a war path."

"I could tell." Laurence saw relief on his brother-in-law's face.
"Listen, would you consider offering me a drink at this hour?"

"I'd like one myself." Colin capped his pen and pulled open
the desk drawer where he kept a bottle and a highball glass. He
gave the glass to Laurence and poured his own two-finger measure in his empty coffee cup.

Laurence took the heavy tumbler from him and held it in
both hands. He paced, so sure of what he'd come to say, he was
afraid to say it, afraid its truth would fade when spoken.

"I went to Sheila's house this morning. And I found something, Colin." He explained the cup and the newspaper and how

they proved that Sheila was alive when he left; only she would have taken them inside. Only she would have washed the cup.

"I understand your point," Colin said, "but it's subtle. And refutable."

"It is?"

"Think of it from Boyd Sparks's point of view. You can't prove that the cup in the drainer is the one you used."

"It's from that china set of Mother's, white with a blue border and gold rim. Rhetta never liked it so she put it in the cottage when I moved in. I took it to Sheila's and I always used one of those cups. Now the whole set's back at the cottage, except that one piece."

"Can anybody verify that you used that one, that day? And where you left it? And how it got inside?"

"It's possible Rhetta saw me put it down when she drove up." He felt his throat close up. "Listen, if Sheila hadn't taken those things inside, they'd still have been on the porch when Rhetta and I got back. She would have seen them then. So would Chief Bland and the other people who came." He remembered the drink in his hands and took a gulp. Colin stared past him and Laurence knew he was posing more questions to himself and coming up with his own answers.

"I'll do what I can with it," Colin asked. "Have you said anything to Rhetta about it?"

"No."

"Good. Don't. I don't want her tempted to tell another lie."

JANUARY 2, 1964

Jabel knew it was morning when the door opened and some-body called "breakfast." That meant bologna sandwiches and tepid coffee in paper cups. Later in the day, the church ladies provided beef stew or chicken and dumplings that had to be eaten out of paper cups with spoons. Then family members began to show up and deputies took men out for short visits. Jabel was afraid Granny would be the one to come see him but it was Raymond, Dex's father, who brought each of them a paper bag with clean clothes.

Clyde Raeburn came into the cell block, looking like a man who'd had no sleep and no change of clothes himself in days. He called out four names, including Jabel's.

"You're going to get to shower before you go in front of the judge, and he's a stickler, so use some soap. Then put on the cleanest clothes you've got. Dex, you'll have to be their mama and be sure they wash their ears."

"Just don't expect me to scrub their behinds." Everybody laughed, except Clyde.

"You've got no records," he told the four, "so Judge Horton is going to burn you a new one, fine you each one hundred dollars and let you go. It took every ounce of my being to get that done, so I'll personally skin the one that says anything besides yes sir and no sir. Got it?"

"What if I don't want to get out?" one of the men said. "If my brothers got to stay in jail, I'm staying, too."

"Hey, man," Dex said, "we ain't got room for you no more. Get on out of here so the rest of us can spread out."

The judge was a long-faced man with strands of hair slicked in a semi-circle around his dome. He made no effort to keep the look of disgust off his face as he looked down on them. By his order, they remained handcuffed.

"You boys," the judge said, "you've been sadly misled by your elders, your so-called leaders, including the one who's supposed to be a man of God. If any one of you shows up here again in the next twenty-four months, you'll do five years at the work camp and I'll make it my business to have Mr. Raeburn here disbarred because he's vouching for you today."

With that, the handcuffs were removed and they were marched down to the Clerk of Court's office where Raymond Long and Granny stood, waiting to pay Jabel's hundred-dollar fine with five new twenty-dollar bills.

JANUARY 17, 1964

"The burden is on the State." Colin had explained it all to Rhetta before. He was shaving, trying to focus on his face in the mirror rather than Rhetta's, flickering in and out beside his. "Sweetheart, please be still. I don't want to show up with nicks all over my chin."

"But you'll put on some sort of defense." She sat down on the closed toilet lid. "Aren't you worried that Boyd has some sort of bombshell? Otherwise, would he have gone this far?"

"Too much Perry Mason." He rinsed his face and buried it in a towel. The idea of the bombshell came close to his worries.

"I think you need to fight more," she said. "And I know how."

He hung up the towel and went to the bedroom to dress.

She took off the robe she wore over her slip. "Just say it. The boy who's telling the lie is the killer."

Colin didn't answer. He took his dark gray suit out of the closet.

"It's the logical conclusion." Rhetta pulled a gray dress over her head. "Jabel had been to their house. He painted the baby's room. He went back to rob them when he thought nobody was home."

They'd been over it before. He had pointed out to her, nothing was stolen. Laurence and Sheila gave Jabel a car. They'd been kind to him and Jabel was known to be a gentle person.

"Just say it," she said again. She turned her back so that he could zip her dress.

"Let's see how the hearing goes." Colin wondered when she would realize how little he told her, how he always answered her questions by referring to procedure or by saying back to her things she had said to him.

They were ready to go, sober in dress, serious in demeanor.

"We get to go in the front door this time." Laurence felt giddy, as if he were here at the courthouse to hear the judge say that Boyd Sparks had over-reached and that the scion of the Vance family was released, reputation restored, with the Court's apologies. And then he was going to pack what belongings would fit in his car and go far, far away.

He knew his mood was more than ridiculous. It was ludicrous and dangerous. If the judge wore half-moon glasses and peered over them, if a bailiff called "oyez oyez oyez," if somewhere a steel door clanked, he was afraid he'd melt in hysteria.

Judge Horton was on the bench. Laurence sat, head bowed, and listened to the lawyers go through their opening gambits. Then someone spoke Sheila's name and his incipient mania collapsed inside his gut. He swallowed, alarmed to find he was nauseous. He felt Rhetta's presence behind him, behind the barrier that separated the well of the courtroom from two rows of benches, full of people he did not know. He felt their presence, too. He looked to the mural depicting Mangum County's history spread across the wall behind the judge and tried to take a deep breath.

Boyd Sparks stood up. "Your Honor, we have a witness who will testify that Mr. Laurence Vance said he would pay to have Mrs. Sheila Vance killed. Mrs. Vance was then seven months pregnant …"

Laurence felt sorrow rock through him, as if her body was there in front of him again.

Colin was speaking. "Your Honor, we submit that this is not sufficient evidence to support a murder charge. If this one witness is all …"

"Mr. Sparks, have you got somebody to corroborate this story?" the judge asked.

"Solicitations to commit murder are usually private conversations."

"Then did he tell anybody?" Judge Horton said. "Call the police?"

"He and his family have a long-standing relationship with the Vances and it made him reluctant. In truth, he was stunned and preferred to think he'd imagined it or misunderstood. But once he heard that Mrs. Vance had been murdered, he did tell his employer who urged him to come forward. Being of good character and conscience, he did so."

Colin jumped up. "Your Honor, the person of so-called good character has recently appeared before you in the courtroom."

"Is that so?"

"On misdemeanor charges," Sparks said. "having nothing to do with this matter."

"Charges in connection with the New Year's Eve trespass, or should I say, riot at Little Dixie," Colin said.

The judge took off his glasses and cleaned them on a handkerchief. His lips began to purse. Laurence thought he was going to spit but he put his glasses back on and nodded once toward Sparks.

"Irrelevant, Your Honor. The witness has no reason to lie and many reasons why he might have kept quiet."

"But Mr. Vance had no reason whatsoever to do what the witness alleges," Colin said. "It's a despicable suggestion that causes my client extreme pain."

"It's our theory, Your Honor, that the defendant felt trapped into marriage, felt that his wife wanted only his money, and he wanted a way out."

"Your Honor, these statements will be easily refuted," Colin said. "There are many people, friends of both Mr. and Mrs. Vance, who will testify to their mutual happiness and their compatibility. In addition, Mr. Vance has an alibi that cannot be questioned. The medical examination shows that Mrs. Vance died after ten o'clock in the morning, by which time ..."

Laurence felt the air in the room press in on him. Too much talking, too much talking.

"That timeline can and will be challenged, Your Honor." Sparks interrupted at last. "And the witness has other testimony that sheds light on motive."

"Well?"

"This is a sensitive issue." Sparks glanced at Colin and Laurence and then scanned the crowd of people on the benches behind them. "May we be heard in private?"

"Come up here." Judge Horton waved the lawyers forward.

Laurence saw his long face and balding head above and between the lawyer's shoulders. The lowered voices disappeared into the room's boggy acoustics. Sparks spoke, Colin reacted and all the time, the judge shook his head, sometimes in a wide arc, sometimes barely moving at all. Minutes went by. Then Sparks and Colin went back to their tables.

As he approached, Colin seemed determined to give nothing away by his expression, but Laurence knew what had gone on.

"I'm going to deny your request, Mr. Phillips." Judge Horton's voice quavered. "A jury's going to render judgment in this case."

A trial date was set for early September. Bond was continued.

The strangers in the gallery were reporters who now filled the corridor. They wanted to know who the mysterious witness was, what the bench conference was all about and, as one piercing voice put it, "if you didn't do it, Laurence, who did?"

Two bailiffs pushed them aside so that Laurence, Colin, and Rhetta could get to the elevator. Just as the doors closed to confine them, a flash bulb went off.

Colin led the way back to the car, so deep in his own thoughts that when Rhetta tugged at his coat sleeve, he was startled.

"What was the conference about?" she asked.

"Something Jabel said early on." He caught Laurence's eye.

"Don't they have to make it public?" Rhetta asked.

"They have to tell the defendant and his attorney, and now they have. The public has to wait for the trial."

"But I'm not the public."

Neither man answered her.

Colin drove Laurence and Rhetta home and walked back into town to his office, glad to have the time alone, and then glad to have other pressing work to bury his worries in. When he got home, at about six o'clock, he found Rhetta in the kitchen as usual, but there were no signs of supper being prepared.

"Why didn't you tell me?" was her hello. "Why did you leave it to poor Laurence?"

There was no point pretending not to understand her. "Until this morning, it wasn't clear that Boyd would use that part of Jabel's statement."

"Jabel." She loaded the name with contempt. "I could kill him myself." She pounded one fist into the palm of the other hand.

"It's entirely possible that Boyd won't bring out the most scurrilous stuff at trial. Juries don't like being made to squirm. It could come back to haunt him come election time."

"So saying a man is a queer is worse than saying he killed his wife?"

Colin found Eden in his study. She sat on the floor, her back to the door, a large dictionary opened in front of her, so intent on the book she didn't sense him. He watched her run her fingertips over the thin pages to turn them, then move her head ever so slightly up and down, side to side, until she found her word.

"What are you looking up?" Colin asked.

Eden slammed the dictionary closed. She jumped up, her face red, and a slip of paper floated away from her. Colin picked it up and glanced at it as he held it out to her. The words froze him. Faggot. Queer. Hommosex. In Eden's rounded script.

"This is disgusting." Colin crumpled the paper in his fist and raised it and was amazed to see her flinch.

"I'm sorry." Her voice was low and he saw she was ashamed. She began to cry.

"I'm not angry at you, sweetheart." He rubbed her back and dug a handkerchief out of his pocket. "I guess we need to talk, huh?"

He stepped back to close the door.

"Sit here," he said. She took the ottoman and he his big leather chair. Once she'd dried her eyes, he drew a deep breath and jumped in. "Tell me where you heard those words."

"It's what kids at school say," she whispered. "I know they're bad, but I don't know what they mean."

"You don't need to know those words." Maybe it was just kids trying out curse words they didn't understand.

"But they say them about Uncle Laurence."

The way word spread in a small town still amazed him. "Did the dictionary help?"

She shook her head and twisted his handkerchief around her fingers.

"The first two are just ugly," he said. "Decent people don't say them."

She looked up at him, puzzled.

"Your friends," he said, "They just say what they hear at home, right? Or they're showing off."

"So they don't know any better," she said. That's how Rhetta always explained other people's bad behavior to the girls. People who don't know any better deserve our pity.

"I know. I don't blame the kids." He stopped to see if there was any chance she'd say, okay, thanks Daddy, and go skipping out. No. She was waiting, her face clearing from the tear-in-duced mottle.

"You feel all of this pretty deeply, don't you?" he asked. "I wish you were a little younger or a little older."

She looked puzzled.

He sat back and she sat up straighter. ""Okay, I'll give it a try. When a man and a woman fall in love and get married, there are three ways they love each other. With their minds and their hearts and their bodies. That body part, that's the tricky one, the one nobody can truly understand. Or explain."

She looked down, then back at him. "I know where babies come from, Daddy."

"Babies are part of it, but not all of it. There are mysteries. Like, a few, a very few people fall in love with somebody like themselves. A man can have those feelings for another man. He's called a homosexual."

"But Uncle Laurence loved Aunt Sheila, so he isn't one." Her unasked questions played across her face and he suspected the unspoken answers played across his. "Why do they say those things about him?"

He shifted to the front edge of his chair and took her hand, the one with the damp handkerchief wrapped around it. "People who live here think Piedmont's a special place. They want to think we're all safe here. What happened to Sheila, it made people think, if it can happen to the Vances, it can happen to my family. That brings it closer than they can bear and they start trying to push it away. One way to do that is to blame somebody quick and then label that person as being different. So they blame Laurence and call him names."

Eden began to nod and he realized this was a speech he'd make to the jury. He put a hand behind her head and kissed her on the forehead. "I hope I've helped you. You've helped me." She hugged him and slipped out of the room.

The idea had come to him as he talked: he could turn

everything upside down by uttering the word "homosexual" before Boyd Sparks did and by applying it not to Laurence but to Jabel. He'd been reluctant to try to tie the murder to Jabel because he simply couldn't believe it of the boy, but this was different. Jabel could be made to look like a spurned suitor who saw an opportunity to get even when he heard about Sheila's death. He had no illusion that this was fair or right. But he had to separate Jabel, the boy he liked, from Laurence's accuser. He closed the dictionary and returned it to its place on the bookshelf. Eden's crumpled note lay on the floor where it had fallen. He picked it up, tore it into pieces and dropped them into his trashcan.

When I get through this case, he thought, I'll never take another criminal trial.

One way or another, Jabel Clark's name became known and was in all of the newspapers, along with the story of his arrest at Little Dixie, his school records, his grandmother's name and address. Boyd Sparks called Colin and asked to meet.

"I want to say immediately," Colin said, anticipating what Boyd had on his mind, "we had nothing to do with the release of Jabel's name."

"Maybe not directly," Boyd said. "There are plenty of people interested in connecting dots, though, and you did say that the mystery witness had been in front of Judge Horton. That was a big dot."

"Don't forget you're the one who said why."

Boyd nodded. "And I said that there was a connection between the families. But I didn't go into details. But all the newspapers have the same information this morning. Do you think they shared? Do you think they all had the same epiphany? Or did they all get the same phone call?"

Colin started to respond but Boyd held up a hand.

"It's a rhetorical question," Boyd said. "Just do me one favor, whether you think you need to or not. Tell your client that any such interference is as good as a guilty plea."

FEBRUARY–MARCH 1964

Marie seldom felt at loose ends. She dealt with troubles by keeping busy, as if she could scrub or stitch or polish her life into order, but she hadn't even washed her breakfast dishes. She sat back down and nibbled at the corner of a cold piece of toast.

The knock on her front door startled her. She wrapped her arms tight across her breasts and went to answer. As soon as she opened the door a crack, Rhetta Phillips slipped in, with little Wren behind her.

"Marie, I had to come." Rhetta put her arms around Marie.

"Why's that now?" She pried herself free enough to step back. Wren held her mother's coat tail and looked scared.

"Because I know all of this has been awful for you," Rhetta said. "I want you to know, I don't blame you at all. You're still as dear to me as ever."

"You better come in." Marie didn't like Rhetta's habit of claiming other people's troubles as her own whenever it suited her, and she knew from long experience that the only way to deal with it was to go through it. If you tried to go around it, it just got bigger and bigger.

She leaned down to smile at Wren. "You look pretty today, honey."

"Say thank you." Rhetta prodded the child.

Wren murmured the words. Marie felt a twinge of impatience. The poor child knew something was wrong but had no way to understand what. Rhetta should not have dragged her into it.

"Maybe you'd like a piece of chocolate cake, honey. You come with me." She took Wren's hand and led her to the kitchen. She put her at the table, cut a piece of cake, and poured a glass of milk. "You stay here, now, so your mama and I can talk."

"Yes ma'am."

Marie studied the top of the girl's head for a moment, the perfect part in her hair and the barrettes. She'd fixed Rhetta's hair just like that so many times, and she'd spent hours on her own daughter's braids and bows. This is what we do for our babies, she thought, and what does it come to?

She shivered and went back to the living room. Rhetta sat on the couch, holding a needlepoint pillow on her knees.

"Marie, I'm so sorry about all of this. I know this must be very hard for you, with Jabel telling these stories."

She seemed to expect Marie to sit beside her but Marie knew Rhetta's moods were quicksand. She took her favorite chair on the other side of the coffee table. "How do you mean, stories?"

"You and I are the ones who know Laurence best and you know he never did this thing."

"Laurence is a grown man now. It was a boy I knew."

"He hasn't changed. He's just as gentle and quiet …"

"And you're still talking for him."

"He's devastated, Marie. I can hardly stand it, but I have to be the strong one. Just like when we were little." Her threatened tears dried up.

"Rhetta, people thought you were the strong one, but the whole time, Laurence always got his way. Nobody noticed because you were doing your song and dance."

"Marie." She sounded wounded.

Marie thought, I'm going to ask Dexter, if we get our civil rights, will she have to call me Mrs. Minton?

"Why are you really here, Rhetta?"

"Please, talk to Jabel. Get him to take all of his lies back."

"What makes you say they're lies?"

"What else could they be?" Rhetta began to sound frantic.

"The truth."

Rhetta's head snapped back. The kitchen door hinge squeaked and Marie turned to see Wren come in, her mouth smeared with icing.

"Let's wash your face, Miss Wrenny Bird." Marie took her to the bathroom and, as she expected, by the time they came back, Rhetta was on her feet, ready to go.

∽

A month after his days and nights in jail, Jabel still felt bruised inside, as if the blows aimed at him at Little Dixie had gone through his body into a core that wasn't flesh and blood.

Reverend Jones appeared at the house one morning. Granny was out, but Jabel was sure she was behind the visit. The two men sat at the kitchen table with reheated coffee for the visitor. Jabel got out a tin of fudge, too.

"How're you doing?" Reverend Jones asked.

"I don't know. It seems like I want to sleep all the time, and then I think about Dex and them and wondering if they even have a bed. I slept on the floor up there."

"It's not so crowded now. Chief Bland helped there, you know. He told the judge something had to give."

"You're getting in to see them, then?"

"Every day, and the church ladies are still sending food."

Jabel looked at the piece of fudge on the napkin in front of him and picked out a piece of pecan.

"So," Reverend Jones asked, "you back working yet?"

"No. I'm scared to call anybody even, to see if I can get work. Those newspapers—they made me feel like I'm on trial."

"What part of what you've done do you want to take back?"

Jabel shook his head. "Nothing, I guess."

"Then you need to give up feeling guilty." Reverend Jones rapped his sugar spoon on the table. The word and the sound together made Jabel look at him.

The Reverend went on, "Guilt is the most useless, wasteful thing a person can let himself bog down in."

"I've been thinking, I should pick up where Dex left off with the demonstrations. It seems like I'm letting him down."

"But there's another side to the coin, Jabel. We can say we're holding off on more demonstrations until our boys are shown some justice. Besides, the Good Neighbor Council decided last night to ask the Board of Aldermen to pass an ordinance to out-law segregation. We're giving them a chance to get that done."

"Do you think they'll do it?"

"We can count on three votes and we need four. There're two people we know won't ever go our way, so that leaves two we've got to work on." He slid his chair back and stood up. "If you want to do something, come to the next Council meeting. I'll figure out something for you."

⌐

The white men who had been among the Little Dixie pro-testors never spent a night in jail and then the charges were dropped.

That left Dex and half a dozen other young black men in jail. Judge Horton set a date for their trial in February. In February, he moved it to March. Every delay brought Clyde Raeburn to the steps of the court house, pleading to the public to bring pressure for fair treatment, or for a reasonable bail to be set at the very least.

Finally, in March, the judge let a court date stand. The night before the trial, Reverend Jones called his congregation to the church.

"We want to get to the courtroom early so we can fill it up. We need you older folks especially, not just the young ones. Everybody dress your best and be solemn and quiet."

At eight o'clock the next morning, the Reverend led the Minton family into the courthouse and up the stairs to the balcony. Dex's parents, Dee and Raymond Long, went first, with Jabel and Marie right behind them, and then a dozen cousins and aunts and uncles of all ages. Jabel sat between Reverend Jones and Marie on the lowest row, with the room laid out underneath them. When the balcony was full, black people began to take seats below, filling it from the back. When Jabel saw it, he held his breath; they'd never been allowed downstairs before. But it was an orderly process and made Jabel think of rising water, moved by a law of nature.

"There're no white people here," he whispered to Reverend Jones.

"Who did you think would come?"

In a while, the district attorney came in from a side door hidden in a paneled wall. When he looked at the audience, his shoulders jerked back. Jabel had to smile a little.

Then Clyde Raeburn came in, lifted his hand and smiled to Reverend Jones before taking his seat. Two bailiffs appeared; behind them, the seven defendants in jail garb and chains, followed by two more bailiffs. The officers uncuffed the defendants and pointed them to chairs just behind their lawyer. They looked around and smiled at seeing their people.

"Here's a white man for you." Reverend Jones nudged Jabel. "You know him? He's a reporter." The man slid into a spot at the end of a row and balanced a notebook on his knees.

"All rise," said a disembodied voice and everybody stood for the judge's entrance.

The judge looks like a turtle, Jabel thought, like he could pull his skinny neck inside those robes. Then he remembered how frightened he'd been when he stood in the well of the room before this same man.

The judge began to read aloud the agreement that had all seven men plead guilty to four misdemeanors. When he finished, the judge frowned and tossed the paper aside. "Mr. District Attorney, this is how you protect the public?"

Beside Jabel, Reverend Jones drew a breath in, a hiss through his teeth. On the other side, Granny gripped his hand.

"Putting fear into the hearts of right-thinking people of both races is not a misdemeanor. I'll just have to correct your mistake." The judge motioned for the seven men to step forward. "Dexter Long, I'm sentencing you to three years at the county work farm. Hampton Ames, I'm sentencing you to three years at the county work farm …"

By the time the judge finished, several women were sobbing and Clyde Raeburn, yelling, "You racist old son of bitch," was being hauled out of the courtroom by a bailiff. No one stood when Judge Horton left his bench and disappeared.

APRIL 1964

Jabel walked the three miles out of Piedmont to the farm where Dex's parents lived. It had been a month since the sentencing and he told Granny he would do for them what Dex always did. But embarrassment and fear had held him back. They'd been so good to him all his life, but he knew he was a poor second next to their son.

He usually walked into the house without knocking. Now he stood by at the kitchen door and rapped on the frame. They both came to greet him, Raymond in overalls and Dee carrying her broom.

"I wish I was there and he was here," Jabel said without even a hello.

"Don't talk like that," Dee said. "You could both be in that place. Then what would we do?"

She was snappish when she said it, and it did more to comfort Jabel than softer words would have. He had to swallow hard.

Raymond slapped his shoulder. "Boy, I'm glad to see you. I'm going to turn over her garden today and start some potatoes. And I got two dead pine trees I need to get down."

The two men worked all day, then cleaned up and sat on the back porch drinking a cold beer each. Dee made a beef stew and an apple pie. When she put them on the table, she said to Jabel, "You better eat every bite because it's Dex's favorite."

It was dark by the time Jabel said, "I'd better head on home."

"I'll drive you," Raymond said.

"No sir, I can walk. You didn't wear me out that much."

"Get in the truck, son." Raymond nudged him and Jabel bent to let Dee hug and kiss him.

As they drove into town, they talked about other work Jabel could help Raymond with. Then, as he turned into Sweet Side, Raymond asked, "You're being careful, aren't you?"

"What do you mean?"

"This murder business. You don't think about it all the time, what kind of risk you're taking?"

"I guess I put it out of my mind, after Dex got sent off." Not true, but he didn't want to complain about his own situation.

"Now listen, Dex'll be okay. He's strong and he has the fire. Besides, Clyde Raeburn's going to file his appeal by the end of the month." Raymond reached up and adjusted the rear view mirror. "You need to have sense enough to be scared for yourself."

Jabel sighed and turned to look out the passenger window. "I ought to have been with Dex from the beginning instead of just going along, getting along, living my life."

"Live is the key word. We all want to live, but it's got to be for something." They were in sight of Marie Minton's house. "It's dark. Ain't she home?"

"It's Wednesday. She's gone to church."

Raymond stopped his truck and put a hand on Jabel's arm. "Sit still a minute."

A car passed them and turned at the next corner, red tail lights disappearing.

"Whoever that is," Raymond said, "they been behind us since we left my house."

"Following us?" Jabel's arms prickled with gooseflesh.

"Like I said, you got to be careful."

The letter came addressed to Marie. It was a plain envelope, sealed with tape, with her name printed on the outside. There was no stamp; someone had slipped it into the mailbox. She stood on her front step and opened it. The message was typed,

"To Marie Minton. Any harm coming to you, blame belongs to your filthy lying boy."

Marie felt her heart beat harder and she looked behind her. It went against her sense of herself to be fearful, or to show it, but her hand fumbled at the doorknob and having to step back to let the screen door swing outward made her feel exposed. She had left a pot of beans cooking and meant to go straight back to the kitchen, but needed to sit in the living room for a moment to get her breath back.

This piece of paper, she thought, it can't hurt me. I'm acting like a foolish old woman. Just like he means for me to. Whoever he is.

She looked around her. The walls of the room were hung with family photographs, going back to one of her own grandmother in slavery days, holding a white baby in a long white christening dress. A Vance baby, the picture a gift from old Mrs. Vance, Laurence and Rhetta's grandmother. And then there were the framed school portraits of Jabel from age six until his high school graduation. When have I seen him smile like he did that day? she wondered.

She took the letter to her bedroom and put it out of sight.

∽

"You must be hungry." Marie watched Jabel attack his bean soup. "You eat it like it might eat you first."

He buttered another wedge of cornbread. "I've got to go out, Granny."

"This evening? Why's that?" She put her spoon down and he heard a shake in her voice that made him look up.

"The Good Neighbor Council meets at the church tonight."

"I'm proud of you for that, but ..." She leaned closer across the table. "You remember what the judge said would happen to you if you get in trouble again."

He crumbled the last of his cornbread into the empty soup bowl. "I've got to be doing something and if I don't help out with this, I don't know what I'll do." He brought his fist down on the table. "I hate to sit around feeling scared."

His granny picked up her own bowl and set it inside his so as to clear the table. "I got to say, I hate it, too."

He followed her to the kitchen. "Don't worry, I'll be careful."

"There's no such thing as careful, as best I can tell." She began to draw water in the sink. "It's come to me late in life, but being careful is whole lot like being scared, isn't it?"

The sun was down. Children had been called inside for bedtime baths, so the yards and porches Jabel walked by were quiet. Two cars passed him and both times he tensed up, thinking about the one that had followed him and Raymond the night before, but tonight friendly voices called him by name and people waved greetings. He tried to relax and told himself to buck up. Tired of being scared? He thought. Then don't be scared.

The meeting lasted a little more than an hour. It lifted Jabel's spirits to be among people so full of determination. He walked home hoping he could live up to them. A car passed him and he lifted his hand without looking to see who it might be. He focused on things unseen but deeply felt and on trying to sort them out.

It wasn't until he got to Granny's street that he lifted his eyes. Her house was at the end of the block. If you turned right at the edge of her yard, you were on a narrow dead end road, the outer edge of Sweet Side. So it was odd to see two, no three, circles of light moving along that road. They looked like flashlights held low to the ground. Now they were even with her yard. From where he was, halfway down the block, he could see that the only light on in her house was the kitchen. She'd be at the table, reading her Bible or doing a crossword puzzle.

Jabel picked up his pace and all of sudden the three gleams
went dark.

He took off running. He veered onto the grass of the neighbors' yards so his footsteps were muffled. As he got to the last
yard before Granny's, he slowed down. The dark figures of three
people huddled under her big oak tree. They looked huge to
him. His breath sounded like drumbeats to him but the men—
they had to be men—didn't hear. He dropped behind a row of
boxwoods that separated the two houses and crawled along
until he could dash around to Granny's back door. The screen
door was latched. She never latched it. He knocked and called
as loudly as he dared, "Granny, let me in."

He heard her unlock the door. "Jabel, what're you doing?"
She opened the screen for him to come in.

"Granny," he panted. "Stay here. There're three men in the
front yard."

He headed for the front closet, where a .22 rifle was propped
in the corner behind the winter coats. There was no time to
fumble with loading it. He opened the front door a crack and
flipped on the porch light. The men froze in place. They had
black caps pulled down to their eyebrows, and scarves over the
lower part of their faces. He could see just enough to be sure
they were white.

"Hey," he yelled. "Who's out there?"

They had a bundle, what looked like a bundle of old clothes,
and rope. Jabel slid the rifle bolt back, then forward, then locked
it down, hoping the sound carried. He stayed behind the door-
frame, but eased the barrel out so they could see it.

"Get the hell off my property."

The men began to run, dropping whatever they carried.

"Jabel, son, what is it?" Granny was behind him.

"Stay out of sight till they're gone." He motioned to her with
one hand and stayed at the door. A car came around the corner,
its headlights dark, and it sped up the street.

Jabel reeled around and leaned against the door jamb. He thought he might throw up. Granny came to him and took the rifle.

"Not loaded," he said.

She leaned it against the back of the couch and put her hands on his face. "You scared me to death. What's going on?"

"I need to sit down."

He went to the nearest chair, propped his elbows on his knees and pressed the heels of his hands against his eyes. "I saw flashlights. I saw these men." He remembered then. "They dropped something outside."

Granny went to the door and looked out. "I'm going to call the police."

"They were white men, Granny."

"Then I'm calling Reverend Jones first."

By the time Abraham Jones arrived, Jabel had washed his face, changed his shirt, and felt close to normal. He was glad to see the Reverend's face, serious and calm, glad to see resolve on Granny's face.

When Reverend Jones heard the story, he nodded. "You did fine, Jabel. Now, I'm going to get Chief Bland."

In fifteen minutes, they heard sirens. "I'll go out and talk to the chief," Reverend Jones said. "I want them to examine whatever it is the men dropped."

Jabel stood with Granny at the front window and wrapped his arm around her as they watched three patrol cars park. Chief Bland and three uniformed officers met Abraham Jones under the tree.

"I should be out there," Jabel said. She took his hand to hold onto him.

"The Reverend's the one to deal with it."

So he just watched, almost as if the scene wasn't real.

The men all leaned over the bundle. Chief Bland nudged it with his foot, then reached down and picked up the length of rope that lay over the top. As he lifted it higher and higher, the cloth unfolded and took form: a noose around the neck of a figure made out of black fabric, wearing a long skirt.

Reverend Jones said something and the chief nodded. Bland let go of the rope as he talked to the officers. Then he and Abraham Jones walked toward the house. Jabel moved away from Granny and let them in.

"Marie," the chief said, "I'm sure sorry about this." He took off his hat.

"They were going to hang that thing in the tree, weren't they?" Granny asked.

"I think so. I think it has to do with you, Jabel."

"Then why did they put a skirt on it?" he asked.

"We'll figure that out," Bland said. "My men will see what evidence they can find. And they'll be here all night. Can we sit down and talk?"

They sat at the dining room table with the police chief at the head of it.

"Thank you, Marie." He took the mug of coffee she offered him. "So y'all tell me everything that happened here."

Jabel took a sip of his Coca Cola before he started talking. "I went out about quarter past seven and came home about nine o'clock. I saw three lights that looked like flashlights in Granny's yard. The lights went out and that didn't make sense so I ran to see what was going on. I saw the three men, more just like three big shapes, under the tree out front so I sneaked in the back door and got my .22 and managed to scare them off."

"Marie, what did you see?"

She shook her head. "Not a thing. I was in the kitchen and Jabel came to the back door. He told me there were men outside and the next thing I know, he's yelling out the front door and he's got the gun."

"There's something else," Jabel said. "Yesterday, I was at my aunt and uncle's and my uncle drove me home. He said somebody followed us the whole way."

"You didn't tell me," Granny said.

"I didn't want to worry you."

She pursed her lips and sighed. "I guess I need to tell something, too." She got up and left the room. Jabel shook his head to indicate to Chief Bland and Reverend Jones he had no idea what she meant.

In a moment, Granny came back with a sheet of paper in her hands. She gave it to the police chief.

"You didn't tell anybody about this?" He handed it over to Jabel. "That explains the skirt on the effigy. Somebody's trying to scare you, Jabel, by threatening your grandmother."

When his fear had waned, he'd felt as if the whole night was unreal. Now the words on the page reached inside him and grabbed his heart in anger. "If something happens to my granny. If something happens."

Jabel met Bland and Boyd Sparks the next morning, in the D.A.'s office. As Mr. Sparks read the letter and listened to the stories about being followed and the effigy, his face turned red then drained of color.

"I reckon somebody doesn't want me to testify," Jabel said.

Chief Bland grunted and nodded.

"Could be." Sparks narrowed his eyes. "Let's assume for the moment that it is. You wouldn't back out, would you?"

"I'm going to do the right thing," Jabel said. "I won't let people down."

Now Sparks turned full attention to Chief Bland. "Now who would be doing this to my witness?"

Chief Bland frowned. "You think the Vances? Colin Phillips?"

"Intimidating a witness," Sparks gestured toward Jabel, "It's as good as an admission of guilt and Colin is way too smart for that."

They continued to talk as if Jabel wasn't there and he just waited, impatient but curious, too. Mr. Sparks called Jabel his witness, a prize to be kept safe. But then what, after Jabel told all he could tell? Who would take care of him then? What did these white men want from him?

Jabel was on his way out when Mr. Sparks said, "Oh, I almost forgot. Jabel, I was going to call you anyway. I have something to discuss."

As Jabel walked home from the courthouse, he followed the same route he'd taken the night before. He remembered the car that had passed him. It could have been those men.

Suddenly, he heard another car coming from behind him. He wanted to disappear or throw himself in the ditch, but turned to see. It was a police cruiser, going slow. It stayed behind him all the way to Granny's. He wondered how the cop felt about watching the ass of some young black guy who probably looked like the one the cop had last arrested.

Jabel opened the front door and Granny called from the kitchen. "What happened?" She came out, wiping her hands on a dish towel.

"The police are going to keep an eye on things." He hung up his coat. "They've already started." He told her about his escort. "And Chief Bland, he said to tell you not to worry. He'll take care of you like he would his own mama."

"Lordy, a policeman in Sweet Side in broad daylight. I doubt we've ever been that well taken care of." She half smiled but her eyes were cloudy, the way they were when she worried.

"Mr. Sparks gave me something else to think about," he said.

"Mr. Phillips wants to talk to me."

"Do you have to?" She clinched her hands.

"Mr. Sparks said I don't."

"I want you to stay away from the Vances and Colin Phillips." She was close to tears, not something that happened often, and Jabel hugged her.

"I'm going to change my clothes," he said. "I can do a half-day's work over at Marvin's, washing windows. Would you make me some lunch to take?"

⌒

"Thank you for meeting with me, Jabel." Colin stood when the young man came in. They were meeting in a small, plain room in Boyd Sparks' suite of offices. When Colin had asked for the meeting, he was sure Boyd Sparks tried to talk Jabel out of it. A witness was not obligated to cooperate with the defense. Yet it hadn't been a surprise to Colin when Jabel agreed. It was in keeping with his character.

Jabel shook Colin's offered hand and sat down.

"A lot has happened since I saw you last," Colin said.

"Yes, it has."

Colin noted the lack of a "sir" as well as the way Jabel met his gaze. He was used to seeing Jabel in the clothes he wore to work on the Vance properties. Now he wore a starched and pressed white shirt, a solid blue tie, and dress pants.

There was a tape recorder set up on the end of the table. Colin moved the microphone so that it was upright between them. "This is so I won't have to take notes, and we can just talk. Are you ready?"

"I am."

Colin pressed the button to start the machine and cleared his throat. He gave his name and the date of the recording. "Would you mind stating your name, sir?"

Jabel did.

Colin resumed. "Mr. Clark, you understand that I represent Laurence Vance who has been charged with the death of his wife, Sheila Vance. Is that correct?"

"Yes."

"And you are a witness against Mr. Vance. Is that correct?"

"Yes."

"You have agreed to be interviewed out of your own free will. Your answers will help me to do my job. My ability to offer a strong defense is essential for justice to be done, but whatever you tell me is not for the record and not for public use. You may stop it at any time. Do you understand?"

"I understand."

Jabel's voice was calm but Colin wondered if there was a vibration of anger in it. "Then, I only ask that you tell me what you told District Attorney Boyd Sparks concerning your knowledge of Mr. Vance's involvement, if any, in the death of Mrs. Vance."

"You'd like me to tell you the whole story." Jabel rested his forearms on the table and clasped his hand. "I can do that. Mr. Laur ... Mr. Vance hired me to paint the nursery room for their baby."

"And when was that?"

"In October last year. And one evening, he drove me home. Mrs. Vance wanted him to, even though I could have walked. They gave me a car in payment for the painting—you know that, right? But I didn't drive it that day. My auntie was taking my grandmother to the doctor, or maybe it was shopping, but either way, I left it for them to use.

"So Mr. Vance drove me home and he started talking to me about how good Mrs. Vance is—was—and I said yes, she'd been real nice to work for, and then he said something about how he didn't want to hurt her, and maybe it would have been better for her if he'd never met her." Jabel stopped and Colin saw his mouth set into a line, as if sewn up.

"What was your reaction to him saying that?" Colin asked.

"I didn't want him to tell me things like that. And he knew it. He said something about a boy like me—meaning race, at least that's how I took it—was too young to know how to talk to him man to man, regardless of color."

"Are those the statements of Mr. Vance's that caused you to go to Mr. Sparks?" He heard his own voice rise, the change suggesting—is that it? Is that all you've got?

For the first time, Jabel hesitated and shook his head before he spoke. "No. It was what happened later on. I was still working for Mr. Shipman. The dealership was closed after the President got shot, that whole week. But folks still needed to get their cars fixed, so once we opened again, we were putting in long hours to try and catch up. That suited me fine because I wanted to make up the money.

"I was driving the car Mr. Vance gave me back and forth to work most days. I parked it way far back at the end of the employees' parking lot behind Shipman's. I was about the last person to leave the shop that night. It was dark when I got to the car and all of a sudden somebody jumped out at me. At least that's how it felt. 'Don't be scared,' he said. 'It's me, Laurence.' I opened the car door and that gave a little light so I could see him. I said something like 'Mr. Laurence, what are you doing out here?' I was scared but I tried not to show it.

"'I had to see you again,' is what he said. I had my hand on the top of the door and he put his hand over it. 'I keep thinking about you,' he said, and I think I tried to get my hand away but he held onto it tighter and then he said, 'I'd give anything, pay anything, to be free, to be out of my marriage.' His face was right up to mine and he whispering. He said, 'Would you free me, Jabel?'"

Jabel closed his eyes, then opened them and looked into Colin's. "And then he kissed me. He grabbed my face and he kissed me."

It was a moment before Colin remembered the tape recorder and shut it off.

"You're going to say this in court?" he asked. "Under oath?"

Jabel unraveled the fingers he'd had locked together while telling his story. "Mr. Phillips, it's what happened. I'm sorry."

Colin wanted to say, I'm sorry, too, it must have been awful for you, but held back. He couldn't offer anything—confidence, faith, or belief—to this young man.

"You realize that all I have to do is plant the idea with the jury that you're not trustworthy. That you're the one who initiated physical contact. Think about which of you they'll be inclined to believe." Colin began to rewind the tape and he focused his eyes on the reel as if it depended upon his attention to function. When he looked up again, he saw that Jabel was watching him in the same way.

Both Rhetta and Laurence were sitting in the sunroom when Colin got home. They had tea cups and a plate of cookies on the coffee table, but had moved on to drinks. They looked at Colin at the same moment and froze, hands lifted.

Rhetta recovered first. "What did he say?"

Colin put his brief case down and went to them. "We need to talk in private, Laurence."

Laurence glanced sideways, as if something had caught his peripheral vision.

"Listen," Rhetta said, "if you two think you can keep secrets, you're mistaken. I want to know what that boy said."

"Wait." Colin put his hand on her arm. "Sweetheart, I've got to separate family feelings from my professional duty. What Laurence says to me is privileged. That doesn't extend to you."

She shook his hand off, crossed her arms across her chest and gave them each long looks.

"I have to take Colin's advice," Laurence said to her.

She stood up. "I've got to start supper. You can both go to hell."

Colin and Laurence went to the study and Colin slid the door closed.

"Sit down," he said. They took the chairs that flanked the fireplace. Colin knew that usually he would give a client a moment to settle, to take a breath for strength, but he found he was lacking the patience he usually had. "Jabel said that you went to Shipman's parking lot one night to find him and that you grabbed him and kissed him and told him you'd pay anything to be out of your marriage. That's what he's going to say in court."

Laurence claimed a few seconds by looking into the glass he'd brought with him and then at Colin. "He misunderstood me. I never meant I wanted Sheila harmed in any way." Laurence turned his glass up and drained it. "I'd never have left her for just that reason. I told the truth in my statement about the day Sheila died. I did leave Rhetta and go sit in the park. But I didn't quite tell everything. I went to meet somebody. Adam. He didn't show up."

"Who is Adam?" Colin moved to his desk and took the bottle of bourbon and two glasses out of the drawer.

"That's not important." Laurence waited while Colin poured. "When Sheila became pregnant and we decided to get married, I told him it was over between him and me. I really thought he'd honor that decision, but it seems he just waited a few months to see if I would waver.

"One night in October, I drove Jabel home from our house and I realized I was … drawn to him." He curled his lip to show some self-deprecation.

"As luck would have it," Laurence went on, "that was the night Adam called the house and spoke to Sheila. He upset her.

My nerves were—well, never mind." He shook his head. "I'll get to self-pity later, no doubt.

"Adam started showing up in places I went, sometimes when I was with Sheila. I'd look up and there he'd be. If I went a few days without seeing him I'd start to wonder if I'd dreamed it, or hallucinated him. There was pressure I can't describe."

"And I can't imagine it." Colin felt shame that he'd given little thought, ever, to the cost of being Laurence Vance.

As if he'd read the thought, Laurence said, "There are a lot of people who'd bar me from the house, declare me unfit to be around their children. Family be damned."

"You know Rhetta would never do that, and I'd like to think I wouldn't, either."

"You're still here, pouring whiskey for me. I'm glad you're an attorney, Colin, and I'm glad you're the one person who has to listen to me." He sipped and went on. "I had this idea that I should see Jabel, too. Just see him, not approach, not speak—certainly not touch him in any way. I thought I could put my feelings to rest or some crazy thing. So I found the car, the one we'd given him, and I waited. When he walked out of the dark, walking easy and right toward me, I lost my self-control. I lost myself. I hated myself for it. And there was still Adam.

"I decided I had to confront Adam, so I made the plan to go to Raleigh with Rhetta. Not nice of me, was it? Using her as cover that way. I called Adam and we agreed to meet in a public place. Daylight. When he didn't show up, I was so relieved. I convinced myself I'd be okay.

"I resolved, I would focus all of my attention on Sheila and the baby. I told myself that if she was happy, I was happy. I wanted that happiness, for both of us."

In the silence that followed, Colin began to put bits and pieces together. "Laurence, you need to tell me who Adam is. He had a motive. And he knew you wouldn't be home ..."

Laurence reacted as if to an electrical shock and sloshed his drink onto his lap. "No. He'd never ... No. And I don't want him dragged into it."

"But think about it. All we need is reasonable doubt and it wouldn't all have to rest on Jabel."

"He's married. He has children." He stood up to leave. "Enough people have suffered because I'm a queer."

JUNE 1964

Jabel sat down for a haircut at two o'clock on a Saturday afternoon, just as a police cruiser drove by the barber shop. The shop was full of men waiting their turn or, having just had it, waiting to see who else would come in.

Marvin, the barber, said, "Son, I never feel safer than when you're around."

Jabel laughed as loud as any of them. They joked about how regular the patrols were, at four-hour intervals from six in the morning until midnight. And it hadn't taken long for Sweet Side people to find out that he and Marie were the ones being protected.

"Maybe those cars are the decoys," somebody said, "and the real cops are here undercover." That brought big laughs and big shows of looking under the sinks and rubbing each other's necks to see who was in blackface.

"No, now, y'all need to take it seriously," Marvin said. "I hear some of those white police aren't so happy about playing guardian angel to our boy here."

"Must be working," somebody said, "Hasn't anything else happened, has it Jabel?"

"Not yet," Jabel said.

"Hey, son," Marvin said, "we got your back. Ain't nothing going to happen to you or Miss Marie." The other men nodded and murmured their own promises. Jabel smiled but saw in the barber's mirror that his doubts were in his eyes.

As the weeks had gone by, Granny seemed to worry less and he was glad about that—but he was on edge. It was June. Laurence Vance's trial wouldn't start till after Labor Day. Three months looked like forever. The thought occurred to him, maybe the police chief knew who was behind the attack and the threats.

Maybe he had put the word out that whoever it was should lie low for a while. Maybe the patrols were nothing but show.

In the barbershop, talk had turned to politics and whether or not the Good Neighbor Council was right to keep pushing the town of Piedmont to pass its own civil rights regulations when, Lord willing, the U.S. Senate just might come through. "If Mr. Robert Byrd and Mr. Strom Thurmond would be so kind as to drop dead," somebody muttered.

The talk got heated fast and Jabel was glad when Marvin finished running clippers on his neck.

He had dropped the idea of working with the Council because they met at night and he didn't want Granny alone. It was one more time he'd failed to do something with meaning greater than himself, but he'd promised his great-uncle Marcus he'd keep her safe.

Marcus wanted the two of them to leave Piedmont and come to New Jersey where he lived, but Granny flat refused. Marcus wrote a letter to the two of them, "It is simple minded to think Jabel's got to give this testimony. What is a dead white lady to us? What are the Vances to us? What are we to them?"

"He might as well say, what's my grandson's word worth." Granny tore up the letter.

On June 19, the Senate of the United States voted "aye" on the Civil Rights Act. The church was crowded that night, and the mood was jubilant. Jabel got Marie seated and then went to stand with the other men who filled the side aisles and back of the sanctuary.

"Brothers and sisters," The Reverend's face glowed dark and it seemed to Jabel it was like the day's events had deepened his blood. "Eighty-nine years ago on this very day, our forefathers and foremothers then abiding in Texas received the glorious news of freedom. What do we call that sacred day?"

"Juneteenth." It was a strong male voice that answered, followed by a few amens but more people, including Jabel, whispered, "What? What'd he say?"

"Juneteenth," Reverend Jones's voice dropped. "Every one of y'all should know and revere it. But when have we even whispered that word? Did you teach your children?" He pointed to people in the front row. "Today, Juneteenth has regained its meaning. In the last ninety years, the Lord has tested America and America failed to seize and hold the gift He'd given us through that greatest of men, Abraham Lincoln. We let Satan in. Satan in the form of Jim Crow, making a mockery of sacrifice and toil and bloodshed. The Lord has given America another chance."

He paused for response, but the congregation only murmured its amens.

"Tomorrow night, the Piedmont Town Council meets," Reverend Jones went on. "Our town fathers and mothers did not see fit to pass the ordinances we asked for. They ducked. They dodged. They danced. They wiggled off that hook. I want us all to attend that meeting tomorrow, so they'll know we will remember come next Election Day. We'll teach them to know the meaning of Juneteenth."

He went on to lay out his plans for a march from Sweet Side to City Hall, with all the black churches joining in.

Hearing him, Jabel's heart beat fast and his lungs pressed against his ribs and he felt faint.

The choir began "Lift Every Voice and Sing." The people around Jabel stood for the anthem and pressed forward. He slid backwards through them into the vestibule and outside into the night so he could think. He walked out to the sidewalk and turned to face the church. The light that poured from it was hazy in the humid night air. The singing ended, there was quiet, then it changed into "Onward Christian Soldiers."

Jabel let go of the breath it seemed he'd held forever. With that long exhale, he was alone, on his own, for the first time. He put the palm of his hand flat on his chest and felt strong.

⤺

Word of the march spread into pockets of white Piedmont. It was Clyde Raeburn who told Colin. "Just letting you know," Clyde said. "So you can decide where you want to be."

Colin was touched and surprised that Clyde hadn't written him off. Maybe taking part in the march would be a small redemption for what he was prepared to do to defend Laurence. He called Rhetta and told her he needed to stay in town that evening for a meeting. He let her think it had to do with a case.

He met up with a group of twenty or thirty white people who stood on the steps of the Episcopal Church and waited. They would fall in with the black marchers when the procession reached them.

The mood was edgy, as Colin himself was. He guessed he wasn't the only white person who'd supported the movement from behind closed doors, not the only one feeling sheepish at coming forward now, when the sense of danger had passed. The priest offered a prayer that Colin didn't listen to. He waited for the sound of feet, imagining that the march would take place in silence, but singing, clapping, stomping, and shouting rounded the corner first.

Reverend Jones was at the front of the march, a row of young men behind him like an honor guard, Jabel Clark among them. They were followed by the flow of hundreds of people in full voice and full rejoicing. Clyde passed by, both his elbows hooked with fellow marchers.

It was a hot night and Colin wore lightweight trousers, a white shirt with no tie or jacket. As he slid into the march, the black people around him were dressed as if to go to church, wearing their best, their faces glowing.

"Mine eyes have seen the glory ..." they sang all the way up Court Street.

Colin had to move along the outside of the crowd and could see that ahead of them, the sidewalks were full of spectators, some cheering and waving signs; some cursing and yelling ugly words. A Confederate flag hung from the upper windows of a store.

A white man stepped off the sidewalk to fall in beside Colin. He even caught Colin's eye and nodded. Then he raised a hand and Colin heard himself yell, "Gun" even before his eyes had registered it.

The man fired and fired again. Until that moment, Colin had not seen any policemen but they swarmed over the shooter, taking him to the ground at Colin's feet. The man yelled in pain and cursed when one of the officers stomped his hand to free the gun.

Colin had to sidestep, almost lost his balance, and found himself spun around, facing the way he'd come. Around him, the march broke. People screamed and ran in all directions. He heard glass break as store windows smashed and saw Reverend Jones standing in the middle of the street, trying to calm and reorder his people.

Then he heard sirens and recognized them as fire engines. People began to scramble out of the street and Colin had a vision of fire hoses used on demonstrators. His heart rate was so high he couldn't breathe, but the three trucks roared by him, headed south out of town. The sirens changed tone and faded. The sidewalks emptied. It was over.

The Town Council meeting was canceled but Colin stayed downtown, hanging around the courthouse until some mix of rumor and news added up to make sense. When he got home, Rhetta met him at the door. "Where have you been?" she asked.

"We saw the riot on TV." She held him in a tight hug.

"What did they say?" Colin returned her hug. He looked past her to where Laurence stood.

"That there was a shooting and a riot and a big fire somewhere," Laurence said.

"It was a starter's pistol," Colin told them. "They were blanks, but they did the trick. I could use a drink." They followed him through the kitchen into the sunroom.

"I'd call it a panic, not a riot." Colin said as he poured bourbon. "Windows got broken and people took leave of their senses, running and yelling. I told Chief Bland I'd swear that it wasn't the marchers who did the damage and he agreed."

"And the fire?" Laurence asked.

"Little Dixie. Junius Shinn said he'd burn his place to the ground before he'd integrate, and that's what he did. He held off the firemen with a shotgun to keep them from saving the building. It took most of the police department to arrest him."

"I'll never understand." Rhetta sighed. "I need to see about Eden. She caught on that something had happened. If she's awake, I'll tell her you're okay."

Colin suspected his daughter was at the top of the stairs, listening. "Kiss her goodnight for me," he called.

Once he heard Rhetta's footsteps on the stairs, he relaxed.

"I expected her to be furious with me," he said.

"Maybe she's mellowing." Laurence sat down beside the glass of whiskey he had apparently left when he went to greet Colin.

"Your sister? Never."

"I'm sorry for her, you know. And you, too, Colin. I feel tension between you and I know I've caused it." He flexed the fingers on his left hand and looked at it as if it had changed since he last saw it. "I'd rather die myself than be responsible for you two coming apart." He looked up at Colin, his eyes full.

"There's no chance of that. None. We'll all get through this."

Rhetta reappeared. "Now, Colin, explain what the hell you were doing in that mob."

The next morning, as Colin walked to the courthouse, he passed the glass company's truck parked in the block where windows had been broken. He greeted the owner, Joe Beech. "You'll have full day's work, I see."

"Hey, Colin. Yeah, what's that they say? It's an ill wind blows no good?" He grinned.

Beech's black workmen took a sheet of plate glass off the rack and glanced at their boss.

Two police officers stood at the top of the courthouse steps, flanking the door. Clyde Raeburn stood beside one of them and harangued. "I'm going up there to tell your boss you're all incompetent."

"What are you doing, Clyde?" Colin asked. "These guys had a rough night."

"They ought to be out looking for whoever burned the crosses last night."

That stopped Colin. "What?"

"You haven't heard?" Clyde took his arm. "Come over here a minute."

They stepped out of the flow of people and stood behind a column. "Two crosses were burned in Sweet Side last night. One at Reverend Jones's church and one at Marie Minton's house."

"My God. How much damage?"

"They didn't have time to stick the crosses in the ground. They laid one on the lawn in front of the church and propped the other one against the roof of Marie's house. Did it while the whole damned fire department was wasting time with Junius Shinn. Neighbors heading home from the march got there in time to put the fires out."

Colin looked down the length of Court Street. "I feel like

I went to sleep and woke up in some place that looks like Piedmont, but isn't."

"Ha. You better believe it is. You think we don't have the KKK all around us?"

"You think it was the Klan?"

"Cross burnings? What else?"

"Could be someone who wants to make it look that way."

"Colin, sometimes I think you're too sweet and naïve to live and sometimes I think you're the canniest country boy I ever met." Clyde slapped his shoulder. "Listen, I'm going up to give Bland a piece of my mind. Want to come?"

Colin laughed and shook his head. "Don't enjoy yourself too much, Clyde."

He stopped into the café for a cup of coffee and to see what else he could learn. As he was leaving, twenty minutes later, a woman called his name. He stopped and watched her cross the street. She was middle-aged, thin, wearing denim pants that were too big for her and a pink flowered blouse. Her hair looked as if she'd just rolled out of bed and the rims of her eyes were swollen and red.

"Mr. Phillips, do you know who I am?"

"No ma'am. Have we met?"

"I'm Debby Shinn. My husband's Junius Shinn and they got him at the jail." She ran her fingers through her ragged bangs. "He wants to talk to you." Her voice took on a skeptical tone.

"He wants me to represent him?"

She looked at him and pursed her lips to let him know she had no time for stupid questions, not after the night she'd had. "He says you got to get him out, or he's going to tell everything he knows about your wife."

Colin knew Junius Shinn by sight, and like everybody in Piedmont, by reputation. Before the push to integrate started, Junius was said to be a bad-tempered jokester who didn't take to being the butt of jokes himself, and who ran Little Dixie without much regard to law. After the demonstrations started, his image sharpened to a single word: mean.

In an interview room, Colin eyed the grimy-faced man in an orange jump suit. "Your wife said you asked for me."

"That's right." Shinn pulled up the knees of the jumpsuit as he sat down and jammed his legs under the table. "You're the man who's going to get me out of here."

"There'll be an arraignment, probably today, and bail can be set then." Colin remained standing. "The court will appoint you a lawyer if you can't afford one."

"I can afford you." Shinn leaned back and crossed his arms over his barrel chest. His eyes were as red and swollen as his wife's and the smell of smoke got stronger every time he moved. The room seemed to fill with it.

"It's not a matter of money, Mr. Shinn. I won't agree to represent you."

"What's wrong with you?" Shinn's voice rose and his jaw set. "You think I'm going to play the fool?"

Colin took a breath and forced his shoulders to relax. He wanted to tell Shinn to go hell. He wanted to get out of the airless place. "I don't know what you're talking about."

"You telling me you don't know who's been paying me?" Shinn's eyes disappeared into slits and his face turned red. He stuck his hands deeper into his armpits and rested his elbows on the table. Then he laughed. "Ha. That makes you the fool."

Now that he thought he had some advantage—or so it seemed—Shinn let his hands fall onto the table and he stretched his legs out. "All right, Mr. Phillips, here it is. Somebody's been paying me to harass that Clark nigger, and I figured you knew all about it."

"Do you mean Jabel Clark? The cross-burning?"

"That and everything else."

"But last night, the crosses. You weren't there."

"I wasn't there for any of it. I got somebody else to do it. Just like she did. 'Don't hurt him,' she said. 'Just scare him out of town.' But I figured that's just so if it turned out worst for him, she could say it wasn't her doing."

"Her." It wasn't a question.

"Yeah." Shinn grinned. "Her."

It was beyond Colin's belief, yet he believed it. Was she sane, his wife?

He left the jail and walked down the dingy, echoing stairs to the basement. He went out the back door and crossed the street to Clyde's office.

"Clyde," Colin called, "are you here?"

"Come on back."

Clyde sat at his cluttered desk, a legal pad in front of him, a pencil behind his ear and one in his hand. He blinked when he looked up, as if his eyes had trouble changing focus.

"What brings you?"

"I've got a problem, Clyde, and you're the only person I can think of to talk to." He sat down and told Clyde Junius Shinn's story. Clyde frowned, linked his hands behind his head and gave close attention.

"Miss Rhetta has taken leave of her senses," Clyde said when he finished.

"You know her. She'd do anything for someone she loves."

"Anything. Well, it's something all right." He flipped to a new page on his legal pad and wrote on it.

"I have to protect her. For my daughters' sake, and for my own. If I lose my reputation over this, I lose everything."

Clyde ran a hand over his head, exposing his receding

hairline and rearranging ragged curls. "Yeah, nobody will be-lieve sweet Miss Rhetta went out to Little Dixie and conspired with old Junius over a couple of beers. They're sure to think you're behind it. You and Laurence."

Colin nodded. "That's why I'm going to have to withdraw."

Clyde bounced his pencil's eraser on the desk. "Boyd's not going to like that. He wants to do this trial before elections, and any new defense lawyer's going to need a delay. It's going to be clear to Sweet Side that the sitting D.A. didn't do much to take care of his prime witness. Or his witness's granny."

"But if I don't withdraw and word gets out that Rhetta was involved, everybody will believe I was, too. That means the jury pool will be contaminated. If Boyd gets a verdict, an appeal law-yer will go to town on it. And the Bar's Ethics Committee will go to town on me."

"What'll kill you is trying to cover it up. And you don't want to wait. If Junius decides Rhetta is the ace in the hole he dug last night ..." Clyde had deep brown eyes that Colin knew he used to his advantage in the courtroom. Now, as Clyde leaned forward, his eyes widened and gleamed as if they were lit by an idea. "Okay, if we're going to take Boyd a problem, we need to take him the solution, too."

"I'm listening."

Clyde nodded. "I don't know what-all evidence Boyd has against your brother-in-law but I know he thought about it long and hard before he charged the heir of the oldest money family in this town with a heinous crime. He must be real sure of his case because if he loses, he's done. Now, if he charges the defendant's sister with two or three conspiracies, he's going to look like he's piling on the Vances. It could give voters a reason to go against our buddy, Boyd.

"On the other hand, if he finds out about Rhetta conspiring to intimidate a witness against her brother—and a black witness at that—and he doesn't do anything about it, well, I guess that's what we call a rock and a hard place and a steam roller.

"So this is what comes to mind. Rhetta throws herself on Boyd's mercy, agrees to plead guilty and take probation for a year or even two if he decides he needs to be tough. But Boyd puts that off until after Laurence's trial."

Colin swallowed as if to get all this down. "Okay, but what about Shinn?"

"I've had some dealings with him. He's not a stupid man. Suppose Boyd doesn't charge him with the conspiracy. Just arson and gun charges and threatening to shoot firemen and what not. That way, he'll have good reason to keep his mouth shut on the subject. Why volunteer for more felony charges?"

"And you think Boyd will see enough benefit to make that deal?"

They both sat quiet for a moment. Colin recognized the silence—it was where the lawyer gave the client time to absorb just how much trouble he was in. "You'll represent Rhetta, I hope."

"If she'll agree to it."

Colin shrugged. Rhetta had said more than once that their old friend Clyde defended the scum of the earth and she was glad because it kept Colin on the higher ground. What she didn't realize was how well Clyde did his job.

"She'll agree." He didn't plan to give her a choice.

An hour later, Colin welcomed Boyd to his office. "Thanks for coming on short notice."

"What's going on?" Boyd sounded both bemused and annoyed. "Well, here's Clyde, too. Why do I feel like I'm being set up?" They shook hands.

"Please have a seat," Colin said. "There's one more person we're expecting and she should be here any second."

Colin heard Rhetta's voice as she greeted his secretary, then she appeared in his office door. She wore a light gray skirt and a cream colored blouse with her pearls. What Clyde had said about her sitting down with Junius Shinn flashed across Colin's mind. Who would believe it? Eventually, everybody.

When she saw the men, she stopped. "I'm interrupting … I'm sorry. Colin?"

He'd called her and Boyd and asked them to come as quickly as they could. "It's vital to the case," he'd said—true enough, and sure to get them both here in a hurry. Rhetta had asked him questions but he was in no frame of mind to answer them on the telephone; he was afraid of what he might say to her.

Clyde and Boyd both stood as Rhetta entered and Clyde went to escort her to the chair beside his. Rhetta gave him a look that suggested she was surprised by his show of manners.

When they were all seated, Colin said, "Clyde, I'll leave it to you to explain why we're here."

"First off, Boyd, I'm here to represent Mrs. Phillips," Clyde began. Rhetta sat up straighter and she stared, first at Colin, then at Clyde, who smiled at her and then turned to face the district attorney.

"My client," Clyde said, "has been accused by somebody I won't name right now of hiring said somebody to harass and pester and bother Jabel Clark. You're aware of the anonymous letter, the threats, the effigy, and the cross burnings. Now, we're not making any admissions but we wanted you to hear about this from us, since some folks might interpret these things as attempts to intimidate a witness. A very serious charge."

Colin knew that what Clyde said was meant to inform Rhetta as much or more than Boyd, and her face showed shock. She glanced at him and then looked down, drawing back in her chair, not unlike Wren when caught with her mother's lipstick smeared across her cheeks.

"Serious isn't a strong enough word," Boyd looked past Clyde. "Mrs. Phillips, if there's any truth to this, after the lie you told in your first sworn statement …"

Clyde moved to block his view. "Like I said, we're not making any admissions. Let me point out the obvious. If these accusations get around, they'll be so prejudicial against Laurence Vance that Colin's going to withdraw. And trust me, a new defense attorney is going to want a delay and then go for a change of venue."

At the word "withdraw," both Boyd and Rhetta looked to Colin, who nodded. She opened her mouth and then closed it and he knew she was beginning to comprehend.

Clyde paused—the same way he had when he talked to Colin earlier—this time, Colin understood it was for Boyd's sake.

"Okay," Boyd said, "we can agree that nobody benefits from that chain of events. What do you have in mind?"

Clyde outlined his plan and Colin had to watch his wife fade and withdraw, her hand over her mouth as if she might be sick. He felt ill himself.

As Clyde talked, he slipped into the shorthand language of two lawyers who understood each other. Every time Junius Shinn's name came up, Boyd groaned and Clyde said, "Yeah," and that was enough on that subject.

"So there you go," Clyde said when he was done. "Did I forget anything, Colin?"

"You covered it very well."

Boyd stood up. "Mrs. Phillips, I hardly know what to say to you. If you understood the damage you've done, you wouldn't have done it. And you'll have to answer for it. Clyde, you better have her in my office the day after her brother's trial ends. No matter what the verdict is."

When he was gone, Clyde turned to Rhetta. "Is there anything you want to say to me, Rhetta?"

"Colin didn't know anything about it," she said, "and Laurence certainly didn't." Her voice was low, but her posture showed some recovery.

He patted her hand before standing up. "You ought to come by my office sometime in the next few days."

"She will," Colin said. He walked Clyde out and when he returned, found Rhetta dabbing at her eyes.

"You and the girls and Laurence are my life," she said. "Who wouldn't do anything she had to, to save her own life?"

He didn't go to her. "Did you park out back?"

She had only her purse to pick up, but looked around as if she might be missing something, then she followed him out. His secretary called a good-bye.

At the car, she asked, "When will you be home?"

"I've lost a lot of time today. I'll be late."

She began to say something else, and he was afraid it would be "I love you."

"We'll talk tonight," he said before she got those words or any others out. He saw her into the car and watched her drive away.

∾

After the cross burning, Granny had been so shaken that Jabel had put her to bed with one of her own toddies, warm milk with brandy and sugar. Then, he'd called Raymond and Fred Franklin to let them know about what had gone on.

As soon as they could get there, Raymond and Dee, then Fred and Louise swept in. Fred carried their little girl, sound asleep in his arms. The women took the child and went to Marie's room. The men had their hunting rifles in hand.

"I've never seen her like this," Jabel said.

"You're doing fine," Fred said.

"And you're not alone." Raymond patted Jabel on the shoulder.

Somebody knocked on the front door and all three men froze. Then Jabel went to a window and peered out. "It's okay." He opened the door and a neighbor, Tyrus Archer, stepped in.

"Y'all okay?" Tyrus asked. "I just came from the church and it looks like it'll be all right."

"We were lucky," Jabel said. "But I'll have to see about the roof tomorrow."

"I want y'all to know, some of us will be out in the neighborhood all night, just to keep an eye on things."

When he was gone, Raymond said, "You're the man of the house, Jabel. You tell us what you want."

Jabel looked at the men, Raymond serious, Fred grinning just a little. "How about we switch off every hour or so? One of us out back, one on the front porch, and one of us close to the ladies and by the telephone?"

"Good plan," Fred said. "I'll start out front."

Raymond pulled a wooden chair out onto the back stoop.

Jabel found Louise and Dee sitting on either side of Marie's bed, holding her hands. Little Janelle was snuggled in beside her.

"These girls are taking good care of me," his granny said.

"If you need anything, one of you call out," he said.

He pulled the curtains on her windows closed and hugged all three women. Then he went to all the other rooms in the house, closing blinds, turning out lights, and made his way to the kitchen. It was ten o'clock. Damn, he thought, it's going to be a long night. He sank down to sit on the floor, his knees up, his back pressed flat against the wall. His resolution to make his own path in the world seemed foolish now. What good was that in a world where crosses got burned, where peaceful marchers were victims, where he brought trouble to the people he loved?

Once the sun was up, Jabel pulled a ladder out of the shed. He carried it to the front of the house and climbed up. A few shingles had been scorched, as had the limbs of an oak tree that grew near the door, and grass on either side of the sidewalk. The charred cross lay off to one side and the ground underneath was marked by its flaming shape. The people who'd put out the fire had dug into the soft dirt of Granny's flower beds, so here and there, pink and purple petunia blossoms showed through the destruction.

"Sure could have been worse," Fred said.

"Yeah, y'all were mighty lucky," Raymond said. "You buck up, son." He slapped Jabel on the back and went inside, Fred after him.

Jabel lingered on the front steps, closed his eyes, and imagined flames rising up around him and the siding beginning to blister. He imagined for a minute that anything he touched would burn.

"Jabel?" Dee spoke to him from the door. "Honey, I've got breakfast ready."

He went to the kitchen and found everybody else sitting at the table with bowls of scrambled eggs and grits and a plate of bacon in the middle. He took his place and Raymond said, "You want me to say grace, Marie?"

Marie nodded. She was still in her nightgown and bathrobe. Her hair was combed and smoothed into a knot at the nape of the neck, but her face was askew, her lower lip pulled to the side. Louise held her hand. To Jabel, the hand looked both weak and heavy. Raymond thanked the Lord for the new day, for the food, for bringing them through a night of peril and fear into the sunshine, Amen.

Louise began to serve a plate for Janelle, sitting in her lap.

Dee set a pan of biscuits on a trivet. "Butter them quick, while they're hot."

"Listen here." Fred had the radio on, the volume low. Now he turned it up and the local station was reporting on the night before.

"At the very moment Little Dixie was burning, the fire set by its owner, Junius Shinn, two wooden crosses were set aflame in the southwestern section of Piedmont, the Sweet Side neighborhood. One cross was burned on the lawn of the Church of the Living Lord. The other was burned at a private residence a few blocks away. The church has been a center of organizing racial protests in Piedmont and its pastor led the march on City Hall last night. Our reporter was not able to ascertain why the private residence may have been targeted. The Piedmont police department would not allow anyone into the area, nor would Police Chief Lewis Bland speculate as to whether or not the cross burnings were the work of the Ku Klux Klan or possibly someone adopting KKK tactics."

Fred turned the radio off.

"It was the worst feeling I ever had," Marie said. "Coming down the street and realizing what I smelled and what I saw was my house burning."

"You want to tell us about it, honey?" Louise asked her, and Jabel saw Granny pull herself up a little straighter.

"We were coming home from the march, from all that crazy goings-on, and I think it was Jabel says, 'You smell something burning, Granny?' We turned the corner and then, yes, Lord, I smelled it and I saw fire in the sky, just beyond the house nearest this one and I knew it had to be mine that was burning."

"We'd have been here sooner," Jabel said, "but I had to find Granny. That's what scared me—losing her in that mob."

"And folks were already here trying to put it out," Marie said.

"Who?" Louise asked.

"People doing what we were doing," Jabel said. "Going home from uptown and saw the flames. The cross was leaning up against the roof, right at the front door, so one of the men broke into the shed and got a ladder. He climbed up and knocked the cross down. And somebody else found the hose. They used my rakes and shovels, too." He realized he was seeing it all over again, three men and two women, laboring away in the dark as if on some strange crop.

"Then somebody driving by yelled out that the church was on fire and as soon as they smothered the last spark here, they took off. My tools went with them, so I sure hope they remember where they got started."

"Oh, they won't have no trouble figuring that out," Fred said and Marie gave a little moan.

"What did they do to my sweet house?" she asked.

"The siding's a little smoked. A few shingles need replacing," Fred said.

"Don't you worry," Raymond said. "It won't take us long to get everything set right."

Jabel took on the job of cutting up the cross while Raymond and Dee started washing the siding with soapy water and sponges. Fred used long-handled clippers to lop damaged limbs off the oak. Louise stayed inside with Marie and little Janelle. It was a humid morning and Jabel had to wipe sweat out of his eyes every few minutes.

He knew Granny would call Marcus, or else Louise would. Marcus would see what Jabel himself saw, that there was only one reason why this house was a target. It might look like it was part of some raggedy-ass bigots' answer to Lyndon Johnson's new law but that wasn't it. Jabel was the reason, Jabel and what he had to tell about Laurence Vance.

Seeing Granny brought so low was the worst. He put the saw blade to the blackened, scaled wood and bit into it with all the strength he had. He felt something he'd never known before: time was getting short.

He knew what he had to do. Now he had to figure out the details.

SEPTEMBER 1964

The Labor Day weekend was three days ahead and Laurence's trial a week away.

The Reverend Abraham Jones was leaving Piedmont to work with Martin Luther King, Junior, and the ladies of the church were planning a send-off, a reception to be held that evening, after his last Wednesday night service.

Marie and Louise and the other women busied themselves in the church kitchen making deviled eggs, finger sandwiches, lemonade, iced tea, and receiving the cakes and pies that people brought as they arrived for the service.

"Have you seen my grandson?" she asked folks as six o'clock rolled around. "Is he here yet?"

She usually sat up front, but Jabel's tardiness bothered her so she waited until the choir had started the call to worship and then took a seat in the back pew. That way, she'd see him when he slipped in. When he still didn't come, she began to feel more anxious. Nothing bad had happened since the cross-burnings, but she saw he was on edge. If he didn't go home after work, he didn't find her note and he was—where? Doing what? And when was the last time he didn't go straight home?

Marie tried to convince herself Jabel had picked this evening to be irresponsible and wouldn't she give him a piece of her mind? But as Reverend Jones began his farewell sermon, it was fear that overruled her other feelings.

Nevertheless, she had duties and it was almost eight o'clock before she embraced the preacher and traded blessings with him and asked Louise to drive her home.

"I thought surely Jabel would be here tonight," Louise said. "Where is he?"

"I don't know." Marie heard the worry in her own voice, saw

how Louise glanced at her, and felt the silence they kept be-tween them until her house was in sight. There were no lights on, though twilight had faded altogether.

"I'll come in with you." Louise turned off the motor.

"I never thought the day would come when I was afraid to go into my own house."

"It's all right. This too shall pass." Louise offered her a hand then called out, "Haints and boogeymen, get from here. You don't want to mess with us."

Marie laughed. "You always were a bold child." They went up the front steps and she reached into her bag for the key. When she put it in the lock, she found the door was open. "I must have forgot to lock it." But she knew she had not.

"Or maybe Jabel's here after all. Could he be out back?" Louise reached around her and turned on the table lamp just inside the door.

They went through the living room to the kitchen, lighting the way as they went. Marie opened the back door.

"Look," she said. "He's been here all right. He left his work boots on the back porch like he always does." Her relief made her giddy and she shook her head at her own silliness. She glanced at the table and saw her note. "Young fool. He never even read it."

"That's not like him …"

"I'll know how to deal with him." She smiled as she said it and suddenly she wanted Louise to go so she could think. "You don't need to wait, honey. Fred and Janelle will be looking for you."

"I can call him. I don't mind staying a while."

"No, you go on."

"Well …" Louise looked around as if she wanted a sign to tell her what to do. "Will you call me when he gets home?"

"If it's before I go to bed. I'm feeling kind of weary now that I think about it." She walked to the door with her niece. "Thank you and I'll see you Sunday. We'll see how that supply preacher does."

When she was by herself, Marie went to Jabel's bedroom and saw that the top of his dresser was clean, no comb, no hand-kerchief, no loose coins. She opened one drawer, then another, then the closet. They had not been cleaned out but she knew that things were missing—maybe two or three of everything from underwear to the shirts she had ironed and hung for him. She sat on his bed, picked up a pillow and hugged it to her.

If he plans to be gone long, he'd have taken more, she told herself. He's got to be back by Tuesday for the trial. Maybe he just needed a little vacation.

She put the pillow back and smoothed the tufted bedspread over it. The word vacation soothed her. She'd never done such a thing herself, never stepped away from duty, but she knew that younger people did. Fred and Louise liked to go to Florida and spend a week at the beach where black people were welcome.

In the kitchen again, Marie stood in the middle of the room and did a slow sweep. Work boots left for her to see; the fruit bowl where there had been four apples, empty; the bread box open and empty; the carton of Coca Colas gone; the percola-tor washed and upside down in the dish drainer along with its basket and lid.

The percolator. Jabel didn't drink coffee. She had put it away after she washed the breakfast dishes. It came to her then—all these things were signs and the coffee pot most of all: Marcus had been there. First thing Marcus did whenever he came to her house was make a pot of coffee. He wanted it stronger than she did, so he made his own. And then he saved the leftover in the ice box because he liked to drink it cold, the only person she knew who did that.

Marie opened the refrigerator and saw the Mason jar of dark liquid, its lid screwed on tight.

Jabel's gone, she thought. He's with Marcus. He's all right …

It was as clear to her as if she'd stood at the back door seeing them off with a picnic lunch to get them on their way. To where?

And what ought she do now? Louise would call first thing in the morning, count on that, to find out what Jabel had been up to, that he broke a promise. Marie hated to tell a lie but as soon as she thought of Louise, the story began to form: Jabel had been there all the time. He came home with a touch of a stomach flu bug and just went right to bed. He heard them come in but he had no thought that they didn't know where he was or that they'd worry. So she was going to keep him home and make sure he got rested up for Tuesday because she thought maybe it was the pressure that made him sick to his stomach. Did Louise remember how Miss Wallis Williams used to throw up every time the least little thing went wrong?

And by Tuesday, she'd sort out what she needed to do about Mr. Boyd Sparks. Sorrow rose from deep down and she pressed her hands against her stomach.

"Not now," she whispered, "I got to do what I got to do."

It was trial day. Marie went to the courthouse by herself, wearing one of her church dresses and a small white hat that fit snug over her head with no brim or veil or anything that might not be businesslike. It seemed the minute Mr. Sparks saw her, he knew what she'd come to say.

"He needs to be here, Mrs. Minton. I told him to be here on time."

She told him the truth—that she'd last seen her grandson when she packed him a lunch to go to work on Wednesday and that he'd gone off with a few of his clothes and a little food and a carton of Cokes. Then she bent the truth—she'd expected he'd be home by now because he didn't take much and because it wasn't like him to worry her so or to fail to do his duty.

"Who else knows he's gone?" Mr. Sparks asked.

"Nobody. If anybody asked me about him, I told them he was feeling under the weather and was home in bed."

Mr. Sparks told her to wait and he went out. In a few minutes, the police chief came in to talk to her. "Marie, we need to go to your house and look for Jabel."

"I think you need to have a search warrant. Isn't that right?"

"Ma'am, he was subpoenaed and that means he can be arrested if he doesn't appear. If you want me to get a search warrant, I will."

Once he had the warrant, she went with them and watched every minute as they—Chief Bland and two young officers in uniform—went into every room, opened all the closet doors and looked under all the beds. She wanted to ask them how stupid they took her grandson to be, but she didn't mind letting the skinnier boy slither headfirst into the crawlspace even though he told his chief spiders scared the daylights out of him.

Whether Chief Bland believed her or not, he gave her a lecture intended to make her quake in fear of the power of the law. He warned her he wouldn't have scruples about arresting her if it turned out she knew more than she was telling.

"It's hard for me to believe he'd take off and not tell you or leave a note or something, Marie."

"You mean because he's honest and true? That's just why he wouldn't leave a note or tell me anything about it. He wouldn't put me where I'd have to tell you any lies."

Chief Bland was red in the face when he left her house.

﹏

Colin Phillips escorted his client through back halls and into the courtroom by way of a side door.

"We're at this table," he said. He put his briefcase down.

"Is it like a wedding?" Laurence asked him. "Bride's side and groom's side?"

Colin ignored his flippancy. "I have a legal pad for you." Colin took it out of his bag. "Do you remember what I said about making notes?"

"Do it so the jury sees I'm engaged. Don't do it so much that they think I've stopped listening." Laurence sat down and took his fountain pen out of the inside pocket of his coat. "Stay alert. Don't make faces. Clasp my hands and look down when Sheila is named so they know I'm mourning, but avoid overdoing it. Play to the audience, but keep it subtle. I can't be cold and heartless, but I can't break down. Does that cover it?"

Colin put a hand on Laurence's arm. "I'm sorry if I've given too many instructions. I hope you'll follow them anyway."

"You're telling me how to be human."

There was no irony in his voice now and Colin squeezed his arm.

Just then, a bailiff came through the same door they had used and leaned over the table to whisper, "Mr. Phillips, the D.A. says he needs to see you right away."

Colin tried not to act surprised. "And Mr. Vance, too?"

"Just you." The bailiff straightened up and Colin stood. He nodded at Laurence, to confirm everything was fine.

Left alone, Laurence felt his nerves rise to the surface. He'd come to depend on Colin in ways he'd never imagined and that dependency just underlined how solitary his life was.

His first visits to this grand old courtroom had been with his father who had shown him the pecan paneling, made of wood milled nearby, and pointed out the murals of historic scenes of Mangum County going back to the Lords Proprietors. And then he pointed to the massive raised desk at the front. "Look there, way up there, that's where the judge sits. That's where justice is done."

Laurence got a little older and learned the Apostle's Creed. He always thought of this judge's bench when he said the words "from thence He shall come to judge the quick and the dead." Was the judge God? Was God the judge?

He didn't believe in either anymore.

Uniformed bailiffs came through the courtroom, in one door and out another, walking with purpose but the purpose wasn't obvious to Laurence, unless it was to sneak a glance at him, something each one did. He kept his own eyes straight ahead and took deep breaths.

"Hi." Rhetta's voice broke his thoughts. She put both hands on his shoulders and leaned down to kiss his temple. "Are you okay?"

"I'm ready to get on with it." He hadn't realized that the benches behind him had filled with spectators. On the other side of the central aisle, a secretary from the D.A.'s office was arranging papers on a desk. He had encountered her before and she'd been businesslike and pleasant. Now she glanced over at him and her mouth was set in a tight frown.

None of them care about Sheila and the baby, he thought. And he had to behave according to a prescribed list to convince the jury that he did care. Apparently actual feelings weren't sufficient.

"Where's Colin?" Rhetta asked.

Before Laurence could answer, the side door opened. District Attorney Boyd Sparks came in and crossed in front of Laurence, but did not look at him. Colin followed and came around the desk. He squatted so that he was between Laurence and Rhetta and took their hands.

"Don't react to what I'm about to tell you." His voice was low. "It seems that Jabel Clark has disappeared."

"What?" Rhetta and Laurence spoke at once.

"Boyd wanted him here at nine o'clock this morning but he didn't show up. Marie Minton came instead and told Boyd she hasn't seen or heard from him since Wednesday." He released their hands and rocked back on his heels.

"What's going to happen?" Laurence asked.

"The judge has issued a warrant for him and Chief Bland is threatening to arrest Marie, too."

"Oh no," Rhetta said.

"He wants to talk to you, too, I'm afraid. He wants to know if you had anything to do with it."

"All rise," the call came, and the judge entered the room.

Colin tugged at Laurence's sleeve to get him to turn around again, but he had to watch to see if Rhetta stumbled, or sank, as she disappeared into the standing, pressing crowd.

"I'll see the lawyers in chambers," the judge said.

He harangued the lawyers for fifteen minutes, demanding to know what either of them knew about the disappearance of the prime witness. When he finally let them go, it was with the warning, "You're going to get one chance to convict this man, Mr. Sparks, and you better not waste it." Then he said court would resume the following Monday.

When that Monday came, when the jury pool was waiting, when the benches in the courtroom had filled up to overflowing again, when Rhetta and Laurence sat straight and still, Colin stood and addressed the judge.

"Your Honor, the Defense calls for the dismissal of all charges."

"Mr. Prosecutor?" the judge asked.

"The State requests a delay of a month."

The judge's long neck allowed his chin to thrust well forward of his shoulders. "The State is incompetent, as best I can tell, and is wasting my time. But that's what I'm here for apparently. You've got four more weeks."

Word spread that Jabel Clark was missing and that the police were looking for him. No one in Sweet Side had any information. The police monitored Marie's house and with the judge's approval, carried out three more searches.

But when the month passed and Judge Horton was on his bench high above the packed courtroom, it was Boyd Sparks who rose.

"Your Honor, as you know, the State's most important witness is not available to testify. For that reason, we must request a further continuance."

"Mr. Prosecutor, when do you expect this witness to be available?"

"We have no way of knowing, Your Honor." Sparks's voice was high and tight.

"Mr. Phillips." the judge's gaze swiveled from Boyd to Colin. "Any comment on Mr. Sparks's request?"

Colin rose. "Your Honor, my client has had to endure the agony of the senseless loss of his wife and unborn child, and the distress of being accused of causing their deaths. He suffers from insomnia, from nightmares, and from many dark hours of the soul. The prosecution brought this unnecessary suffering on him by relying on the testimony of one individual. That person has proven his unreliability by disappearing on the eve of trial. We ask Your Honor to dismiss all charges so that Mr. Vance can attempt to put his life back together."

"Save your closing arguments, Mr. Phillips," Judge Horton said. "Mr. Sparks may yet be able to reinstate the charges, but as of now, they are dismissed."

Laurence closed his eyes and pressed them with the palms of his hands. Lights burst and trailed like meteors behind his eyelids. He felt someone—Colin—pull on his elbow until he stood, and he heard noise rush around him like a wind.

Then Rhetta's voice: "You're free, it's over."

And she embraced him, crying into his shoulder. He held her and began to wonder if he'd gone blind. Then it occurred to him to open his eyes and the room came into focus.

The judge was gone, Boyd Sparks was gone, almost all the people—those who'd come to see him convicted as well as those who'd come to support the family—had filed out of the court-room. The bailiffs smiled at him now as they went about their business, ushering the lingerers out and closing doors.

Laurence had known what would happen. Colin had told him, but it wasn't until the judge had uttered the last words that the reality set in. Not just the reality of the moment, but of what he must do next.

"It's been a horrible time." Colin had a soft smile on his face. "I'm glad it's over for you."

"For us all." Rhetta wiped her eyes with the handkerchief Colin handed her.

"I don't have words ..." Laurence's throat constricted.

"Let's go home," Colin said. "Let's just go home."

Colin felt weightless, as if he had floated over the morning, watching from above.

"Let's eat in the garden," Rhetta said. She was busy making sandwiches and a salad. "Would you carry the tray out?"

Even more than usual, he was struck by her resilience, and her reliance on food to keep people close.

Rhetta followed him with a pitcher of tea and a plate of cook-ies. It was a pleasant day, the air dry, the sun warm, and a breeze moved over the roses and blew the scent toward the house.

"Should I open Champagne?" she said.

"I wouldn't," he said.

Laurence had gone to the cottage to change out of his suit and when he came out, Rhetta served them. She had her hair pinned up. Colin watched tendrils work loose and dance on the back of her neck.

Suddenly, she reached for their hands. "We've survived. We have our lives back."

"Wait." Laurence said. "I need to tell you something Rhetta. I can't stay here."

"You mean in the cottage?" She let go of Colin's hand so she could hold Laurence's with both of hers. "That's okay. I'll help you find something ..."

"I can't stay in Piedmont."

"But why?" She looked at Colin. "Did you know about this?"

"I haven't discussed it with Colin," Laurence said. "But I'm sure he understands. There are people who'll always think I got away with murder, aren't there?" He looked at Colin, who nodded. "I'll never be able to have a life here again."

"But you're a Vance," she said. "You hold your head up and depend on the people who believe in you." Her voice didn't match her strong words.

Laurence smiled at her. "You and Colin and the girls? If there is anybody else, they haven't made themselves known. Rhetta, I don't have the fortitude for the stares and the whispers. I've got to go away."

She turned toward Colin. "Can't you make him stay?"

"No, he can't." Laurence said. "Your lives are here, the two of you and your children. Mine has to be somewhere else."

Two weeks later, Laurence slipped into the house through the sun room, put a note on the kitchen table and drove away. It was just before dawn and he was heading for New York. He wanted his last recollection of Piedmont to be this house, where he had grown up, where the child Jabel Clark had followed him around, where his own child would have had Christmases and birthdays, and where Sheila gradually would have come to feel welcome.

As he closed the door, he heard a sound. It could have been the rip of fabric, or the rasp of stifled breath, or just the sound of an old house giving up something of its own.

Until Proven

PART 2

FEBRUARY 2003

Eden Phillips changed from her work flats to a pair of heels. She handed her keys to the parking valet and started up the steps of the Mangum University president's house.

Above her on the veranda, a man stood in silhouette against a lighted window. She couldn't see his face but he was likely to be someone she knew so she prepared to smile and speak. As she got closer, she saw that he was a black man with cropped graying hair and light skin—a stranger. She smiled a neutral smile and said, "Hello."

"Good evening," he said. Their eyes met.

"Eden, wait." It was her sister's voice. She turned and waited while Wren, their father, and Wren's husband Kenneth came up the stairs.

"Hi," Eden said. "I thought you'd be here ahead of me." She and Wren met with a half-hug. She gave Kenneth a peck on the cheek and then tugged at her father's tie. "Dad, you look great."

"New suit," he said. "The first one I've bought since I retired."

"I bullied him into it," Wren said. "Isn't he handsome? Mother would approve."

As they went in, Eden glanced at the man again. He had turned his back to them.

President Boone and his wife met them at the door. Someone took their coats and they were drawn into the party.

The reception was an annual event for the board of trustees, their spouses, and people known as Friends of Mangum. Eden's grandfather, her mother, and now her sister served on the Board, so family attendance was mandatory. The guest list changed little from year to year, so the party had the air of a reunion. Eden never looked forward to it but once she was there, she had a good time. She circulated, a glass of wine in hand, nibbled boiled shrimp and mini quiches, and caught up with people she hadn't seen since the last reception. Then she spotted State Senator Dexter Long across the room, introducing a newcomer around. She was sure it was the man from the porch and she was curious. President Boone and her father were in the men's path, so she strolled over to link her arm in her father's.

"Colin is telling me how well you're doing, Eden," President Boone said.

"Dad," she stage-whispered, "didn't I tell you not to brag about me? He'll expect a larger contribution this year."

They laughed, and suddenly Dexter and his friend were beside them.

"Colin and Eden," President Boone said, "have you met Professor Marcus Minton? He'll be our Distinguished Visiting Professor next year. And between you and me, I'm doing my best to lure him home from New York for good."

"Home?" Eden asked. "So you're one of the Piedmont Mintons?" She realized that even as he shook her hand, Marcus looked at her father.

"Mr. Phillips and I knew each other years ago," he said.

Her father's face was blank and Eden felt tension rise between him and the newcomer. Beside her, Dexter cleared his throat. So he felt it, too.

"Jabel," Colin said. "You're Jabel Clark."

∽

"You could have given me a little advance notice," Marcus Minton told his cousin.

"About what?"

"You know what. Seeing Colin Phillips."

"It's been forty years, young cousin." Dexter drove toward the center of Piedmont. "I didn't give it a thought."

"Like hell. You think about everything." He laughed to take the edge off the words. He was in Piedmont for the first time since he was eighteen. He had turned down two earlier overtures from Mangum University. Only his granny's great age, failing health, and inability to travel made him accept this time.

The little town he had known was still there, but it was an island he got glimpses of among rising and falling waves of the new strip malls and big box stores that surrounded it. This road, he thought, this was a narrow twisty thing back then, nameless as far he could remember. Now it called itself University Boulevard. Mangum had grown from a respectable college on the edge of town into an internationally-known research institution, so of course Piedmont widened and straightened the road and brought the school within its limits.

"Let me tell you about Colin Phillips," Dexter said. They were at a traffic light, ready to turn onto Court Street. The grand old courthouse with its lit façade and columns loomed ahead. "I didn't know it at the time, but when I got out of the work farm and wanted to go to college, Mangum was going to turn me down flat but somehow Mr. Phillips heard about it and made sure I got in."

He drove south. "And he's contributed to my campaign fund every time I've run, including the first two times when I lost."

Marcus shifted in his seat and adjusted his seatbelt. One of his touchstones was that Dexter was still a radical. It didn't feel right to hear him rationalizing. Especially not for Colin Phillips.

"And," Dexter went on, "I long since lost track of how much pro bono work he's done for the community." Meaning the black community, their old Sweet Side neighborhood, Marcus understood.

"Guilty conscience," he said. Dexter snorted.

They turned into Sweet Side and drove past the church their family had helped to found in the 1890's. Even it had changed. The Christian Education annex was twice the size of the original building and the small parsonage was gone, replaced by a parking lot.

"It's good to see the church thriving," Marcus said.

"It draws everybody back, even those who've moved out to the suburbs. If they don't come, they still send money."

A group of young men occupied a corner on what had once been the business block. They were solid shadows in dark jeans that pooled over their feet and oversized black jackets with hoods up. They turned to watch Dexter's car go by, and even then their faces were hidden.

"Granny never told me how things have gone down around here," Marcus said.

"The old folks who are hanging on went through enough hell to get what they've got. They're not going to let a few drug dealers run them out."

Marcus grunted a laugh. "In her day, Granny would have run them off single-handedly."

They stopped in front of Marie Minton's house but Dexter didn't turn off the engine. "Aren't you coming in?" Marcus asked.

"I need to get home. Kiss Auntie for me. Tell her I'll see her Sunday."

Marcus let himself in the front door. A woman who looked to be in her forties sat in the living room, flipping through a cooking magazine. She smiled when she saw him.

"Hey, Marcus." She stood. "I just dropped by, hoping to see you. I'm Janelle."

They hugged. "Janelle. I remember you in pigtails." In the last few days, he'd had so many of his relatives introduce themselves, it was an embarrassment. "I know you're a faithful visitor here. Thank you for that."

"Aunt Marie was an angel when my mother was sick. I'm glad to do what I can." They both sat on the couch. "Don't tell her, but some of us have a little rotation we do. Somebody checks in at least once a day."

"And you think she doesn't know that? She told me all about it, says she only puts up with it so she won't hurt anybody's feelings."

The kitchen door opened a crack and Marie called, "Is that my baby home? One of y'all come carry this tray."

Marcus took the tray with a tea pot, cups, and a saucer of cookies on it. Marie reached up to pat his cheek. The bones of her hand were light on his skin.

"I didn't used to have to reach so far," she said. "Set it over there. Janelle brought the cookies."

"I don't know if I need caffeine this time of the evening," Marcus said.

"Pshaw. This is green tea. Everybody knows it's good for you." She eased into her chair and closed her sweater around her thin frame. "I wish somebody'd told me about it when I was sixty. Imagine how long I might live if I'd started it sooner." She laughed.

"You've got a long way to go yet," Janelle said. "If I can be like you when I'm ninety-nine, I'll drink my share and Marcus's."

He took the cup Granny poured for him, watching the slight tremor in her hands. Until she was ninety, she had traveled alone back and forth to New York to visit him. After his wife died, when his daughter was a young teenager, Granny had stayed two or three months at a time twice a year. When she quit traveling alone, she would find someone to fly with her, and eventually agreed to the wheelchair in the airports. Then her visits became much shorter and farther apart, and finally stopped. That's why he'd accepted the visiting professorship.

"How's Sydney?" Janelle asked.

"Wonderful. It's hard to believe she's in the middle of her senior year." He took a cookie and bit into it. Besides the shock of seeing the Phillipses, he'd had enough heavy hors d'oeuvres and wine that he would have preferred a glass of seltzer water and early bed. "How is your son doing?"

"Anthony's a sweet young man" Granny said. "You should see him with his baby."

"Baby?" This was news Marcus had not heard. "Is he married?"

"No." Janelle put her cup down hard. "He wanted to marry the girl, but … Well, I don't have much good to say about her. She didn't want the child."

He recalled that Janelle's son and his daughter were about the same age. He shuddered to think of Sydney with a child to raise, dreams gone. "Did Anthony go to college?"

"He finished a year at State," Janelle said. "Now he works evenings when I can take care of Shayna. And he puts her in daycare three mornings a week so he can go to the community college. They both live with me."

Marcus studied her face a moment. She was more than ten years younger than he was, a late child born to his cousin Louise and her husband, Fred. They were so proud of her for getting her pharmacy degree and now she was a regional manager. But it seemed her son would have to work hard to patch together an education. And to raise a little girl as a single parent.

"I look forward to meeting him," he said.

Janelle had maintained a half-smile since they sat down. Now her eyes registered warmth. "You could be a big help to him, since you've raised a daughter."

After Janelle left, Granny insisted on cleaning up the kitchen, then went to bed. Marcus sat alone in the living room with a book on his lap and thought about Janelle's reaction to his interest in her son. He had never reflected on what he had missed after he left Piedmont and all the family, other than Granny, or on what his role might have been in other circumstances. Selfish, he thought. He knew he had flaws but hadn't considered that to be one of them. In fact, he'd been inclined to think the opposite. After all, he was about to spend a year in a place he didn't want to be, for Granny's sake. Now he was less impressed with himself than he had been a few minutes earlier. Maybe he could make amends for time lost by helping Janelle's son and grandchild. And by not wasting any more of it worrying about Colin Phillips and the past.

ᔧ

Wren insisted on riding in the back seat, so Colin sat beside his son-in-law on the way home.

"Was that really him?" Wren asked, leaning as far forward over the console as she could. "How does he dare come here?"

"Of course it's him." Colin was irritated at the questions. "He has a perfect right to be here."

"But isn't he some sort of fugitive?"

"No."

"Well, it doesn't seem right. When you consider what he did to us."

Colin didn't answer.

"This is the guy who accused Laurence?" Kenneth asked. "And he's just reappeared out of the blue?"

"Please," Colin said. "He has done well in life. He has family here. It has nothing to do with us."

"Daddy, want to come in for some real food?" Wren asked when they got home.

Rhetta had left her family home to Wren and Eden, with the understanding that Colin had a life interest. He had, instead, moved into the cottage behind the house so that Wren and Kenneth could raise their children there.

"No thanks. A bowl of cereal and a book are waiting for me." He kissed her goodnight and walked through the rose garden to his cottage. No doubt Wren would have her sister on the phone before he could get there, wanting to talk about Jabel. He hoped that she wouldn't obsess. He hoped that he himself wouldn't obsess, but wasn't optimistic.

MARCH 2003

Eden answered the telephone and heard Dexter Long's voice.

"Ms. Phillips. What an honor it is to speak with you."

"Senator." She responded in kind. They had come to know each other well, but he always began with formalities, before jumping to his purpose.

"Eden, I'm calling on behalf of my cousin, Sydney Marie Minton. She hopes to find a law firm to intern with for a year and I thought of you."

"She's in law school?" Eden was working at her computer. She forced herself to keep her free hand off the keyboard. "She can certainly send me a résumé."

"She is an undergraduate at Harvard and will earn her BA this spring. She is interested in the law but wants to gain some experience before making such an important decision."

"You have a legal department, Dexter. Is there a reason why you aren't hiring her?"

"The girl isn't interested in the legal issues that percolate up in an insurance company like mine. She said she'd rather sue them when they trample on people." He laughed. "I couldn't take offense. She's young and earnest and her father has kept her in the dark about a lot of family history."

"Who's her father?" Her interest rose, and she anticipated the answer.

"My cousin Marcus. You met him."

Eden tried to keep her voice steady. "And you think she should work for me?"

"You do the kind of advocacy law she's interested in," he said. "And I know you won't hold old stuff—sins of the father and such—against her."

"Of course I won't." She knew Dexter was daring her to say

the opposite. "But with your connections, you could get her a job anywhere."

"I offered, as a matter of fact. Philadelphia or Washington, but she wants to be in Piedmont. Hey, I have sons. How am I supposed to know what a twenty-one-year-old girl is thinking?" He laughed again. "So she's writing you a letter with recommendations and so forth. You'll like her, Eden."

The letter came and Eden handed it to her assistant, Jessica, to read. "She says she'll be here on spring break. Make an appointment for her to interview."

"A Harvard girl? Oh goody." Jessica gave a fist pump. "You need to hire her."

"Sight unseen?" She smiled.

"She needs my help to explain the real world to her. I mean, she's coming to Piedmont on spring break for God's sake."

Sydney Marie Minton was on time to the minute. Eden took in the navy blue suit, the deep pink scarf, and pearl earrings, then registered long wavy hair, almost the same color as her pale caramel skin. Her eyes were like her father's, green lit with gold. It was clear to Eden that her mother had been white.

"How do you do, Ms. Phillips? Thank you for seeing me." They shook hands.

"Let's sit over here." Eden had a pair of wing chairs that faced each other over a small table in a corner of the office. "Now, tell me about your interest in Phillips and Phillips."

Sydney was practiced and poised. She had her speech ready and went through it with confidence in her voice, but Eden noticed that her right foot rocked on the heel of her pump, the only sign of nerves.

When she finished, Eden said, "Okay. If you can work for what I can pay, and if you're willing to be the gopher, I can hire you. There won't be any glamour, but I'll make sure you get to see what a plaintiff's attorney really does." She leaned forward and offered her hand. "Now, tell me how your great-grand-mother is."

"Do you know Granny?" She was surprised.

"My mother knew her very well and loved her."

"I love her, too. She practically lived with us for a while when my mom died. I don't know how Daddy would have made it." Sydney was solemn with womanly wisdom. "I plan to stay with her now."

"I'm sure she'll love that. Your father will be here, too, I understand."

"He's renting an apartment. He thinks I'll live with him, but he's mistaken." She smiled. "Granny says I can paint his old room and girly it up a little."

Eden was amused by how easily the proper job candidate mask slipped away. The girl behind it was endearing. Then as if she realized what had happened, Sydney stood and offered her hand again.

"I promise you'll be glad to have hired me, Ms. Phillips."

"Call me Eden, and stay in touch."

JUNE 2003

Eden parked in the lot behind her office and retrieved her laptop bag and briefcase from the back seat. Jessica's car wasn't there yet. It was the day after the long Memorial Day weekend and it was also the morning Sydney Minton was to start work. It wouldn't be the best time for Jessica to come huffing and puffing in, twenty minutes late, a little pale, with a story about a faulty alarm clock or a line at the ATM.

Eden went in the back door, put her bags down in her office, then went into the reception area. When she drew the drapes on the front windows, she saw a young woman sitting on a bench across the street, a large Starbucks travel cup beside her, head down and eyes closed. It was Sydney.

Eden opened the front door, waited for a car to pass, then crossed the street.

"Sydney, good morning." She touched the girl's shoulder.

"Hi." Sydney sat up straight and blushed. "How embarrassing. Note to self, don't let the boss catch you sleeping on a bench."

"The boss is impressed that you beat her here." Eden smiled.

"One of my cousins gave me a ride and she had to be at work early."

"We'll get a key made for you."

Sydney stood and smoothed her skirt. She wore a peacock blue blouse that lit up her green eyes and the pearl earrings from the interview. Eden had the sense that they were once her mother's.

They walked into the office just as Jessica came through the back entrance. Eden was relieved to see she had found time to fix her hair, do full makeup, and wore a new pantsuit.

Jessica came forward with her hand out. "Girl, am I glad to see you."

Eden saw Sydney's confusion. "You remember my right-hand woman, Jessica Sprunt? She's got first dibs on your time."

"And I'm a slave driver," Jessica said, then her eyes grew wide and her mouth went slack as she remembered Sydney's heritage.

Don't say another word, Eden thought, but Sydney was either oblivious or too poised to react. "I want to do everything there is to do," she said. "I want to learn all I possibly can."

"I've got to get ready for a nine o'clock client," Eden said. "If you can spare her, Jess, I'll take Sydney to lunch today. Till then, she's yours."

At 12:30, Eden and Sydney slid into a booth at the Village Grill.

"So what have you learned so far?" Eden studied the girl's face and thought her eyes looked a bit glazed.

"How to make coffee. How to answer phones. How to greet people. How to email documents to the copy shop. Who knew it was so complicated to do simple stuff?"

"I can see what's coming. Jessica will want a raise because you're proving it takes two people to do what she usually does."

The waiter came to take their orders. Sydney asked for a salad and yawned as she handed him her menu. "Excuse me. It's like this morning when you found me. I stay sleepy all the time since I got here."

"If your college career was anything like mine, you're coming off of four years of sleep deprivation." Eden reached for the glass of iced tea the waiter had put in front of her.

"Eden, may I ask you something?"

"Sure."

"You've known my family here a long time, right? Do you know any secrets about my father?" Her voice was soft.

Eden stirred a lemon wedge down to the bottom of her glass to buy a little time. "In my experience, everybody has secrets. Have you asked him?"

The waiter put their plates in front of them.

"Papa wasn't excited when I told him you'd offered me a job and I can't figure it out. It seems perfect. I want to spend time with Granny and I want to get to know this huge family that's here. So I asked him straight out, why?"

"What did he say?"

"Just that there are bad memories. But he won't say what." She picked at her salad, sorting out the radishes.

Eden couldn't help wanting to know what Marcus had told his daughter. "You're not convinced?"

"It just feels as if there's more. This past weekend, on Saturday, there was a big family gathering to welcome me and I kept asking people to tell me about Papa when he was a boy. They'd tell all these great stories, but then it was like there was a wall and when the story came too close to the wall, it just stopped." She jabbed the air with her fork. "So what I want to know is, did Papa do something wrong? Against the law, maybe?"

"Now how in the world do you get to that conclusion?"

"Does it sound crazy?"

Before she could answer, Eden felt a hand on her shoulder. "Hi. Aunt Eden."

She looked up at her redheaded nephew Sean. "Where did you come from?"

He leaned down to hug her. "I went by your office and Jessica said you're here." He turned to Sydney. "You must be the intern. I'm Sean Laurence Caldwell."

"Sydney Minton." Sydney extended a hand.

Sean insinuated his long legs onto the bench beside Eden, all the time making eye contact with Sydney. Yikes, Eden thought, yikes.

"Jessica tells all," Sean said. "You just graduated summa cum laude from Harvard." He shook his hand as if he'd touched something hot. "I'm going to be a senior at Mangum. If you can stand to hang with a local yokel, I'll show you around town."

Color rose in Sydney's cheeks and she glanced at Eden.

"If you spend any time with this yokel," Eden said, "you'll discover he's smarter than he looks and his mother, my sister, taught him some decent manners."

"Did you want to order something?" The waiter leaned over Sean to refill Eden's tea glass.

"Burger and fries. And I'll take the ladies' check, too."

"Big spender." Eden was amused.

"Aunt Eden." He jostled her with his elbow and pretended to whisper. "You're messing up my play here." Then, to Sydney, "I don't start my summer job till next week. Maybe we could do lunch again tomorrow?"

"I'll have to see what Eden needs for me to do."

"She's a softy." He put his arm around Eden's shoulder.

As they walked back to the office, Eden said to Sydney, "My nephew is what they call irrepressible, but if you don't want to go to lunch with him, you don't have to. It'll have nothing to do with you and me."

"Thanks. That was a little awkward."

Ha, Eden thought. The only thing making it awkward was old Aunt Eden, and maybe a few of those family secrets.

Colin had retired five years earlier, but kept an office at Phillips and Phillips. It was a small one, furnished to his plain taste. He teased Eden that she'd hardly let him get out the door before she redecorated the rest of the suite. She had, in fact, raided the Vance family attic for a silk French rug, a pair of wing chairs, a brass chandelier and some glass front bookcases from her grandparents' day. Some interior designer had managed to turn these bits of history into a setting worthy of a magazine spread—except for his office.

He accepted that his idea of a law office being an austere place was out of date. It was harder to accept the new legal assistant, Miss Sprunt, who had now worked for Eden for a year. Miss Sprunt was given to bright clothing and various hair dos that he had trouble overlooking. She seemed efficient, he acknowledged, and Eden swore by her, called her "the fixer."

When he walked into the office, Jessica Sprunt greeted him, "Hey, Mr. Phillips" and handed him whatever mail had accumulated, the envelopes slit opened, organized by date.

"Thank you, Miss Sprunt." He glanced towards Eden's closed door. "Is she in?"

"No sir. She went to a deposition, and she took Sydney with her."

"So Miss Minton has started."

Eden had told him about her summer intern. He knew his reaction was unreasonable, but having Jabel Clark's daughter in the office made him uneasy. Not that there was anything she might find; there was nothing on paper to show that he'd been ready to throw Jabel to the lions forty years earlier. The evidence of that was in his heart and mind.

"The first of the week," Jessica said, "and guess who's sweet on her? Sean."

"My grandson? But how?"

"Magnetism." She laughed but it was a nervous laugh, no doubt in response to his reaction.

"All right." He turned and went into his office. It had been a pleasure to watch his grandchildren grow up. First the only girl, Caraleigh, both quiet and independent, reminding him so much of Eden. The youngest, Peter and Terence, were twins, double-bonus babies their father called them. Colin thought of them as puppies, needing only food, naps, and love—and constantly surprised that anyone would object to the latest way they'd found to occupy themselves.

"I don't know what I did to deserve this," Wren said to him

more than once when the twins used a beloved rosebush as a soccer goal. "Thank God for Sean."

Sean was the middle child, between Caraleigh and the twins. He was named Sean Laurence for his uncle, and looked like him, right down to their baby pictures. But from early days Sean had an easy-going nature and openness that his namesake had struggled to find. Also from early days, Colin saw that the boy was Wren's favorite. That made him grateful for the twins. With them to keep her busy, she didn't have time to dote on Sean the way Rhetta had doted on Laurence.

The twins had been born a year after Rhetta died, and Colin believed that there was some connection, that the pregnancy was part of Wren's grieving, though he wasn't sure how or why. Maybe Rhetta and I should have had more children, he thought—a boy to make up for the loss of her brother. But then again, Peter and Terence in no way threatened Sean's place as prince of the family.

He snapped himself out of it. Sean and Sydney ... there was something to make Wren fret. Wren's best friend since girlhood was Susan Lyle Fallon, married to U.S. Senator Avery Fallon. According to Wren and Susan, their children, Sean and Brooke, were all but engaged.

~

That evening, after she'd eaten the salad she'd picked up on her way home, Eden took a glass of white wine out to the screened porch on the back of her house. A large oak tree shaded the porch during the day and with the ceiling fan on, it was comfortable after dark, no matter how hot the day had been. The deposition she'd had that afternoon ran long. When she got back to the office, Jessica told her that her father had been there, had waited a while to talk to her, and had left seeming worried about something.

Ever since, Eden had struggled with whether or not to call him. Jessica was prone to overstating things and it was Eden's role to be the daughter who didn't worry about him, or at least didn't worry him with her worries. She sipped the wine and tried again to think of a valid reason to call him and check on his frame of mind, and suddenly her own phone rang.

"Hi, Aunt Eden. It's Sean."

"Hi." It had been a long time since he'd called her and he sounded almost the way he had when he was a kid, calling to ask if she'd take him swimming in the river.

"Hey. Umm, listen," he said, "if you're not too busy, could we come by?"

"Who's we?"

"Sydney and me. We'll take you for ice cream."

She was aware she delayed before she spoke. "Sure. Come on out." She said it fast, to make up for any hesitation.

Sean and Sydney must have been almost to Black Haw when he called. Eden barely had time to change from her baggy cutoffs to black linen shorts, put on a white linen blouse, and comb her hair before she heard the front door open and Sean call, "We're here."

"I see you are." She came to give him a big hug and Sydney a light one. "What are you two up to?"

"Out on the town." Sean grinned.

"I told him, you see enough of me and we shouldn't interrupt your evening," Sydney said. She glanced up at him, her cheeks a little flushed.

"It's okay," Eden said. "The promise of ice cream gets me every time." They all laughed and Sean made a show of opening the door wide, bowing them through.

They walked up the street toward the town's small business district. The Mill Town Provisionary occupied the building that had once been the store run by the Black Haw Mill for its employees. It was now a gourmet grocery, café, used bookshop, and ice cream parlor.

"I was telling her, they give you these little wooden paddle things to use for spoons," Sean said. "And how we used to take them back to your house and try to eat our cereal with them the next morning when we slept over."

"I'd forgotten that," Eden said, and then to Sydney, "Sean and his sister and brothers used to love to come out here for a weekend, but it's been a while."

"Did you know it's a full moon tonight?" Sean asked. "I thought maybe we'd walk down by the river with our ice cream."

"You think you can find the path again?" Eden teased.

"You can show us," he said.

"I'll just point you in the right direction."

Sean bought for all of them. Strawberry sorbet for Sydney, Mud Puddle for himself, and with a trace of irony, Eden ordered Rocky Road. The Provisionary had a row of chairs on the front porch, and they were full of people eating ice cream, enjoying the early summer evening and the old timey ambience of Mill Street with its row of galleries and shops.

"This is cool." Sydney paused to look around. "It's like a little oasis."

"It's Mecca for the creative class now, but people thought I was nuts when I moved out here."

"Why?" Sydney asked. They began to stroll up the street.

"The mill had closed down. The town was half deserted. I had just gotten divorced and just gone into practice with Dad, and I somehow thought I had time to fix up an old house. People do crazy things when they feel like they've lost all control over their lives." She laughed.

"You're never out of control, Eden," Sean said.

"If you only knew. The Law keeps you humble that way." She looked at Sydney, who walked between them. "You've been warned, young woman. Now, I'm going this way. Y'all enjoy the river path. It's a great night for it."

She took a few steps away from them, then turned to look. They were holding hands now and were trying to match strides. She remembered—one of the first challenges of a new love.

Eden was surprised to see that she had a phone message, and even more surprised that it was from her father. She settled back on the porch and called him.

"I just thought I'd ask," he said, "how Miss Minton is doing."

"She's smart. Confident. If she decides on law school, she'll eat it with a spoon."

"What? Oh, I see what you mean."

"Sorry, Dad. It's an expression of Jessica's. She's rubbed off on me."

"And speaking of Miss Sprunt ..." He sounded uncomfortable. "I don't like gossip, you know that, but she did say something about Sean and Miss Minton."

"Did she? Well, she doesn't know what a minefield that is." She thought for a few seconds before saying, "They were just here, Dad. Sean brought her out to get ice cream and see the river in the moonlight."

"Oh. Well."

"My feelings exactly. I hired her because I had no reason not to. Except for the family history, and that just didn't seem right. And I'm glad I did, but." She paused. "There's Wren. I avoided telling her I hired the girl. Now I'm not sure what to do."

"It seems to me someone said that Brooke Fallon is going to England for the summer." He sighed. "I've always thought Sean was too young to be so attached to a girl, even one as fine as Brooke."

"They're both too young. Maybe the thing with Sydney, whatever it is, will blow over by the time Brooke gets home." The ice cream was thick and sludgy in its cup on the table beside her. She wished she'd poured another glass of wine on her way through the house. "Dad, is this what's bothering you? Do you think I was wrong to take Sydney on?"

"If you'd asked me, I'd have said exactly what you felt. It's ridiculous to hold her responsible for what happened so long ago. But having her here among us, and knowing that Jabel will be back any day now … it brings back all the old memories."

She thought of Sydney's question about family secrets. She herself had been twelve when her aunt Sheila died. She had memories but they had been shaped and reshaped over four decades and mostly had to do with her parents' marriage. As an adult, with a divorce on her own record, she looked back and saw the cracks they had plastered over.

"I suppose," her father said, "we kept all of you young people in the dark, thinking we were protecting you. But really, people mostly act to protect themselves."

❧

Sean had never driven into Sweet Side before, but he knew where to turn in, by the big brick church. Even at 9:15 on Friday night, the stained glass windows shimmered, its parking lot was brightly lit, and a dozen or so cars were there.

"I think it's choir practice," Sydney said. "There's always something going on."

He heard a degree of wonder in her voice and glanced at her.

"It's really different here," she said. "I knew it wouldn't be New York or Cambridge, of course, but I'm still wrapping my head around what it is."

"My big sister couldn't wait to get away from Piedmont. Or maybe from Mom." He laughed. "But—this may sound totally stupid to you—I like it here." He hesitated a moment, but felt safe saying a little more to her. "I feel like it's where I'm supposed to be."

"Yes." She turned under her seatbelt to face him. "That's what I didn't expect. To feel that."

They drove by a group of young people gathered in the

parking lot of a closed gas station with fat lettered graffiti on the plywood windows. Rap music beat from somewhere and there was a partying atmosphere. Sean's foot pressed harder on the accelerator. He hoped she didn't notice.

"You turn at the next corner," Sydney said. "Then Granny's is the last house on the right, at the end of that street."

"I have to say, this doesn't seem like a place you'd belong in." He was looking at the houses with cars parked in the yards. Street lights showed sagging porches and unkempt yards.

"It's not so much the place as it is the sense of place. Like the church. You go in and you feel all the history of it. Did you know that it was like Civil Rights Central for Piedmont? And the family. I grew up with just Papa and Mama and Granny, then just Papa and Granny. Now I've got cousins and aunts and uncles and all these great stories."

He turned where she'd told him to. "My mom is always saying be careful what you wish for."

"What do you mean?"

He laughed. "Family. It can be the best and it can be the worst."

He stopped in front of a small house at the end of the street. The porch lights were on and the windows on the front of the house glowed.

"You know what you need to do?" Sydney asked. "You need to come around and open my door for me, help me out of the car, walk me to the door, and come in to meet Granny."

"Really?" He was surprised.

"I promise, she's watching and it's a good idea to show what a gentleman you are." She unlatched her seat belt and nudged him with her elbow.

He leaned past her and saw a slight movement behind a curtain. "How old did you say she is?"

"You're not scared of a ninety-nine-year-old lady?"

"Heck no." He got out, bounded around the car in exaggerated slow motion, opened her door and bowed her out. "Milady."

By the time they got to the front door, it was open for them. Sean had no idea what a person so old would look like until there she was, angular and soft at the same time—pointed face bones with skin that pillowed on either side her mouth, cottony white hair and sharp green eyes.

"Introduce your young man, Sydney."

"Ms. Marie Minton, may I introduce my friend, Sean Caldwell?"

"How do you do, Ms. Minton?" He was suddenly glad for his mother's insistence on knowing old fashioned manners.

"You two come on in," she said and led the way into the living room. She motioned for him to sit on a straight-backed chair. Sydney sat on the couch, on the end nearest to him, and Ms. Minton sank into an arm chair that was clearly hers. "Now, Sean." She made a mouthful out of his name.

"Yes ma'am."

"Your grandmother Rhetta and I had a serious falling out." She pressed her elbows into the chair arms to straighten herself.

"You did?" He'd never heard that. "My mom says you practically raised her mother and uncle."

"Did she say I was like part of the family?" She snorted. He was puzzled. That's exactly what his mother said.

"Granny," Sydney said, "Sean doesn't know any more than I do about whatever happened way back then. Nobody tells us."

From the look she gave him, Sean thought Ms. Minton wasn't buying it. Then the look melted and she smiled at him.

"Get us some lemonade, Sydney, and when you get back, I'll educate you young people."

She began, "Your papa will be unhappy with me, Sydney, but I'm going to do it anyway because he won't."

When she finished her story, Ms. Minton rose, her hands a little shaky on the arms of her chair. Sean and Sydney both stood and reached out to her.

"Just hand me that cane from over there." She pointed to an umbrella stand. Sean jumped to do it.

"All right then," she said. "I'll leave you two to say your good-nights." She straightened herself and went down the hallway.

When he heard a door close, Sean turned to Sydney, who had cried off and on but had not said a word during the last hour.

"It's okay," he said. That sounded stupid, but he had no idea what else to say.

"It isn't." Sydney shook her head. "How can you say that? They've lied to us all our lives." She looked up at him. Her eyes looked darker and a vertical line appeared between her brow. Her mouth was tight and narrow, her jaw line thin as a blade.

He wanted to soften the harden muscles of her face, wanted to be the one who could lighten her eyes. He'd never felt it before—this urge to just hold somebody.

"What I think I meant was, we're okay. Aren't we?" He put one hand on her shoulder and she stepped into his arms. They had not done much more than hold hands and kiss a little, but he was overwhelmed by the rightness of the fit. He wrapped his arms around her and stood still until she relaxed, inhaled and exhaled, and then when she released herself, he stepped back.

"We're okay," she said.

Sean had planned to meet some buddies after he took Sydney home, but he wasn't in the mood for beer and pool anymore. He had moved home for the summer and that's where he headed. It was 10:30. The twins would be out, and his mom and dad were probably in bed already. He was pretty sure his granddad would be up, though. Granddad said it was one of the perks of old age—he didn't need sleep the way he used to.

Sure enough, the big house was dark except for the lights Mom always left on when somebody wasn't home, but Grandad's cottage was lit up. Sean parked and walked into the back yard.

Colin opened the door as if he'd heard the footsteps on the gravel path. "Sean, what a delight. Come in."

Sean stepped inside, suddenly unsure what to say. When he was a little boy, Sean would sneak out of bed and come see Granddad. It had been their secret. But it had been a long time.

"Do you have a beer?" he asked.

"I have to remember, you're of age now." Granddad laughed and led him into the kitchen. "In the refrigerator. Would you like a glass?"

"The bottle's fine." Sean took a pale ale.

"Now what brings you? Is everything all right?"

"I don't know." Sean sat at the table and waited for Granddad to put ice in a glass, pour bourbon for himself, and then take the other chair. "You know Aunt Eden has an intern, right? And you know who she is? I mean her name's Sydney, but you know who her dad is, right?"

"Yes, I know."

Sean shifted and began to scrape the label with his thumbnail. "Okay, so. I met Sydney's grandmother tonight and she said if we're going to be friends, we ought to know what happened back in the '60s. And she told us."

"I've been thinking about all of that lately, with Jabel, or Marcus, coming back, and his daughter. Even without knowing that you and Sydney are friends, I'd begun to think that it's time to quit keeping secrets."

"Is it true? Uncle Laurence might have killed his wife?" He watched Granddad's face and saw a flinch. "And Grandmother hired some guy to set fires at a church and at Ms. Marie's house?"

"Your grandmother let her love for her brother overrule her good sense."

Sean took a draw on his beer and swallowed loudly. "What happened to her?"

"She pled nolo contendre, was given a suspended sentence. It changed her, though. Changed her life."

"That's pretty weird."

"I trust Marie told you that Laurence was never brought to trial. Without Jabel's testimony, there was no evidence."

"So it was never settled." Sean had grown up thinking that the law was a calm and orderly thing, the way Granddad was calm and orderly, and Aunt Eden, too. Now he expected Granddad to say something right away, something about innocent until proven guilty or something else lawyerly and meaningless. Instead, there was silence for a long minute.

"Sean, I'm as sure as I can be that your uncle was not a murderer."

"Then Jabel was lying?" Sean thought of Sydney.

"It wasn't that simple. The truth seldom is." Colin sipped at his drink. "My job would have been to make the jury comfortable with the gray areas. The whole thing was going to come down to black and white, you see."

Sean didn't see, but he knew when Granddad talked that way, he expected you to keep up. "Ms. Marie's story made me sad. And the way she told it, like she was saying, 'Here you are and here's how you got here, so deal with it.'"

Granddad laughed. "Not her exact words, I'm sure, but that's Marie all right. Deal with what the world delivers."

"I don't think Sydney's ready to deal yet. She was mad as hell about it, and her dad gets to town tomorrow."

Granddad smiled. "I can almost feel sorry for him."

"Yeah." Sean laughed a little. Then he finished his beer and started to stand up.

"May I ask you something?" Granddad held out a hand to stop him from going.

"Sure." He eased back into the chair.

"You may want to tell me it's none of my business. I wonder about you and Sydney becoming so friendly. I always thought your affections were … what should I say? Otherwise engaged."

"You mean Brooke." Sean smiled. "Brooke and I are best friends, but we aren't girlfriend and boyfriend. We never have been."

"That comes as a surprise."

"I know. I've tried to explain to Mom, but she and Dr. Fallon have had Brooke and me married off since we were kids. And you know how Mom is." He shook his head and Granddad smiled back. "Here's the deal. When we were about thirteen or fourteen, Brooke and I made this pact. We'd just hang out and do stuff together because we were like brother and sister, except that we really liked each other. We'd just let the world think whatever it wanted to think."

"That's a sophisticated understanding for a pair of teenagers."

"It worked great for a long time. It just took all the pressure off. Since we've been at Mangum, we've both gone out with a few other people but neither of us found anybody we were goo-goo-gaga about. Until sometime last fall, Brooke started getting mysterious, didn't want to spend much time together, almost dropped out of sight."

"Was she goo-goo-gaga?"

"That's what I thought, and I asked. She said no, she was just busy. I didn't buy it." The truth was, it had hurt more than he expected when Brooke withdrew from him. "Anyway, she's going to be in England till mid-August." They had finally had a long talk and she'd promised him that when she got back, she'd tell him what was going on.

"And what about you and Sydney?" Granddad asked. "Goo-goo?"

"Totally. But keep it to yourself, okay?"

⌒

Marcus Minton had leased a three-bedroom condominium in the Highgate development just north of Piedmont. Janelle

Huey had told him about it. That was where her son, Anthony, worked as a night security guard. Marcus was doubtful that Highgate needed much in the way of human security; the rental agent assured him that there had never been a break-in and the police had never had reason to answer a call. It was gated, had a complicated system for getting in, with motion lights on the perimeter and an alarm system. The security people could even trip a siren to warn people of any emergencies.

"What are they afraid of?" Marcus asked. One corner of his mouth lifted.

The agent's shoulders stiffened and he took a step back. "We were under construction on 9/11."

Marcus turned his head away and smiled in full. The young man showing him around would find burning crosses and Little Dixie as unlikely as he found the idea of Al-Qaida in Piedmont. But he took the apartment, in part because he still hoped Sydney and even Marie would move in with him, in part because of his intention to get to know Anthony.

An interior designer who worked for the developer furnished the place like a hotel suite and he moved in on Saturday, June 7. Sydney was there to meet him. He'd been so reluctant to come back here, even more reluctant to have her here, but now he realized it would be the first time in four years that he might see her every day. He hugged her, held her a moment longer until he could force tears back down. Then he realized she was stiff in his arms.

"So how are you?" he asked.

"Same as I was when you called me from the airport an hour ago." She stepped away. "I want to talk to you."

"Something serious?" He followed her into the living room. Sydney turned to face him. "Granny told me all about Jabel Clark."

His breath deserted him and his chest caved.

"You should have told me, Papa." She planted her feet and crossed her arms.

"Why did she? Did somebody else say something?"

"Laurence Vance's great-nephew is a friend of mine. He didn't know either. She told us both."

He nodded and met her gaze, not knowing what to say.

"You had this other name. This other life." She flung her hands up in front of her, her fingers extended as if she'd failed to catch something. "You should have told me."

"I see that. Yes."

"You accused a man of murder and then you ran away."

He waited until she sat. Her arms were tight against her ribs and her face tighter.

"Sweetheart, I left Piedmont because I was afraid, partly for myself, but more for Granny. Someone wanted to drive me away, and they were willing to use her to do it. I didn't want her to suffer."

"But she did suffer. She said she didn't know where you were for a while."

"I didn't know if the court here could drag me back. I didn't know what would happen. Great-uncle Marcus helped me get papers in my new name, Marcus Minton II, and then into the Army. Every time I saw a policeman, or an MP, I wanted to run. Basic training was a nightmare." He bounced the heel of his hand off of his forehead. "I didn't feel safe until I got out of the country. Can you believe that?"

He could see his daughter's breathing was shallow and quick, and on her face, something like shock. "Sydney, I am sorry. Maybe if your mother had lived, she'd have known how to handle it."

"Did she know?" When he nodded, she doubled over, her face in her hands, and cried. His feet moved a step toward her of their own volition, but his brain overruled them. She wouldn't want comfort from him.

When she had cried herself out, she stood with shaky dignity. "We have to go to Dexter's house. Granny's there. It's a barbecue to welcome you home, so you should change clothes." Then she moved off to the powder room.

Marcus was in no mood for a party, but he lugged a suitcase into the master bedroom and found khakis, a sport shirt, and loafers. By the time he was ready, she had washed her face, smoothed her hair, and the red was fading from her cheeks if not her eyes.

"Ready?" he asked.

Dexter and his wife, Phoebe, lived in a big brick house on a large lot in a development near the university. Marcus had visited there in the winter, and couldn't help but think of the farmhouse where his cousin had grown up.

"They lived to see it, you know," Dexter had said, meaning his parents. "Mama said I should be whupped for getting above my raising." They both laughed, knowing that meant she couldn't be prouder.

Phoebe opened the front door before Marcus could find the doorbell.

"Here you are." She took Marcus's hands and kissed his cheek. "Sydney, I'm so glad to meet you." She kissed her. "Come right through. Everyone's waiting."

The broad hallway went straight through the house to French doors, onto the patio where Dexter held court in Bermuda shorts and a Hawaiian shirt, a drink in hand. Beyond him, the extended clan flowed out onto the lawn. Sixty people, including the children, cheered when they saw Marcus.

Dexter came to embrace them both, saying, "Y'all took your sweet time," then stood aside for Granny.

Marcus stooped to hug her, her warmth a relief after his daughter's chill. "How I have wished for this day," she whispered.

"You coming home."

He wanted to remind her, he wasn't here forever, just a year, but before he could frame the words, cousins and in-laws, some known and some not, surged around him.

Sydney stood back, as did the youngest family members, little children two generations removed from her father and his story. She turned and looked out to the back yard. A catering company had set up a stainless steel portable kitchen and three people in white stood at attention, waiting for someone to give a signal

"Hey, Cousin." It was Anthony, holding his little girl. "Shayna wants to say hi."

The little girl wore pink from the barrettes on her braids to her tiny sandals.

"Can I hold her?" Sydney held out her arms and Shayna went to her with a smile.

"Want me to get you something to drink?" Anthony asked.

"White wine?"

"You got it." He patted Shayna's fat diapered bottom as he left to go to the bar.

The little girl held tight to Sydney with one arm and reached the other hand out toward Anthony.

"Your daddy will be right back," Sydney said, and danced her around a little, trying to get a smile from her. Just holding the baby made her feel better.

Finally, the barbecued chicken and steaks, salads and garlic bread and baked beans were served, along with plenty of beer and wine and sweet tea.

"Not like the old days, when we snuck off to take a drink," Dexter said and all the people of a certain age laughed.

"If it was my house," Granny said, "I'd take the broom to all of y'all." But she waved her hand as if brushing off a fly, sharing the joke.

Sydney and Anthony sat together to eat.

"I just met your dad a little while ago. He's a nice guy. Why did he stay gone so long?"

She glanced at him. "Some deep, dark family secret, maybe."

"For real?" He laughed. "I thought everybody knew everybody's business in this family. And the history? Wait till the old folks get started on that."

"You think you know all the stories?" She doubted it.

"I've heard them all about a thousand times." He laughed again. "Mom says I'll treasure them one day, and that our generation will tell ours just the same way."

As the evening went on, Anthony, his mother and daughter, and other people with small children left.

Dexter and Phoebe's youngest son, Johnny, called out, "Anybody want to shoot some pool? Play video games? Come on downstairs."

Phoebe happened to be near Sydney and touched her arm. "You should go on with the young people. Johnny's got a whole arcade in the rec room."

"Thanks. Let me just see about Granny first."

She found Granny sitting in a lawn chair between Dexter and her father.

"Pull up a seat, honey," Granny said. "I want Dexter to tell you about the time he spent on the prison farm."

Sydney felt her mouth drop open. More she didn't know. Someone provided her with a bench and other people drew up until there was a circle of listeners.

"Not much to tell," Dexter began. "We dug holes and filled them up again. I did a little organizing as best I could with a bunch of men who didn't trust their own shadow. There was this one guy …"

Sydney watched her father's face. He leaned back, looking down at the ground in front of him. Granny held one of his hands, the other was loose on his lap. He looked as if his mind was elsewhere, but she knew that was how he looked when he was listening with all his energy.

"So that's how I wound up in solitary the first time," Dexter said. "But it's all right. I'm still here." He began to laugh. "I'm still here and organizing."

After that, the stories turned tender and humorous, about run-away mules and folks long dead. Sydney loved the responses around her, the murmurs, the laughter ahead of a punch line. Her father was relaxed now, but when he smiled, Sydney thought it had a sadness to it, the way he smiled when they talked about her mother. She wanted to stay mad, but began to soften.

"And then," Dexter said, "there was the time Jabel—I mean this one ..." He pointed with his thumb. "This one and I drove Daddy's truck into the creek and got it stuck."

"You were the one driving. You nearly killed us both, going over that bank." It was Marcus, speaking up suddenly, as if he'd just arrived. There was a moment of silence and then the laughter rose louder than ever, like the lingering chord of a hymn.

Finally, the group began to break up with a round of "past my bedtimes." Sydney went inside to locate her Granny's purse and cake plate. Two cousins, women in their twenties, stood in the kitchen, their backs to the door.

"White girl trying to pass for black," one said.

"She thinks listening to the old folks to tell their stories will make her one of us," the other said.

Sydney felt as if she'd been slapped but rebounded fast. I won't cry over them, she thought. "Excuse me."

They jumped and turned, both shame-faced. She walked between them and took the plate out of the drainer, then gave them each a direct look before stalking out again.

⌐∽

Sunday morning. The fight with Sydney, then the party, the stories, Granny's fine-boned hand, the strange apartment, the sterile bed. Not since he left Piedmont all those years ago had Marcus felt so unmoored and alone.

He got up at seven o'clock. While he waited for coffee to drip and wondered where to go to buy the Times, he heard a buzzer. It was from the downstairs door—a touch of city living. He went to the panel with the tiny screen that showed him who his visitor was, Anthony Huey in a tan and green uniform.

Marcus buzzed him in and opened the front door of the condo for him. "Good morning."

"I hope I'm not waking you." Anthony was soft-spoken with a good smile, as Marcus had observed the night before. "Mom said I ought to drop in after my shift, to see if you need any help."

"I was up. I'm making coffee. Will you have a cup with me?"

"That'd be nice." He yawned.

"Come on in then." They went through the living room into the kitchen. "Do you work all night every night?"

"Sometimes it's from five o'clock till eleven. Sometimes it's eleven to seven."

"A tough schedule." Marcus opened cabinet doors until he found dishes in the place the designer had thought they should be. "Cream? Sugar?"

"Just black thanks." Anthony accepted the mug Marcus filled for him. "The schedule works good for me. I can take care of Shayna during the days, except when I go to class and then I have her in daycare. Mom says it's good for her to be around other kids because I spoil her." He laughed.

"When do you study?"

"At work. The folks who live here aren't exactly night people so especially on that late shift, I can study a lot."

"You have it all sorted out, as long as sleeping isn't something you care about." He'd made the coffee strong and enjoyed the first jolt. That and the guest lifted his spirits. He took eggs and cream cheese out of the refrigerator.

"Sleep? Man, what's that? But Mom worked, raised me, and went to Pharmacy School fulltime, so I don't complain."

"She's proud of you, you know. Proud that you've stepped up to raise your daughter."

"There was never a question." His voice stiffened and Marcus glanced up from breaking eggs to see the young man's pride. "I knew from the first minute I heard Tasha was pregnant, I couldn't live without my child."

"It's hard, raising a daughter alone. Sydney was twelve when her mother died." He thought how hard his wife had fought to live, to stay with them. "Eggs? Bagel?"

"A bagel would be good. Thanks." Anthony sipped his coffee. "I guess I'm glad Tasha took off when she did. My little girl won't ever know she was rejected."

But you know it, don't you? Marcus thought. And you feel it, for your baby and yourself.

Anthony was good company, but yawned several more times and they agreed they'd get together again soon.

"Come up anytime," Marcus said.

"And you're always welcome at the guard shack."

Marcus went to the sink to rinse dishes. The window over it looked out onto a manicured stretch of grass and flowers, and a portion of the curved drive that led to the parking lot. He saw Anthony come out of the building and head across the lawn. He stopped and turned, as if someone had called him. A young woman joined him there and began talking. He stood with his head down, his hands in his pockets while she stood close to him. Then she held out her arms and they hugged for a long moment before she turned and walked away. Anthony watched her go, and so did Marcus until she was out of sight. She was young, white, with blond hair pulled up high on her head in a ponytail held by a red ribbon.

Marcus drank a second cup of coffee, then spent an hour putting clothes away and setting up his laptop. The password the university had issued him didn't work, and no one answered the telephone in IT. He was sure that Granny would be going to church and that Sydney would go with her. He had time to get there, too, but he decided instead to drive around town on his own for a while, to reorient himself.

When he stepped out of the building, he saw the girl Anthony had embraced. She stood at the curb, a large suitcase and a carry-on bag beside her. He passed her on his way to his car, nodded and said, "Good morning."

"Are you Dr. Minton?" she asked.

"Yes, I am."

"Anthony told me you'd be moving in," she said. "I'm Brooke Fallon."

"How do you do?" As he shook her hand, a woman driving a Mercedes pulled up beside them. She put the car in park, the engine running, and got out.

"Mom," Brooke said. "You know Anthony, the guy who works here? This is Dr. Minton, his uncle. Dr. Minton's going to teach at Mangum."

"Anthony and I are cousins, actually. Second cousins, to be precise." He was struck by the way Brooke referred to Anthony, as if she only knew him as the security guard. But then, she had no idea what he'd seen.

"How do you do? What department?" Susan Fallon was asking.

"African-American studies."

Susan looked him in the eyes and smiled, a practiced smile.

"Wonderful. I hope we get a chance to talk sometime. I've got to get Brooke to the airport and we're running late."

∽

"How was the rest of your weekend?" Eden asked. It was Monday morning and Sydney had arrived at the office early.

"Fine, thanks." She was making a pot of coffee.

"Your father arrived?"

"Oh yes. And we had a big family get-together." Sydney's smile was more controlled than usual. "I should get to work. I didn't quite finish scanning documents for Jessica on Friday."

Did things not go well with Sean? Eden wondered. She got her coffee and went to her own office, resolving to set her curiosity aside and stay out of whatever might be between her nephew and her intern.

Just before lunch, Jessica brought in documents for signature. "What's going on with Sydney?" she asked.

"What do you mean?"

"Last week, she was telling me everything. Today, zip." She drew her finger over her lips.

"Not everybody has your tell-all personality." She smiled up at her assistant as she handed the papers back.

Jessica snorted. "Like you don't want to know how she and Sean are getting along."

"Actually, seriously, I think I ought to stay out of it. Okay?"

"Okay. You won't hear it from me." But she smiled and winked as big a wink as possible.

It was a busy week and Eden kept her two employees running, with little time for chitchat. She kept them late a couple of nights, but not on Friday. By then, she needed a little decompression herself, so she sent them home at five and left the office herself a little after six o'clock. A good portion of the legal community in Piedmont gathered at the bar of The Village Grill on Friday nights, and Eden walked the two blocks to it. The owner, Jack, greeted her as always. "Lady Justice. Come right in. Are you meeting Susan and Wren for dinner?"

"Susan Fallon?"

"She's in the bar, now, waiting."

Susan and Wren were the same age, six years younger than Eden, and were best friends in a way that kept Eden, and almost everyone else, on the outside. Marriages, children, Wren's social life and volunteerism, a medical career for Susan and her husband's election to the United States Senate hadn't lessened their bond.

Susan saw Eden and waved. They hugged and Eden took the stool next to Susan's.

"How are you?" Susan asked.

"I'm great. How are you and Avery?" Eden caught the bartender's eye. He knew she wanted a California Zinfandel.

"He's happy as a pig in slop." She laughed.

Eden laughed too. "I've heard the Senate called a lot of things, but not that." She picked up her wine and tipped it toward Susan's glass. "I hear you're involved with a think tank?"

"We're working on new ideas for health education in underserved areas. It's becoming a passion with me—the way things are, people need to know how to help themselves."

"That sounds like a natural for you. What brings you to town?"

"I came to see Brooke off to England for the summer. She's gone with a group to study at the London School of Economics."

"You must be proud." Eden wondered again about Sean and Brooke. And Sean and Sydney.

Susan held up a hand as if in surrender. "She's been a little distant lately. Avery says she's just growing up and he's right. I'm being a little clingy. I'm going to ask Wren for advice in letting go."

"It has to be different though, with an only child." Eden didn't express her doubts about Wren being the one to advise on that subject.

"That's my excuse." Susan laughed again. "Oh, here she is." She stood and met Wren with a big hug. Wren returned it.

Eden was glad that her sister had a steady husband who made a lot of money, lived in the Vance family homeplace, and had four children. Those were the things that Wren needed—things that Eden did not need. But seeing the warmth of these two friends gave her a twinge of envy. She greeted her sister with a smile and moved so that Wren could sit next to Susan.

Once Wren's mojito was ordered, the two friends began to talk. Susan's first question was, "How's Sean? I don't hear much about him these days."

"Yeah, what's going on with those two?" Wren answered. "He doesn't bring Brooke around."

To Eden's ear, they were curious but not worried; after all, their children belonged together. Just then, Jack appeared to announce he had a table for them.

"Three of you dining?" he asked.

"Oh no," Eden said. "These two need some girlfriend time."

Wren and Susan followed Jack into the dining room, Susan looking back to wave a good- bye.

❧

Eden got to the family house just after two o'clock, a couple of hours before guests were due for Wren's annual Summer Solstice Party.

"You're early." Wren held a big bowl of fruit salad in both hands.

"Put me to work."

"It's all under control. Kenneth and the boys have set things up in the garden. We'll have the bar outside and food in the sunroom, as usual."

"When you give a party, even the weather falls in line." She stole a slice of kiwi. She took in the patio and the rose garden, transformed by tables covered with pastel linen cloths, weighted at the corners, and folding chairs with paisley-print slips over them. The rose garden was awash in pinks and yellows.

"It looks like a sunrise settled over your backyard." Eden managed to take a tray of glasses from her sister and carried them to the bar table.

"Do you think Mother would approve?"

"Maybe she's the sunrise."

"Thank you, Eden. That's a sweet thing to say." Wren's voice went hoarse.

Kenneth and the twins, Terence and Peter, came in. They hugged Eden and Kenneth asked Wren, "What's left to do?"

"I'm still thinking we need more white wine. Where's Sean? He can go to the store."

"He left," Peter said. "Went to pick up his date." He opened the refrigerator. "What can I eat, Mom?"

"What date?" Wren and Kenneth said it in unison.

Peter gave a disinterested shrug and took out a carton of orange juice. His brother elbowed him, probably to remind him that the date was a secret.

"I'll go for the wine," Eden said.

By five o'clock, thirty or so people had gathered in the garden. Kenneth poured wine and sangria, mixed gin and tonics. Wren's daughter, Caraleigh, and her roommate had driven up from Atlanta for the weekend. They passed trays of stuffed mushrooms, sausage balls and boiled shrimp. Eden made sure her father was happy, sitting at a center table talking baseball and politics with several other men. She made her way back to the kitchen and found Wren taking a roasting pan out of the oven.

"Is it time for the real food yet?" Wren asked.

"They're still mostly on their first drinks, so I don't think there's any hurry."

"Is Sean back yet? With this mystery date?"

Just then Eden heard Sean's voice and realized he was coming down the hall from the front of the house.

"Here's my mom," he said. "And your boss."

"How do you do, Ms. Caldwell? I'm Sydney Minton. Thank you for having me. Hi, Eden."

Wren's hand moved forward in greeting but Eden saw her mouth twitch. Not a happy twitch.

"Sean's friends are always welcome," Wren said. "Minton?"

"Sydney's just graduated from Harvard," Sean said. "She's Aunt Eden's intern."

"Really? I didn't know you had an intern." The smile Wren directed at Eden was forced.

Caraleigh pushed the door open with her hip and let her friend in. "We need refills."

Sean introduced Sydney while Wren and Eden put more hors d'oeuvres on the girls' trays. Then all the young people went out and Eden watched Sean escort Sydney as if he had a prize to show everyone.

"She's beautiful," Wren said. She began to arrange asparagus spears on a platter. "Why didn't you tell me?"

"Tell you what?" Eden decided it was time for a glass of wine.

"About my son dating your intern." Wren sounded annoyed and distracted at once. "Would you mind tossing the salad?"

"I'm not sure they are dating. You know they don't do that the way we did." She pulled open a bag of mixed greens and dumped them into the old wooden dough bowl Wren used for salad at her parties.

"Besides brains and beauty, who is she? How did you come to hire her?"

"Dexter Long asked me to." Eden knew the half truth would only make it worse later.

She opened a second bag. "She's interested in law school but wants a little real world experience before deciding for sure."

"And?"

"She's Marie Minton's great-granddaughter." Postponing the inevitable.

"That girl?" Wren squeezed lemon juice over the asparagus. "She looks white."

"Are you surprised? Multiracial is the fastest growing demographic." Eden emptied a third bag and reached for the fourth.

"I'm just surprised. I'm not passing judgment. Which is more than I can say for you."

Eden took a few quick, shallow breaths, trying to dissipate her own rising ill temper. It was an old grievance of Wren's that Eden judged her, and there was no point in answering. Wren carried a platter to the sunroom and Eden followed with the salad.

"Where has Kenneth gone?" Wren muttered. "He knows I need him to slice the tenderloin."

She brushed by Eden on her way out to find her husband.

Eden went back to her wine and stayed to finish it.

Kenneth appeared, grinning. "What did you do to Wren? Can't I leave you two alone for a few minutes?"

"Sorry. I'm to blame for Sean's date, it seems."

Kenneth began to sharpen a carving knife. "Despite what Wren and Susan think, he and Brooke are too young to be serious. I was glad to hear she's spreading her wings a little. And this Sydney is one good looking young lady."

"I think I should tell you, Kenneth, she's also Jabel Clark's daughter."

Colin was tired of listening to the man-talk going on around him. Wren had parked him—or so he felt—saying, "You know that people want to talk to you, Daddy. You just sit here and hold court." A group of men, most of them business friends of

Kenneth's, had assembled at his table and he felt their conde-
scension. They had been through politics and baseball, subjects
they seemed to assume Colin was interested in, and had moved
on to golf and zoning regulations and the coming reassessment
of real estate values. He was glad to see Sean appear on the patio, with a girl Colin didn't know. Sean's wave provided the excuse and the impetus he needed to move from his spot. He met
the young couple halfway down the walk.

"Hi Granddad," Sean said. "This is Sydney Minton and she
wants to meet you."

"Miss Minton, at last we meet." He shook her hand and ad-
mired her eyes. "I see your father and great-grandmother in
your lovely eyes."

"Thank you." She smiled at him and glanced at Sean.

"Y'all find someplace to sit and I'll get us something to
drink." Sean went toward the bar.

"Let's go over here where it's quieter." Colin motioned for
Sydney to go ahead of him down a path to a small table set up
under the arbor, at a little distance from the party. "It'll be easier
to talk."

He hoped she didn't sense that he had avoided her until now.
He had made his weekly visits to the office at off hours, or with
the knowledge that the intern had been sent to the law library.
Now that they were face-to-face, he felt a bit ashamed of it.

Sean found them. He had two beer bottles by the necks in
one hand and a plastic glass of sangria in the other.

"So, Granddad," he said once he was seated, "Sydney and I
keep talking over everything Ms. Marie and you told us about
Uncle Laurence."

"Sean," Sydney said and Colin understood it was the verbal
equivalent of a kick under the table.

"What?" Sean said. "Granddad won't mind. Ask him your
question." He sipped his beer and Colin caught the sideways
glance he gave the girl.

"Mr. Phillips, I don't mean to be disrespectful," she said. "I know from Sean how you feel about Laurence." She leaned toward Colin. "It's just, I took a class on domestic violence and the law. I know that certain crimes ... how few are truly random, how many pregnant women die ..."

"At the hands of their husbands and boyfriends." Colin finished her sentence. "My dear, I am well aware." His voice was altered by the tightening muscles in his throat. "I have even represented some of those men. But our family was visited by one of those very, very rare truly random tragedies."

Wren watched them from the sun room, her father, her son, and Sydney, sitting apart from the crowd and talking. Sean leaned back in his chair and looked from the girl's face to his grandfather's and back again, as if following a verbal tennis game. Sydney was on the edge of her chair, her hands on her knees, her body tilted forward as she listened.

I could go out there, Wren thought, and imagined herself saying "what's going on here?" in a breezy, joking way. There was a fourth chair at the table and she could take it and they would let her into their little circle. She'd find out why Sean was moving away from her and why her father seemed to be so prickly these days and why Sydney frightened her. But she couldn't go. She had guests and somebody was calling her now and it was time she went out and attended her own party. Her mother had taught her the secret to hospitality was to plan, plan, plan, leave nothing to chance, and then to let people see that you're the one having the best time. No matter what.

JULY 2003

Sydney approached Eden late one July morning, with a note in hand.

"Papa wants to thank you for what you're doing for me," she said. The note was an invitation to lunch on the date of her choice.

"That's not necessary, but I'll be delighted." Eden took a piece of letterhead and wrote a quick response. She felt a bit of disloyalty to her family but really, she'd hired Sydney so it was a little late for that.

The next day, she walked down the street to the Village Grill. Marcus Minton was waiting for her in the foyer, talking to the restaurant's owner, Jack.

"Ms. Phillips, I'm so glad you could make time." His hand was dry, making her realize that the two-block walk on a 90-degree day had made hers moist.

Jack led them to a booth, mentioned that the baked flounder in white wine sauce was good, and patted Marcus's shoulder when he left.

"I was glad to find that this place is still in the family," Marcus said. "Jack's father sent some food to the jail on that New Year's Day in 1964. That was when Dexter and I and the other demonstrators had been arrested."

"I remember Big Jack," Eden said. "I didn't know he was quite that enlightened."

"It wasn't talked about, I can promise you that." Marcus unrolled his napkin and laid out the knife, fork, and spoon it contained.

"Not good memories."

The waiter showed up and they both ordered the flounder and a salad.

"And hard to explain to my daughter, I've discovered. She's read all the books. She's studied with Henry Louis Gates, but my experiences came as a shock. I'm not sure why."

"The difference between abstract and concrete, I suppose."

"I'm sure that's it. Anyway," Marcus said, "I want to thank you for hiring her and for giving her such good experience."

"She's a pleasure to have around."

"I hope her friendship with your nephew hasn't caused discomfort. He's a nice young man."

"You've met him? Good." Their salads arrived. "My sister isn't thrilled about it, I'm afraid."

He raised his eyebrows, a protective father.

"I didn't put that very well," she said. "It has nothing to do with Sydney. For a long time, Sean has been close to a girl named Brooke Fallon. Her father's the Senator and her mother and Wren are best friends. I'm pretty sure that whatever there was between Sean and Brooke, it wasn't romance. That part was their mothers' fantasy."

"I've met Brooke. And her mother. Or should I say, I encountered them. They were leaving Highgate on their way to the airport. That was just after I got to Piedmont."

"Brooke's studying in England this summer."

"Ah." He had been looking directly at Eden but now he lowered his gaze to his food. Maybe he was concerned about his daughter being in some love triangle. She wished she'd been more careful with her words. He broke the awkward silence.

"I have been out driving around," he said. "Finding old spots, some recognizable, some not. I even drove to Black Haw one day. I'd never been there before."

"Never? Really? Dad used to take us swimming in the river there."

He laughed. "Sweet Siders didn't go there back then."

The waiter brought their fish and they took a moment to shift salad plates and make room. Eden was glad of the break and wondered how many more times she'd say the wrong thing at this lunch.

He resumed the conversation. "I heard it had been gentrified, the mill turned into a place for artists, and I wanted to see for myself. Part of me wishes something of the sort would happen in Sweet Side."

"I live in Black Haw, you know."

"I do know." He smiled. "What interests me is, where do the old timers go if and when property values start to rise again? Are we stuck with a choice between gentrification or loss of an old, stable community to crime and deterioration?"

The rest of the conversation was the kind of talk Eden most enjoyed—trading of ideas, pros and cons, and stories of worlds colliding with outcomes good and bad. She was late getting back to the office.

As she walked to work, she tried to settle her disorientation. Marcus Minton and Jabel Clark were different people now.

AUGUST 2003

Colin had become a night owl since he retired, and especially enjoyed summer nights because there was always a baseball game to watch. He could reread old favorites—Wallace Stegner now—keep up with the game, and hope for extra innings.

The phone call came during the seventh inning stretch. Colin muted the sound and reached for the handset on the table beside his chair. The incoming number was Sean's.

"Granddad, something really bad has happened." Sean didn't wait for a hello.

Colin heard background noises, voices, and then a siren. "Have you been in an accident? Where are you?" His heart rate rose.

"We're at Highgate." Sean's voice broke. "Yeah, okay." That didn't seem to be meant for Colin. "Granddad, it's Brooke. Brooke's dead."

Sean was crying now. Colin's brain didn't accept the words, but his body did. He was hot, then cold and dizzy.

A voice that wasn't Sean's spoke through the phone. "Hello. To whom am I speaking?"

The voice was quiet, mature, and also shaky.

"This is Colin Phillips. Is my grandson all right?"

"Mr. Phillips, this is Marcus Minton. Sean's upset, but he's being attended to."

"Marcus. What's happened?"

"Sean and my daughter came to visit Brooke Fallon and found her dead in her apartment."

"But she's in England."

"Just home, I gather. Just a few days ago."

Sean came back on the phone. "Granddad, will you tell Mom? I don't think I can and reporters are here."

"Yes, I'll tell her." He turned in his chair until he could see out a window. Lights were on in Wren's house.

"The police say Sydney and I have to stay here a while. We're supposed to give them statements."

Of course. Suddenly he was a lawyer again. "Listen, Sean, don't make any statements until I get there."

He leaned back in his chair to ease his breathing and think for a moment. How like that horrible call from Rhetta, so many years ago, the day Sheila died. His hands shook as he got a dial tone and called Eden. He made it quick: could she come over and be with her sister? Then he stood, smoothed his clothes, and went to tell his younger daughter the news.

In a few minutes, he sat on the couch in the sunroom, holding Wren's right hand in both of his. Kenneth sat on the other side of her and held her other hand. She was pale, her breath shallow, her eyes fixed on something only she was seeing.

Colin looked at Peter and Terence, called down from their rooms, standing on the step that divided the sunroom and kitchen. "One of you get your mother a glass of water."

Neither of them moved, then both at once. Peter presented the water glass to his mother and stepped back, his twin beside him, waiting for an adult to make sense of this, or so Colin thought.

"All right." Wren sipped, then straightened her spine. "I have to be all right. For Susan. And for Sean. My poor boy."

For Sean? Memory's voice was loud in Colin's ears. Rhetta and Laurence. How often had she said poor boy, poor Laurence, my poor brother?

"I'm going to Highgate," he said. "The police will want statements from both Sean and Sydney and I told him to wait until I get there."

"What?" Wren's eyes were huge. "Is he a suspect? Dad?"

"No, no. It's just procedure." He squeezed her shoulder as he stood.

"I'll drive you." Kenneth rose from the couch.

"You should stay with Wren," Colin said.

"Peter and Terence are here, and Eden is on the way, right? I'll drive you."

"I want Kenneth to go," Wren said. "I want him to bring my boy home."

As they got close to Highgate, Colin saw that the police had the entrance blocked. Two television vans and their personnel were already set up to broadcast.

"Don't worry," Kenneth said. "I can get us in." He drove past the development, which his company had built, around a curve in the highway, and used his high beams to find an opening in a row of trees. It was an abandoned construction road, roughly paved and rutted. It took them to the edge of a parking lot where a barrier stopped them.

"We'll have to walk from here." Kenneth turned off the lights and the motor.

They walked across a concrete pad that, like the road, now went unused, and then across a maintained parking lot. They saw slow-turning blue lights and as they got closer, heard voices. A crowd of people gathered at the edge of the parking lot nearest the buildings, kept back by a couple of uniformed officers.

"Let's go this way." Instead of going toward the crowd, Kenneth led the way to the back of the buildings where there was a narrow sidewalk. They followed it until they came to a gap between the buildings. From there, they could go through to the front where several police cars, marked and unmarked, a Crime Scene van, and two ambulances clustered.

"There's Sydney." Colin pointed to the open back door of an ambulance. She sat inside, wrapped in a blanket although it was a muggy August night. A woman in an EMT uniform was talking to her.

"Where the hell's Sean?" Kenneth started forward and one of the officers noticed him. He stepped forward, blocking Kenneth's way.

"Let me by," Kenneth's voice rose, angry, as he tried to get past the policeman. "I want to see my son."

"Kenneth, Kenneth." Colin tugged his son-in-law's arm.

Just then, Colin saw a detective he'd known for years. Bobby Atchison had his back to them, talking on a cell phone and at the same time gesturing directions to a uniformed officer. The raised voices got his attention, though, and he turned toward them. With the cell phone still to his ear, he headed their way.

He ended the call and said to the policeman who was nose to nose to Kenneth. "It's okay, I'll handle it."

"Bobby, I'm glad to see you're in charge," Colin said.

"How did you two get in here?"

Colin tightened his grip on his son-in-law's forearm and answered before Kenneth could say anything. "I'm here to represent my grandson's legal rights. Kenneth is a concerned parent." As soon as he said that, he remembered that Marcus Minton was here somewhere, another concerned parent. "I represent Sydney Minton, too."

"All right." Atchison sighed. "I tell you what, her father's over there on a bench. You can go wait with him, but only if you both stay there and don't interfere. I'll let you know when we're ready to take their statements."

Now Colin saw Marcus on a bench at the entrance to the nearest building, near enough to see Sydney even if he couldn't go to her.

"I want to see my son," Kenneth called as Atchison turned away.

"Be quiet," Colin said. "If Sean isn't okay, Bobby would tell us."

When Eden got to the house, she found Peter and Terence in the sunroom, side by side on the couch, feet on the coffee table, attention full on the TV. Eden leaned over the back of the sofa, her head between theirs, and kissed their cheeks. "It's so awful. I'm glad you boys are still home so I can hug you."

Eden looked at the screen. The local station had its helicopter circling over Highgate. The reportorial voice said, "The police are not confirming but neighbors have told us that the body of a young woman was found in the condo belonging to Senator and Dr. Fallon."

"Where's your mom?" Eden asked.

"Trying to call Susan," Peter said.

Wren appeared in the kitchen door, her cell phone in her hand. "I can't talk to her." She wasn't crying, but her voice was choked with emotion.

Eden went to her and hugged her hard. "Guys, turn the sound down?"

One of them muted the reporter midsentence and both of the boys came to touch their mother and rub her back.

"Sit down." Eden guided her sister to a chair in the sunroom. "What can I do for you?"

"I've never felt so useless. A police woman and the Senate chaplain were with her. The woman said she was too distraught to take the call."

"Where's Avery?" Eden asked.

"In California for some speech. His staff will get him on the first plane. Thanks for coming over, Eden." She managed to smile.

"Sure." She stepped back and watched both boys fuss over their mother. It comforted her to see them, as sweet as when they were small and cuddly. Then she thought of Susan and Avery and shuddered.

Wren's phone rang and she answered, "Caraleigh, you've heard?" She got up and went to a more private place to talk to her daughter.

"Hey, there's the police chief," Pete said. He moved to turn up the sound on the TV. Eden and Terence followed him.

The Chief of Piedmont Police stood under lights, in front of microphones, at the entrance to Highgate. He confirmed that the deceased was Brooke Fallon, that both of her parents had been notified and were en route to Piedmont. He said that the medical examiner would have to discover the cause of death, but if it proved to be a crime, then the department would put all of its resources toward finding the perpetrator. In the meantime, citizens should take "sensible precautions."

"What's that about?" Terence asked.

"It means Brooke may have been killed in her own home, in what should be a really safe place." Eden said. "That's going to panic some people and he's trying to get out in front of it."

The boys were quiet and she wondered if safety had ever crossed their minds beyond admonitions not to speed, not to drink and drive, not to do drugs or smoke.

From his bench, Marcus shifted his gaze to Colin and Kenneth, but slowly as if he had to drag it. He stood and shook hands. "I'm glad you're here. The children shouldn't have to go through this alone." He made room on the bench.

"You sit," Kenneth said to Colin. "I don't think I can stay still." He began to pace the four feet from one end of the bench to the other. "You know what I want right this minute?"

"A cigarette," Marcus said.

"Yeah man." Kenneth stood still, apparently finding a kindred spirit. "You, too? Have you seen my son?"

"I have. He was badly shaken but it was Sydney who went into Brooke's apartment first and found her. She was in shock and he was trying to take care of her and do everything right."

"He called the police?" Colin asked.

"I think Anthony did."

"Where is Sean now?" Kenneth asked, sounding exasperated with Colin's interruption.

"When the police arrived, they separated him and Sydney. They wouldn't let me talk to either of them, after that. The medics attended to them both, and I can at least see her from here."

"And who is Anthony?" Colin asked.

"He is a relation of mine and he works here as the gate attendant at night."

From across the parking lot, Bobby Atchison held up a hand to get their attention, pointed to Colin and gestured for him.

"The detective must be ready to take statements," Colin said. He left Kenneth and Marcus behind.

Highgate had a small business center with a conference room and that was where Atchison had video and audio recording set up for statements. Colin took a seat and asked for a notepad and pen. "I left home in a bit of a hurry." He got them, and then Sydney was escorted in.

She was pale, red-eyed, and she clutched a box of tissues. Colin stood, smiled at her, and leaned in to kiss her cheek. "From your father."

She nodded and sighed, as if composing herself. Colin held a chair for her, then sat beside her, close enough to touch her if he didn't want her to answer something. But the questions Atchison put to her were to draw out only the facts—why had she come to Highgate? What time? What did she do? And after that? What did she see?

She answered Atchison's questions in a soft voice. When he was through, the detective explained that she'd need to come to the station to sign the statement later. "And we'll probably have more questions, but you can go now. The officer will take you out this way."

A different officer brought Sean in after she was gone. Colin saw right away that he was angry.

"I don't need you here, Granddad." He sat, crossed his arms

and stared across the desk at Atchison.

"Calm down, Sean." Colin took the boy's arm and felt it stiffen.

"They wouldn't even let me see Sydney and she was really upset. She shouldn't have been by herself."

"She's okay, all things considered." Colin said. "And by now, she's with her father."

Sean frowned and gripped his hands together, staring at them.

"Mr. Caldwell," Atchison said. "Mr. Phillips is here as a lawyer if you want him. If you don't, I'll request that he leave."

Sean leaned back in his chair and crossed his arms over this chest. "I guess he can stay."

Atchison began his questions. He asked the same ones he'd asked Sydney, and then asked them again in different form. Piedmont's population was close to sixty thousand now, but in many ways it was still a small town. The detective had to know the Vances, Caldwells, and Fallons were close acquaintances and had been for generations. That knowledge was enough to drive the questioning deeper, and as Sean acknowledged he and Brooke saw a lot of each other, deeper still. It was thorough police work and Colin found nothing to object to. It made him anxious.

Finally, Colin and Sean were outside again. Kenneth sat by himself on the bench and got up when he saw them. Colin glanced at his watch. It showed the time to be 12:30, but it meant nothing to him. The two ambulances were gone. Parked where one of them had been was a van marked Canine Unit. Good, he thought, they think there's someone else out there, someone to track.

"Hey, there's Anthony." Sean said.

Colin saw a young black man walking beside a uniformed officer toward the interview room. At the sound of his name, Anthony looked toward them and made a gesture that could have been the last wave of an exhausted man.

"I knew him in high school," Sean said. "Nice guy. Smart. He's been working here for a while. I used to see him every time I came over. He and Brooke were friends, too."

"And he was security guard tonight?" Colin remembered Marcus mentioning Anthony's name and their relationship.

"Yeah. He heard Sydney screaming and came running. He called 911, then he kind of fell apart. He was in worse shape than I was, kept saying something about it being his fault."

"What did he mean?"

"He's security, right? And somebody he knows gets killed."

Colin stopped and looked back. "What's his last name?"

"Huey."

"Tell your father I'm sorry, but I've got to keep all of you here a little longer." He headed back to the interview room. He got to the door just as Detective Atchison opened a Coke can and handed it to Anthony.

"Mr. Huey," Colin said from the doorway, "my name is Colin Phillips and I'm your lawyer, at least for tonight."

Atchison had a ballpoint pen and a notebook, but they seemed to be props. He'd made few notes in the interviews with Sean and Sydney. The digital recorder on the table got the words more accurately than the human ear would. The detective watched faces and eyes, and so did Colin.

Anthony was a good looking young man with a softness about him. It showed in his dark eyes with lids that drooped and a lower lip that trembled when he first spoke Brooke's name.

"I knew her from high school," he said. He glanced at Colin. "I knew Sean Caldwell, too, but him and me weren't friends then. She was a friend to me."

"How so?" the detective asked.

"We had homeroom together every year. That was her joke, that she knew where to go when she saw me."

"Did you see her outside of school?"

"No sir. She had a boyfriend—Sean—and I had a girlfriend." His voice rose a little, defensive in Colin's ear. The officer who sat by the door cleared his throat.

"When did you come to work at Highgate?" Atchison asked.

"Almost two years ago."

"When did she move in?"

"About the same time, a little later. Her parents own the condo and she lived there."

"Alone?"

"She has a lot of friends who came and went." He sighed. "She had a lot of friends."

"Did you and she renew your friendship?" Atchison tapped his pen on the table.

Colin's antennae began to twitch. Should he stop this line of questioning?

"We were friendly, I'd say," Anthony said.

"Okay," Atchison nodded. "So what can you tell us about last night?"

"I came on at five o'clock. That's when I saw the man."

Everyone in the room froze for a moment. Then the officer sat forward.

"Who did you see?" Atchison asked.

"I don't know his name, but he's an older man who used to come see Brooke pretty often."

"Can you describe him?"

"Sure. He used to have to come through the visitor's gate, but I guess she gave him the code for the residents' gate because he started using that."

"What does he look like?"

"He's got lightish hair. I think it's going gray. He's got blue eyes. Thin face. He drives a silver Mercedes and it has a Mangum parking sticker on it."

"How did you know he came to visit Brooke Fallon?"

"Before I open the gate, I get the visitor's name and who they're visiting and I call the resident."

"Then why don't you have his name?"

"He didn't give it. He'd say, 'just call Miss Fallon. She's expecting me.' Then he'd smile like ... like he was in charge. I'd do it, like he said, and Brooke would say to let him in."

Anthony's voice rose and fell and Colin sensed that he was battling some emotion he didn't want to show.

"And you saw this man yesterday?" the detective prompted.

"I was coming from the employees' parking lot and I saw his car. He was stopped in front of Brooke's building and then he drove off."

"You saw the car, or you saw him?"

"Him, inside the car. He had to go right by me and I saw him."

Atchison looked over at the officer by the door and nodded. He asked a few more questions and then said, "We'll want to talk to you again, Anthony. Maybe when you come in to sign your statement."

Colin walked out with the young man. "Anthony, do you understand the importance of what you said?"

Anthony didn't answer. He looked down, then away.

"It's too late to talk more. We're all tired." Colin offered a hand. "Come see me at my office tomorrow. It's Phillips and Phillips, on the square two blocks south of the courthouse."

When Colin made his way in the dark to Kenneth's car, he found his son-in-law dozing in the driver's seat and Sean asleep in the back. Kenneth stirred when the door opened but the boy didn't budge. Without speaking, Colin got in and Kenneth started the engine. It took several attempts at a three-point turn, and a few soft curses, to get the BMW headed out.

Colin whispered an apology for the delay. "But it may have been important that I was there."

"No problem." Kenneth turned onto the state road. "I like him."

"What? Who?" Colin's brain wasn't equal to the non sequitur.

"Marcus. I like him."

"Oh. What did you talk about?"

"Our daughters."

In the dark, Colin nodded. He could have said, I like him too, or even, I always did like him, but he just nodded.

When the police told Sydney that she could go, Marcus drove her to Granny's house. He had already called Marie to let her know what had happened and she waited up for them with her special toddies ready to soothe their nerves.

"You come sleep with me tonight, baby." Marie wrapped her arm around Sydney. "Your daddy can sleep in your bed."

He saw them both into Marie's double bed, satisfied that his granny would comfort his daughter through what remained of the night. His old bedroom had been painted lavender and his old dark wood furniture was now a creamy white. He undressed down to his boxers and socks and lay down on top of the quilt. He had no expectation of sleeping. Someone else's child was dead, a child a lot like his own. He couldn't help being grateful that it wasn't Sydney, and felt heavy with guilt. Then he remembered seeing Brooke and Anthony together. Should he tell somebody? Maybe, but hadn't he done that once? Told, that is. Look how that turned out.

He groaned and rolled over, wishing he dared get out of bed so he could escape these thoughts, but he couldn't risk disturbing his daughter or grandmother.

It was almost two o'clock in the morning when Colin walked through the garden to his cottage. A damp breeze played with the roses' scent and ruffled his hair as a human hand might.

He thought about Anthony Huey. "That's when I saw the man," he'd said. The description of the man, the car, the Mangum sticker. Bobby Atchison couldn't have asked for a greater gift. It was one of the miracles or accidents that solve crimes.

Colin undressed and fell into his bed. He closed his eyes and saw Anthony's face. Then it melted and reshaped as Jabel Clark's.

Eden fell asleep in her sister's guest room, wearing one of her sister's night gowns. She woke in what felt like five minutes and pulled the pillow over her head, hoping it wasn't the end of her rest. She rolled over and opened an eye to look at the clock. The minute hand lurched to 4:46.

She turned onto her back and poked the pillow into a trough for her neck. It would have been good to get up and sneak out of the house, to go home, take a long, hot shower and pretend that nothing terrible had happened.

At daylight, she got up and put Wren's extra bathrobe on over the gown. For her feet, she had the sandals she'd worn the night before. She went downstairs and put a cup of leftover coffee in the microwave. While the machine hummed, she looked out the windows over the rose garden and saw her father walking the paths, his head down, his hands behind his back. When the microwave stopped, she took her cup and went to catch up with him.

She didn't want to startle him by calling, so she waited by the patio until he made another round. He wore an old pair of seersucker trousers, a blue polo shirt and his bedroom slippers. His hair was combed in front but cow-licked in back and she imagined he hadn't used a mirror.

"Good morning," he said. "You're up early."

"We should both still be in bed." She stepped off the patio to join him.

"I envy anybody who can sleep in, or sleep at all this morning." He made a gesture of invitation and they began to walk.

"Have you eaten?" she asked.

"Coffee and cereal. You?"

"Just this." She sipped, trying not to spill on Wren's robe as she walked. "Dad, do you think Sean's a suspect?"

"He should be, if the police are doing their job, but we may have a savior." He told her Anthony's story.

"Oh, Dad." She took his arm with her free hand.

"But we can't take it for granted that the mystery man in the fancy car will do the trick. I think that both Sean and Sydney should have representation. I assume Bobby Atchison will want to talk to them again."

"I've been thinking about that, too. For Sean, I can call a friend from law school who practices in Raleigh now. And for Sydney—who do you think?" She had her own ideas but felt that she should ask.

"I'll tell you exactly. Get Clyde Raeburn."

"But he's older than … I mean he's retired."

"You mean, he's even older than I am, and he is, but that doesn't mean he wouldn't enjoy getting up the D.A.'s nose again. His brain functions very well. And he's got nothing to lose."

She drained her coffee cup and carried it with a finger hooked in the handle. "What about you, Dad? You could advise Sydney."

"I thought about it, briefly, but … it's all the old business about Laurence and Jabel. Marcus. Her father. I like the girl very much, but I can't say that my mind is clear on it all. And I know that representing Laurence, someone so close, was a big mistake."

"I've never heard you say that."

"Nonetheless." Colin said. "Besides, I did come out of last night's events with a client."

"You mean Anthony Huey."

The paths had led them back to Colin's cottage. "You must be ready for more coffee. I know I am." They went up the steps and followed the porch around to the kitchen door.

"We can find someone else for Anthony," she said. "It's great that you were there, but you don't have to go on with it."

Colin rinsed out the cone of his drip coffee pot and put a filter in it. "I know, but I feel an obligation."

Eden caught a note of stridency in his voice. "Why obligation, Dad?"

The kettle began to whistle. He turned his back to her and poured water over coffee grounds. He sighed. "Anthony Huey is Marcus's cousin. There's a chance that I am trying to make up for something and he presents the opportunity."

Eden dressed and drove home. Her morning paper had a banner headline, SENATOR'S DAUGHTER FOUND DEAD. The article told the basics: the body was found by friends the police declined to identify. The police had questioned and released three people they declined to identify. The body was taken to the state medical examiner's office. The Piedmont police chief would make a statement later that day. Then it went on to review the careers of Senator Avery Fallon and Doctor Susan Fallon.

"Questioned and released," she said to herself. The phrase always made her think of fishing.

Eden got to the office, a large latte in hand. Jessica was already there.

"You look pretty rough." Jessica stood and came toward her.

"I feel worse." She accepted a hug. "We're closed for the day, don't you think?"

"I've already cleared the calendar." Jessica followed her into

03333333

her office. "And I've been working the phones. I've tracked down the EMT who helped Sydney. He says she shook for half an hour."

"Is there any word on what the police think?" Eden thought again about the mysterious man in the Mercedes.

"That's harder. They're real tight lipped."

"Understandable." She pried the sippy top off the paper cup. "Considering who Brooke's parents are."

Jessica perched on the edge of the client's chair. "It could be a random break-in gone wrong, couldn't it?"

"Is that the answer you'd want, if you didn't know the people involved? Or would you be hoping for the ex-boyfriend? And/or his new girlfriend? Nice and neat and predictable. Easy for the jury, too." She opened her desk drawer, where she kept packets of no calorie sweetener and added more to her coffee.

"Eden. You're talking about Sean and Sydney." Jessica was shocked.

"Don't you know the person or people who find the body are prime suspects?" She sighed and reached out to squeeze Jessica's hand. "Actually, there is someone ahead of them in line right now. Dad was at Highgate last night, sitting in on their statements. He sat in with the night watchman when the police talked to him, too, and he told about seeing a car there yesterday. The driver was some older man who used to come see Brooke."

Jessica sank down into the chair and leaned forward to get all of the details Eden could give her. When Eden finished, she said, "I bet I can find out who drives that car."

"Bobby Atchison will be all over that, Jess."

"Yeah, but Detective Atchison isn't going to call me and tell me, is he? I want to know who the scumbag is." She stood up. "I've got a friend in Security at Mangum and I'm calling him."

"I don't think that's a good idea. You don't want to get into police business."

"Don't worry. My friend's a good guy."

Jessica came back in five minutes and handed Eden a sheet of paper. It was a group photograph, printed from an online newspaper story. "He's the guy in the middle. His name is Joseph Dantry. He's getting a teaching award." She snorted. "You can tell he thinks his poop doesn't stink."

Eden recognized the university president and dean. They flanked three people and everyone smiled for the camera. She didn't know Joseph Dantry but she saw a man in his forties, with a romantic shock of hair over his eyes. A lean face with high cheekbones. His smile had a twist of smirk to it.

She handed the printout back to Jessica. "But he's still innocent until proven guilty. Of anything. Remember, Brooke was an adult."

"Oh come on. She was a baby. I know his type." She stalked out as if Eden had committed a crime.

Eden ran her hands over her face and set the latte aside. This is going to be horrible, she thought. Just like 1963.

Colin got to the office just before eleven o'clock. Anthony Huey was already there, with a woman wearing a pantsuit. Colin saw a deep vertical worry crease between her eyebrows.

"Good morning," Colin said. "I hope you haven't been waiting long. You must be Mrs. Huey."

As they shook hands, Jessica came out of the break room holding a little girl in a pink dress.

"We found baby sister some good old crackers," Jessica crooned. "Here's Mr. Colin. Say hello to Mr. Colin, baby sister."

The little girl said "gaaa" and thrust out a fist dripping cracker crumbs to Colin. He smiled at her and took her hand in his.

"And Miss Huey, if I'm not mistaken."

"This is Shayna." Anthony said.

"A daughter is a wonderful thing for a man," Colin said and

Anthony rested his hand on Shayna's tight braids.

"You all can go about your meeting," Jessica said. "I'll be glad to keep her."

Colin led his visitors into his office. "Please sit down." When they had all settled, he said, "Mrs. Huey, has Anthony told you about last night?"

"Yes, he did. I appreciate your stepping in. He was very upset."

"Mama, you talk about me like I'm not here," Anthony said.

She turned to him. "You were upset. And I am thankful. But, Mr. Phillips, here's my question." Her gaze shifted again and Colin sensed that she was accustomed to being in charge. "Is my son a suspect in this murder?"

"The strongest suspect at this point is probably the man he saw. You saw, Anthony. But if the police do their job, they should consider anyone and everyone who knew Brooke." He cleared his throat. "That includes my own grandson, so I don't say that lightly."

Janelle was quiet for a moment. "I called my cousin, Marcus Minton, this morning, to see how Sydney is doing. I asked him about you, too, and Marcus says that whatever happens, we're in good hands."

It was Colin's turn for a pause. "I appreciate his confidence, but I intend to be clear. Anthony, it is your choice, who represents you. I was there last night, but it doesn't mean you're obligated."

"But you'll do it if I want you to? You aren't saying no, are you?" Anthony was anxious.

"I am not saying no. But you may want to think about it, talk it over with your mother."

Mother and son looked at each other. She smiled a slight smile and nodded.

"Mr. Phillips, my son made it plain that he wants to stand on his own here. It's hard for me, but I'm going to leave now."

She rested her hand on Anthony's head, much as he had touched his daughter's, then she stood. Colin rose to escort her out.

"There's no reason for you to worry, Mrs. Huey."

"I'll try to believe that." Her voice let him know that since Anthony came into the world, she'd done nothing but worry.

"Now," Colin said. He took his place at the desk again and pulled a legal pad over. "Let's talk a little, Anthony. Have you thought of anything important that you didn't tell the police last night?"

Anthony looked down and swallowed hard. "Just one thing." When he looked up, his eyes were wet.

Suddenly Colin doubted that he'd read this young man at all well. "What is it?" He fumbled for the handkerchief in his trousers pocket. By the time he offered it across the desk, Anthony's tears had overflowed.

"What I tell you …" Anthony gulped and wiped his face. "Anything I say, you keep it a secret, right?"

"Yes." A wave of anxiety constricted his chest.

"It's just, seeing her like that. Oh God. And there's nobody I can tell how I feel. She's the only one I could tell and now …" He looked at Colin at last. "It's just, I loved her."

"Ah." Colin's shoulders eased. "Yes, well, that's a word you don't want to use with a detective."

"I'm so used to keeping it in, but I thought I'd go crazy if I didn't tell somebody."

"Your mother?"

"No." He shook his head. "I can't lay more on her."

"All right, then. I'm listening."

"Like I told the police, I knew Brooke in middle school and high school. She was always friendly to everybody, a real sweet girl. I got admitted to N.C. State and started school there, but my girlfriend, Tasha, she didn't like me being away. She wanted me to work and support her, and like a fool, I did. Then Tasha got pregnant. She wanted to get an abortion, but we talked her out of it, my mom and me. I told her we could get married, but she was just all over the place. Emotional, kind of crazy, told me she never wanted to see me again. I thought maybe once we had the baby, we could get back together. I wanted to do the right thing, you know?

"The baby came and Tasha said, you take her or I'm going to leave her at the fire station. So I took her, and I thank God for her every day. Mom talked me into taking classes at the community college and the job at Highgate is perfect. It's pretty quiet and I can study some. Mom got her degree and worked when I was little, so I can do it, too." He sounded defiant. "Then Brooke moved into her folks' condo. She recognized me and she stopped to say hi."

"Is that enough for you to fall in love?" Colin knew it could be.

"Just about." Anthony smiled and wiped his eyes again. "I took a few nights off when Shayna was born and when I got back, Brooke asked me what was going on. I told her the whole story and after that, if she was home when I was working, she'd come down and hang out. She wanted to see my baby, so she came to the house one afternoon. We started spending time together. It just happened."

Colin made notes. "When was this, Anthony?"

"Shayna was born November second."

"And your spending time with Brooke began then?"

He nodded. "So Brooke would come over to the house and take care of the baby while I got a little sleep. Then we'd all go to the park." He laughed suddenly. "Lord knows, I never thought I'd be pushing my baby girl's stroller in a park holding hands with Brooke Fallon."

"You held hands?"

"It was her thing. If anybody looked at us—you know, a mixed couple with a baby—she'd grab my hand and call me sugar or darling."

"But you started to take it seriously?"

"I couldn't help it, Mr. Phillips. I had to wonder, why not? You know? Why not us?"

Colin did know, but didn't say so; the young couldn't believe it of the old, that they remembered what love was like in the first few months.

"We could talk to each other," Anthony said, "I told her stuff I never told anybody else, and she did the same with me."

"I'd like to know what kinds of things she told you, these things she didn't tell anyone else."

"I don't want to say anything bad about her. It was her secret and I need to keep it."

"What you tell me is protected. For Brooke's sake, you should answer."

Anthony had settled his gaze on Colin's face while he spoke. He pressed his lips tight together, then nodded. "She told me she'd gone to bed with this older man, who was married. He was one of her professors. She was real ashamed of it, said she couldn't believe she'd been that stupid. He was pressuring her to, you know, do it again and she was trying to keep out of his way. If she ever came down to the guard's booth to talk to me at night, she'd duck down out of sight when a car came through, just because we weren't sure if I'd get in trouble with my boss. One night, she was there and a car pulled up and a man said he'd come to see Ms. Fallon. I was surprised but I tried to keep cool and I just called Brooke's apartment like I normally would and then told him she wasn't home."

"What was Brooke doing?" Colin pictured her, crouching down to hide from her stalker.

"She was squeezing my ankle and when I had a chance to look down, she was shaking her head hard. When I told the man she wasn't home, he said that was funny, she'd told him she wasn't going out. So he takes out his cell phone and calls her. When I saw that, I was scared her phone would ring right there where he could hear it, but she'd turned it off. Anyway, when he got voicemail right away, he says 'damn her' and drives off."

They sat in silence for a minute and Colin made notes to provide breathing space. "Did Brooke tell you who the man was?"

"Not his name, but she said he's the one she'd made her mistake with."

"And this was the man you told the police about the night Brooke died?"

"Yeah."

"Why didn't you tell them about that incident? It sounds as if she was afraid of him."

"It's like I told you. She was ashamed and I don't want anybody to think bad about her."

"But at some point, Brooke did begin to let him into her condo, is that right?" He saw Anthony flinch but had to push the point. "If she was afraid of him, why did she do that?"

"I don't know, Mr. Phillips." His face became that of a betrayed child. "She even gave him the code for the residents' gate, like I wouldn't see him come in that way."

There was a soft knock on the office door. Jessica opened it a crack and said, "Sorry to interrupt but my little friend is getting fussy. I think she wants her daddy."

"Yeah, it's her lunch time." Anthony took his daughter and smiled into her face.

Jessica kissed the little girl goodbye. "You bring her back anytime." When they were gone, she turned on Colin.

"Now why does that sweet man need a lawyer?"

⁓

The Fallons' church was too small for the crowd expected at Brooke's memorial, so they arranged to use the civic center.

Eden walked from her office. As she expected, Bobby Atchison and another detective had stationed themselves at the central doors. They could have been with the funeral home in their dark suits and their mild demeanors, but they would be watching to see who came. By now, she was sure, they would have Dantry's name.

She lingered outside, waiting for her family. Prominent politicians from all over the state arrived. High school friends of Brooke's, and the principal and teachers. A large group of college students. Susan's medical partners.

The university president with two other people trailing him stopped to speak. "Eden, such a sad day. I think you know Dean Wyke, and this is Professor Joseph Dantry. He was Brooke's major advisor."

By reflex, she shook hands with the three and managed to say, "It'll mean a lot to the Fallons that you're here."

"Brooke was one of the most talented young women I've ever known," Dantry's voice was low and somber.

When President Boone and his entourage had moved on, Eden allowed herself a tiny shudder. It could be that she'd just shaken hands with Brooke's murderer.

"Aunt Eden, mom sent me to find you." It was Peter at her elbow. She followed him into the hall and joined the rest of her family in the row immediately behind the one reserved for the Fallons.

The white casket, closed and cloaked in flowers, lit from above, focused and heightened grief—the somber and contained public grief, the jagged and raw private grief—so the cavernous auditorium felt like a chapel. Eden sat beside Colin. His eyes were closed, as if in prayer, but he took her hand and held it.

The service began, made tender by music, gentled by laughter when the minister recalled the charming child Brooke had been. Eden had a view of the Fallons' profiles and they were the epitome of dry-eyed, shatter-faced dignity.

After the service, people milled around, sorting themselves into those who planned to follow the procession to the cemetery and those who had to return to work after lingering for an appropriate length of time. Usually Eden would have been among the second group and she knew their sense of relief and guilt that, for them, life would return to normal. Sean stood to one side, head down. Wren was saying, "Daddy, why don't you ride with Eden?"

"Is that all right with you, my dear?" He took Eden's arm.

"We'll have to walk back to the office to get my car."

But they weren't out of the crowd yet. While Colin paused to greet old friends, Eden felt someone touch her elbow. It was Carmen Loftus, an assistant district attorney she'd worked with on a recent settlement.

"Eden, good to see you."

"You too, Carmen. Do you know the Fallons?"

"I'm here with the delegation from our office. You're close to the Senator and his wife, aren't you?"

"My sister and brother-in-law are closer, but I've known them all my life."

Carmen leaned toward Eden's ear and lowered her voice. "Then you'll want to be available for them."

Eden waited, watching Carmen's forehead wrinkle and clear and wrinkle again while she decided how much to say.

"The medical examiner's report is going to be hard to take," the young woman said.

"Will they get it before it's made public?"

"My boss is going to see them this evening." She turned and made her way out to the street.

Eden looked around and spotted her father. He talked to a young black man and seemed to be consoling him. She waited where she was and in a few minutes, her father joined her. She told him what Carmen had said.

"What do you think that's all about?" she asked.

"There aren't many reasons why a girl like Brooke gets killed."

"Dad." She stopped walking. "You think she was pregnant?"

He also stopped and turned to face her. "Has it really not occurred to you?"

She shook her head and started moving again. "I met Dantry. I shook his hand."

"After this funeral is over, the police will move quickly." He sounded detached now. "If I'm right, they'll go for the father of her baby."

⌣

The next morning, Sean, Anthony, the six male students who had been on the trip to England, and Joseph Dantry were all asked to give DNA samples for paternity testing.

Sean's attorney advised him not to submit to the requested DNA test, as Colin did with Anthony. Apparently the students and the professor received the same advice, because the D.A. had to go to a judge for search warrants and asked to have them sealed, along with the medical examiner's report on Brooke's death.

The violent death of a Senator's daughter had drawn the national press. The chance to sue for information under the Freedom of Information Act cranked interest into a minor frenzy. Colin was taken aback when reporters he'd never met stopped him on the courthouse steps, looking for statements.

He ducked them, but the lawyers for several of the other men whose cheek scrapings were sought were more than willing to give press conferences, usually backed by their clients.

"Why do they want all that?" Anthony asked. "Who wants to be out there like that?"

Colin didn't have a response, and Anthony answered his own question.

"I guess if you're white, you grow up thinking that attracting attention is a good thing." He laughed. "I bet those other lawyers would be glad for me to take the test."

∾

Wren tapped on the door of the cottage. "Daddy?"

"Come in." Colin got up from his chair and went to accept a kiss on the cheek.

"What are you doing?" she asked. "Am I interrupting?"

"Watching a little afternoon baseball. Join me." He sat again and muted the television.

"I want you to come to supper tonight. I'm on my way to see Susan and I'm going to bring her back with me."

Colin knew that Wren had tried to reach her friend by telephone and email many times in the two weeks since Brooke's funeral, but had gotten no response. "You've talked to her, then?"

"No, but it was on the news this morning that Avery has gone back to Washington, so I'm just going to Susan's mother's house and that's that."

Colin couldn't stop himself from frowning. "Her grief is still new, Wren. If she isn't ready, you ought not push her."

"I can't let her bog down in this. I'd count on her to do the same for me."

"Do what exactly?"

"Get her out to be with the people who love her. Her poor mother has round the clock caretakers, so Susan doesn't have to stay there all the time." Wren's voice took on the edge that made him think of Rhetta.

"What time do you want me?"

At six o'clock, Colin let himself into the sunroom. Kenneth was in the kitchen, standing at the work table spooning olives from a jar into a bowl.

"Where's Wren?" Colin asked.

"She left a note saying she's gone to pick up Susan. I just got here myself." He turned to the refrigerator and opened the door. "I don't know what she planned to cook. Maybe I'll just take us all out."

"Do you mind if I make myself a drink?"

"I'll join you."

They converged at the bar where Colin poured himself bourbon and Kenneth made a vodka martini with four of the olives.

"I'm worried about her," Kenneth said and Colin understood he meant Wren. "I'm spending every minute of every day wondering if my son's going to be charged with murder. She's obsessing over Susan instead."

"I suppose that's her way of coping." He felt disloyal discussing his daughter with her husband, but as he took a second sip of his drink, he asked himself, why not? "She's so much like her mother. It took a long time, but I finally understood that when Rhetta focused on one problem, it was because she believed she could do something about it. She blocked out all the things she couldn't control."

"That's Wren, for sure. And don't get me wrong, I love Susan, too, and I can't imagine what she and Avery are going through, but I have to think of my own family. All Wren will say is that Sean ought to take the damned DNA test and get it over with. Then she checks her email again." He took a draw on his martini. "I guess I could use some of that focus of hers."

Before Colin could say anything, they heard Wren's car in the driveway.

"I'd better open a bottle of wine for the ladies." Kenneth chewed on an olive and headed for the wine cooler.

Colin saw Wren at the French doors. Her demeanor, her posture, were those of someone drenched in a downpour, although that made no sense. The sun was out. He moved to meet her and put his arms around her. "What is it? What's wrong?"

She hugged him, then reached for Kenneth who'd left the wine bottle half-opened and come across the room. It was on her husband's shoulder that she let go and wept.

"Honey," Kenneth said, "you've got to tell us what's going on." He dabbed at her tears. "Where's Susan?"

"She's not coming." Wren sat back and closed her eyes until her breath became regular. "She doesn't want to see me or talk to me, she said, until she knows who killed Brooke."

I should have thought of that, Colin thought. Then I could have warned her.

"I asked her what she meant," Wren said. "I asked her how she could think for a minute that Sean could do something like that. She said she can't believe in anything anymore." She blew her nose. "So that's that."

Then she looked at Colin. "I've been thinking that all of this lawyering is stupid, that Sean and the others should just open their mouths for a scraping and get it over with. But now, I get it. What you've always tried to say, Daddy. Being innocent isn't enough."

∽

After a month of arguments, a judge ordered that nine men would submit DNA samples for the purpose of determining the paternity of the deceased's unborn child. The media assumed that once the father was known, the killer would be known, and that was indeed what happened.

When the report came back from the lab, but before it was made public, after negotiation with the district attorney,

Professor Joseph Dantry, escorted by his attorney, turned himself in to be charged with first degree murder.

Just after Dantry's arrest, Colin arrived at his office and found Marcus Minton there. Colin knew from Eden that Marcus stopped into the office from time to time to see his daughter, but the two men had not crossed paths before.

Marcus rose from his chair and said, "Hello, Mr. Phillips. My grandmother asked me to tell you that she would like to see you."

The next day, Colin drove to Sweet Side and found the address. Marie opened the door for Colin. She smiled up at him, leaning on her cane. Marcus stood just behind her, a steadying hand against her back.

"How do you do, Mr. Phillips?" she asked.

"I'm well Mrs. Minton. And I am humbled to be in your presence again after so long."

"Please come in and take a seat." She and Marcus both stood aside for him, then Marcus assisted her to her chair.

"I'll get the refreshments," Marcus said and disappeared into the kitchen. Colin swallowed and discovered that his throat was tight.

"You came here once, when you and Rhetta were courting," Marie said.

"I remember. It was just after Mr. Vance died, I believe, and you were such a comfort to Rhetta."

Marie looked away and rested her hands on the arms of her chair, almost as if she expected to raise herself up again. She glanced at the kitchen door, perhaps anxious for her grandson to come back and ease the tension. He appeared with a plate of cookies and pitcher of lemonade, then had to go back for glasses with ice in them.

"There's a tray, you know," Marie said.

"I don't trust myself not to spill something all over your floors, Granny."

She laughed and motioned for him to set her glass on the little table at her elbow. Then she cleared her throat. "We appreciate you coming all this way, Mr. Phillips. For humoring an old lady."

"When Marcus conveyed the invitation, I realized there was nothing I'd rather do than visit you."

"You better wait till you hear what I want to say." She laughed again, teasing them as if they were little boys.

Colin looked at Marcus, who shrugged; he didn't know either.

"Y'all don't need to be scared," she said. "I want to thank you for helping advise Anthony. He's a fine young man, but not the most grown sometimes. Janelle loves him too much. Of course, the same might have been said about me and Jabel, back when he was Jabel. That choice was taken from me."

"Granny, I was never taken from you." From his chair, Marcus touched her left hand.

She waved him away. "And Rhetta. She didn't want to let Laurence go."

"She was loyal. And protective," Colin said.

"Do you think she knew? About him being on the down-low, I mean?"

"Granny." Marcus sounded shocked, but she ignored him. Her eyes were rheumy but when she looked at Colin with that question in the air, their still striking color intensified, like a light coming toward him through water.

"It may sound odd, but it was not something we talked about. She would tell people that the loss of his wife and child made it impossible for him to contemplate marriage again. He didn't reveal the truth about himself until after she died."

"They call that coming out. It means he could live like he was free." She picked up her glass and Colin followed suit. "The way everybody ought to live."

"Granny, you never cease to amaze." Marcus shook his head.

She motioned for him to hand her a cookie. "These aren't so bad. Not as good as mine used to be."

"Mrs. Minton, you talked about the adults not knowing how to let their young ones grow up. At what age do our young ones forget that we're adults?"

"Ha ha. Now that's a good question. But you're just a young one yourself, Mr. Colin Phillips."

They laughed and, with a silent apology to Rhetta's ghost for his disloyalty, Colin let himself relax and enjoy the company.

NOVEMBER 2004

For once in his life, Colin's sympathies were with the prosecution, but he shared defense attorney Simon Tate's outrage that the judge had not granted a change in venue. It came as no surprise to him that it took a week and a pool of ninety-eight potential jurors to seat the twelve plus two alternates. The trial would be standing room only, and televised. That meant the old courtroom was returned to service. It was larger by far than any of the rooms in the new Judicial Center. If its architect had been able to imagine cameras and live feeds, he couldn't have done a better job with its layout. Talk on Court Street blended civic pride with irony: wasn't it the perfect backdrop for a Trial of the Century?

Colin had heard the chat and tried to ignore it. He knew he was sentimental about the old place, but he did think that its dark paneling, murals, wine-red carpet, and brass fixtures were right for the ritual by which the horror of a murder was transformed into law and order.

He arrived early on the morning the trial was to start and waded through television crews setting up on the front steps of the courthouse. One of the bailiffs who knew him from the old days had kept a bench near the front open for him. Reporters were herded to the back. Friends and family of both the dead girl and the defendant filed in and took their places to the right or left of the central aisle, thus establishing their allegiance.

Clyde Raeburn, in a suit Colin could believe was forty years old, appeared beside him.

"You got room for me?" Clyde asked.

"Sure. I'm glad to have company." Colin expected the rest of his family but there would be ample space.

"For an old man, I'm nervous as a bride groom." Clyde groaned as he sat.

"How would you know how a bride groom feels?" Colin nudged his elbow.

"Lively imagination. I just left Miss Sydney and her father. She's going to be the first witness."

"She'll be fine. I hope my grandson has had advice as good as yours. And I hope the same for my client. Think we've done the young people justice?"

"You and I're as good as we ever were but we're done now. We don't have anything to do but wait."

Soon, Eden, Wren, and Kenneth joined them. Eden took the seat beside Colin, to his right. Wren and Kenneth sat to his left. Only Sean was missing, sequestered until after he testified. Just before nine o'clock, a bailiff escorted the Fallons in and seated them. Colin felt the gravitational pull of their grief.

The Honorable Ricardo Desmond emerged from a door in the paneling behind his raised desk and looked around the room until it was silent. "Let's call them in, Mr. Bailiff."

The jurors filed in and took their seats. Seven women and five men. One of the men, by appearance the youngest, wore black jeans, a white shirt, and narrow tie. Hipster, Colin thought. One of the women and one of the men were black, both white-haired and dressed as for church. The lady wore a small grey hat nestled into her hair. District Attorney Hardison Smith stood to make his opening statement.

"Ladies and gentlemen, it is a great tragedy that brings us together today. We have lost a bright, promising, brilliant child. No, she was not my child, or yours, by birth. Indeed, her parents sit here, their dignity and strength an inspiration to us all, but with her death, Brooke Fallon becomes ours and we must do justice for her."

He stood squarely in front of the jury, his hands clasped behind his back. Colin had seen this before, and knew it worked.

It showed the jury that he didn't need notes, that he was humble in regard to himself, but serious in regard to his work.

"What you will hear from the witnesses and see in the evidence the State presents, is this series of events: Brooke was drawn into a love affair with Professor Joseph Dantry, an older, more experienced man, a man who was in a position of power, power he had abused this way before. He was her teacher, her advisor, her mentor, a man whose reputation was such that he could make or break the careers of his students.

"You will hear that Brooke withdrew from her friends, ended other relationships, became secretive with her parents where before she had been close and confiding. Why? Because this man knew how to seduce her and cut her off from all who would have said, 'Brooke, what are you doing? Come back to us, come back to yourself and the values you were raised with.'"

Smith turned to look at the defendant, and the jurors' heads turned with him. "This man, Joseph Dantry, included Brooke in the group of students he took to England for the summer, so she was physically as well as emotionally cut off from anyone who loved her. Those are the circumstances in which Brooke found herself to be pregnant. DNA evidence proves that the defendant was the father of her baby."

He faced the jury again and reclasped his hands over his diaphragm. "Once they returned to Piedmont, Brooke woke up to her situation. She found the strength of her character. No doubt she confronted Dantry. No doubt she told him she expected him to take responsibility. And no doubt, Professor Joseph Dantry saw his status, his career, his family, all begin to slide away. He was a man who had to be in control and Brooke turned out not to be just another of the girls he had seduced over the years. She threatened him and he could not allow that.

"So he went to Brooke's home, the Highgate condominium her parents owned. He was seen there, ladies and gentlemen, by someone who had seen him there more than once, and you will hear from that person. Dantry went with the intention to kill Brooke, and he did kill her. He slammed her head against the floor three times and caused traumatic injury to her brain. That injury killed her, but not immediately. She could have been helped, but her murderer left her on the floor to die.

"These are the elements of the crime he committed. These are the elements of the crime that the State will prove to you with evidence and witnesses. Then the State will ask you to convict Joseph Dantry of the premeditated murder of Brooke Fallon."

Smith walked back to his table, head down, burdened by the seriousness of his cause.

Simon Tate sat still for a moment and pressed one finger to his lips. Finally, he stood and walked to the jury box. He took time to look at each person, to engage each with a gaze.

Colin glanced at Eden and she rolled her eyes. He read her thoughts: showboating.

Tate wore a gray suit with a chalk stripe, a bright white shirt, and his tie was striped blue, white, and silver. His sandy hair and ruddy cheeks gave him a boyish look, offset by his serious demeanor and tortoise shell glasses.

"Ladies and gentlemen, the prosecutor has told you a tall tale. He has taken a few facts that my client does not deny, and has drawn them out to their thinnest and most stressed length. We might say that is his job and we might express sympathy for him because convicting an innocent man is a hard job. You make it hard by bringing your life experience and common sense to this trial."

He took off his glasses, folded in the earpieces, then held them loosely in his right hand.

"My client had a sexual relationship with the dead woman. He broke his wedding vows. He hurt his wife and family and colleagues, and he regrets it beyond words. He knows and feels the depth of pain he has caused. He understands that people he does not know judge his behavior harshly. He will live with that.

"But, he relies on you to know that poor judgment and human frailty do not add up to murder. That is the most fragile thread Mr. Smith has spun. He stretched it from wall to wall." He spread his arms. "But it can break at any point. Mr. Smith wants you to believe that piling on other instances of bad judgment—which have nothing, nothing to do with the death of Brooke Fallon—somehow strengthen that thread, but they don't. Your common sense will tell you that."

Colin shifted his eyes from Tate to the jurors. The lady with the gray hat had narrowed her eyes. Skeptical? Disapproving?

"My job," Tate was saying, "as you know, is to demonstrate the essential, sacred mainstay of our system. Reasonable doubt. In my experience, jurors wrestle first with that concept. Reasonable doubt is part of our common everyday language. It is responsible for all the courtroom dramas on TV. But what is it?

"Let me explain it this way. You and I, working together, will examine every fraction of every inch of Mr. Smith's thread. It will snap and once it snaps, it cannot be put back together. That is reasonable doubt."

He put his glasses into his breast pocket. "My client did not kill Brooke Fallon. He did not strike her. He did not even see her on the day she died. We all want to know who committed this horrible crime. We all feel outrage and sorrow and sympathy, but strange as it may be, this courtroom is not where we come to express those emotions. It is where we come to test the State's case. That case will fail to withstand your testing, and you will acquit my client. You will deliver justice for him."

The young hipster had been leaning forward. Now he sat back and Colin saw his chest move with a long exhale.

"Mr. Smith," Judge Desmond said, "call your first witness."

As soon as Smith stood to do so, Tate came half out of his chair. "Your Honor, may we approach the bench?"

Judge Desmond nodded and waved them up with the fingers of his right hand. At the same time, he tucked his chin and frowned.

"Tate ought to know Desmond doesn't like a lot of delays," Eden whispered to her father.

"But he's got to keep working on the prior bad acts business." Colin folded his arms and leaned toward her.

"The judge will love that, too, after he's made a ruling."

"It's got to be done, if only to have something to work with on appeal." Colin was outraged that the judge had ruled the prosecution could introduce the affairs Dantry had had with other students over the years. Once a defense attorney, always a defense attorney, he supposed, but he kept his umbrage to himself.

"Here's Marcus." Eden touched Colin's arm. Marcus had been waiting with Sydney. Colin slid down the bench and Eden followed so that Marcus could take the place they had saved for him. When Colin resettled and looked back to the front of the court, he found himself caught in Wren's glare.

She still can't stand it that we show Marcus even a little courtesy, Colin thought, and he wished she could accept a world made up of shades and subtleties. Just as he caught her eye, she faced forward again.

The conference at the judge's bench ended. Simon Tate and Hardison Smith returned to their desks and the bailiff called out "Sydney Marie Minton."

Sydney wore a navy blue suit and pearl earrings. Colin approved. Her hair, usually wavy and full, was straight and flat. He didn't know how that was accomplished and couldn't keep himself from thinking it was the stress that had changed it.

She took the oath, then sat and looked around. Smith straightened papers on his desk, perhaps to give her a moment. She spotted Marcus and Colin saw her relax a bit. Smith cleared his throat and got her attention. He asked questions, simple at first, designed to put her at ease and to let the jury learn about her.

"I'm twenty-two," she told the Court. "I grew up in New York City, graduated from Harvard, and I've been in Piedmont for a year and five months. I work at a law firm, Phillips and Phillips, and next fall I will enroll in law school here, at Mangum University. No, I had never been to Piedmont until last year, but I have family—extended family—here. My father was born and raised here."

To all of this, Smith nodded encouragement. Once she began to speak normally, to sound less choked, he established himself in front of the jury so that she had to face him and them.

"Now, Miss Minton, do you recall the events of August 12, 2003?"

"Yes sir."

"What went on that day that makes it stand out for you?"

"It's the day I found Brooke."

"You are speaking of Brooke Fallon?"

"Yes sir."

"And when you say you found her, what do you mean?"

"I went with a friend to visit her, and she was dead on the floor. I saw her first."

"Where did you find her?"

"In the condo at Highgate. The condo where she lived."

"Had you visited her there before?"

"No sir. I'd met her once, just the day before. She'd been in England. She'd just gotten home."

"Did you have other reasons to be familiar with Highgate?"

"My father lives there. He moved in about the time Brooke went to England."

"Would you have considered it to be safe, secure?"

"Oh yes. There's a lot of security."

"Could you just drive in, the way you might drive into, say, a shopping center?"

"No. There were two gates, one for people who lived there and had a code to punch in, and one for visitors. If you were a visitor, you had to have your name on a list."

"And there was an attendant at the visitors' gate?"

"Yes."

"So, how did you enter Highgate that day?

"We went through the residents' gate. I had the code from my father."

"When you say we, who do you mean?"

"My friend, Sean Caldwell."

"What happened after you went through the residents' gate?"

"We drove around to where Brooke lived, at the back of the development. It was Building M. And then we called Brooke to tell her we were there so she could open the door of the building for us."

"You couldn't just walk in?"

"No. You need another code, or somebody buzzes you in."

Colin paid attention to her voice. She had gone from nervous to calm and now sounded flat, almost rote. As if she had rehearsed the next part to herself a hundred times.

"Once you called her, did Miss Fallon let you in?"

"There was no answer. Sean—Brooke had told Sean the building code I guess, because he knew it. We went into the building and he pushed the elevator button but I made a joke about it and I ran up the stairs. I think somebody must have had the elevator stopped because I got to Brooke's door first."

"What did you find?"

Marcus Minton drew an audible deep breath. Colin saw Eden rest a hand on his back.

Sydney answered. "The door was partly open. I thought she might be in the bathroom, or her phone battery had run down, or something and I didn't want to seem like I was just barging in. I called her and went into the foyer. There's a mirror on the wall and something made me look at the mirror. I saw a bare foot and I didn't understand it. Then I realized somebody was lying on the floor in the living room and I was seeing the reflection. Not of the whole person, just this little part. This foot. With red nail polish on the toes." She began to talk fast, to sound tearful.

"Miss Minton." Smith spoke louder than necessary, and it stopped her, snapped her back to the moment.

"I'm sorry," she said.

"It's all right, Miss Minton. I do realize this is a difficult thing to remember, but please slow down just a little, so the jury can understand you."

Marcus Minton sat back and Colin heard him take an audible, deep breath.

"I went in the living room." Sydney's voice was tempered. "I saw Brooke lying on the floor and I think I started screaming right away."

"Why did you scream, Miss Minton?"

"She was lying on her side and I just knew something horrible had happened."

"What happened next?"

"They say I didn't faint or pass out, but there's a hole in my memory. After a while, I was sitting in an ambulance and somebody was giving me oxygen. I was wrapped in a blanket and that didn't make sense because I knew it was a hot day, but I was shaking. My body and my mind just weren't working together."

"One more question, Miss Minton. Do you know what time you and your friend arrived at Highgate?"

"It was five minutes past six when we tried to call her from the parking lot. I saw the time on my cell phone. And I checked it later."

"Thank you, Miss Minton." Smith turned and nodded at the jury as if thanking them, too.

Simon Tate was ready.

"Good morning, Ms. Minton," Tate said. "You lost a friend on that August day and I'm sure we all extend our sympathies. Now, remind me, how long had you known Ms. Fallon?"

"I met her the day before she died."

"So is it fair to say you hardly knew her?"

"I knew a lot about her." Sydney's voice was soft, embarrassed sounding, and Colin knew that was exactly what Tate wanted. He couldn't assail her facts, but he could show her emotion, all this grief for a girl she hardly knew, to be suspect and make her look foolish.

"How did you come to meet her?"

"Through Sean. Sean Caldwell."

"And that is the same Sean Caldwell who knew the code for getting into Ms. Fallon's building?"

She nodded, then said, "Yes, sir."

"Ms. Minton, when did you meet Mr. Caldwell?"

"In June 2003."

"Were you aware of the nature of the relationship between him and Brooke Fallon?"

"They were …"

"Yes or no."

"Yes."

"Now, Miss Minton, could you tell us what you did on the twelfth of August, up to the point that you went to Highgate."

"Objection." The district attorney half-stood. "Relevance, Your Honor."

"I'll allow it," the judge said.

"It was a Thursday," Sydney said, "so I went to work. I met Sean for lunch and he said that Brooke had called and invited us over for drinks after work. Then I went back to the office until he picked me up."

Tate showed a sheet of paper to Smith and then to the judge before going back to his place in front of the jury. "I have a copy of your statement here, Miss Minton. Perhaps you could read the highlighted line out loud for the jury."

"It says, 'Sean picked me up at the office at about 5:30 or 5:45. He was late.'"

"Did he explain why he was late?"

"He'd gone to register for classes and there was some mix-up. It was okay. I had work to do anyway."

"Do you have any personal knowledge of where he went and what he did? Yes or no, please." He put emphasis on the word "he."

"No."

"Thank you, Miss Minton. That's all."

"Folks," the judge said, "it's time for our morning break. Fifteen minutes."

Sydney came straight to Marcus and the two went out into the hall, his arm around her shoulder. Eden followed them.

Colin realized his back ached from the hard bench. He stood up and stretched. Wren slipped down the bench toward him. He saw that she was distressed, not far from tears.

"It's awful, what Tate's doing. He's going to try and make Sean look guilty, isn't he?" She looked across the courtroom, toward the defense table where lawyers huddled and Joseph Dantry held his wife's hand.

"He'll try. That doesn't mean he'll succeed." Colin kissed her cheek. He felt her tension. Wren was like her mother that way: when she was under pressure, something radiated from her, something that played on his own nerves. "Try to see it from the other side and maybe it'll be easier for you. Tate has a job to do."

Wren turned to him. Her eyes showed anger and hurt. "I don't know how you do it. How do you defend a monster like Joseph Dantry?"

"Don't you believe that everyone is entitled to the best defense? What about your Uncle Laurence? He needed defending."

She wrapped her arms and clasped her elbows. "You know that isn't what I mean, Daddy. Please don't …" She shook her head and closed her eyes.

"I'm sorry, sweetheart." He touched her shoulder. "We're all on edge. Will you and Kenneth go home after Sean testifies?"

"I want to see it through."

"Are you and Susan still, what should I say? Estranged?" He lowered his voice.

Susan and Avery Fallon sat behind the prosecution's desks. They had not moved during the recess but as if she sensed that her name had been spoken, Susan half turned her head and seemed to listen.

"After Dantry was arrested, I thought Susan would apologize, but she hasn't said a word to me."

"She will need you," Colin said. "Be forgiving." Just then, the courtroom doors opened and people who'd stepped out began to file in.

"Forgiving?" Wren said. "I'm sorry, but I have a hard time forgiving a person who thought my son could have committed murder. I saw him—Jabel, or Marcus, or whatever his name is—sitting with you. And about Uncle Laurence? Have you forgotten why he needed defending?"

Eden was worried about Sydney. The girl and her father retreated to an alcove at the end of the hallway and she followed them. She thought Sydney was crying, her face turned to the wall, head down. Marcus's hand rested in the middle of her back and he bent forward as if to shelter her from the view of curious people who filled the hallway, including a clutch of reporters.

Eden put her hand beside Marcus's and leaned toward Sydney to see her face. "You were very good. You couldn't have been better."

"He's an asshole." Sydney's voice came through clinched teeth and she shook off the two embraces. Eden had known the girl more than a year and had never heard her swear. Then she realized it was anger, not tears, Sydney tried to control.

"You mean Simon Tate?" Eden guessed.

"He made me look ridiculous. And he wants to make Sean look guilty."

"The jury sees through all that, I promise." Eden and Marcus looked at each other.

"Where's Mr. Raeburn?" Sydney asked. "I want to know what he thinks."

"Do you want me to go look for him?" Eden asked.

"There he is." Sydney stepped forward to greet Clyde Raeburn. He was an elderly man in an elderly suit, who shuffled a bit as he walked toward them.

"I thought I'd never get out of there," he said. "Don't know why so many people want my opinion. Not anymore." His grin belied that. "Miss Sydney, you did fine." Clyde shook Marcus's hand. "You can be proud of her, Dr. Minton."

"I am," Marcus said.

"We've told her how good she was," Eden said. "but she needs to hear it from you, Clyde."

"You told me not to take things personally," Sydney said to him, "but I can't help it. I hate Simon Tate."

"Well now," Clyde said, "if you follow through on your idea of being a defense attorney, you've got to be willing to get hated that way." He patted her arm. "Besides, I was watching the jury. They liked you and they didn't think much of Mr. Tate, either."

"I'm glad she had you by her side through this," Marcus said.

"And while we're at it," Clyde said, "we'll give Eden credit for asking me to help out."

"It was Dad's idea," she said. "He thought you'd enjoy it, Clyde."

They all smiled because Clyde had taken pride in irritating Hardison Smith by insisting the D.A. prep Sydney himself rather than assigning her to an assistant, and further irritated him by sitting in on the prep sessions and being free with opinions.

"And it's tired me out," Clyde said, "I'm going home to take a nap." They laughed and he shuffled away, stopping every few feet to greet someone.

"We should go back in." Eden led the way and stopped short when she saw her father and sister nose-to-nose. She heard Wren hiss something about Uncle Laurence and why he had to be defended and heard Marcus, close behind her, draw in breath. Then Wren saw them and set her face in a cold stare.

"Dad?" Eden asked. He shook his head and sat down, looking straight ahead.

The bailiffs began to move into their places and the attorneys came in and took their chairs. As the family reassembled, Eden found herself down the row, sitting next to Wren. She squeezed her sister's hand to show some solidarity, knowing that Sean was up next. Wren didn't reciprocate.

Hardison Smith began with Sean as he had with Sydney, letting the witness relax a bit, letting the jury get to know him. Sean told the jury he was twenty-two, had just graduated from Mangum University with a double major in Business and Psychology. He planned to work in his father's real estate development business for at least a year and then possibly get his MBA. He had lived in Piedmont all of his life, as had his mother and her family going way back.

Sean wasn't prone to sitting still and his shoulders shifted as if his hands, out of sight in his lap, were opening and closing and flexing. Eden hoped his energy wouldn't look like nerves to jurors.

Smith stepped to his place at the corner of the jury box, nodded a greeting to the jurors, and took his characteristic humble stance. He led Sean through the events of August 12, 2003. Sean said, as Sydney had, that the two of them got to Highgate a few minutes after six, that she had gone into Brooke's apartment ahead of him and he'd heard her scream.

The D.A. nodded. "Now, you'd known Miss Fallon for a long time?"

"Since we were babies. Our moms have been best friends since they were little."

"Would you say that you were close friends with Miss Fallon?"

"Yes sir."

"How frequently did you see Miss Fallon?"

"Our families went on trips together when we were kids. And I saw her every day, just about, while we were going through school. We didn't have the same classes in high school so much, but we ate lunch together and hung out after school and on weekends. For our first couple of years at Mangum, it was the same. We saw each other a lot."

"Did you consider her to be a confidant? Did you talk to her seriously?"

"Oh, yeah. Yes sir. For a long time, I talked to her more than I did to anybody."

"And did you feel that Miss Fallon regarded you as her confidant?"

"I did, yes."

"Was there a time when that changed?"

"Yes sir." He sighed.

"Can you pinpoint when?"

"Some in the fall of 2002 and a lot more by the winter semester in 2003."

"And in what way did it change?"

"I felt like Brooke was avoiding me. We'd make plans and she'd cancel at the last minute. We used to study together in the library and she changed her carrel to one on a different floor. We'd talked about going skiing over spring break but she said she needed to stay home and study."

"Is it accurate to say that the closeness you'd had was deteriorating?"

"I'd agree with that, yes." He sighed again.

"Did you talk to her about it?"

"I tried, but she'd just say there was nothing wrong and take off."

"And did her behavior toward you change again at any point?"

"It did. She went to study in England for the summer and when she got back in August, she got in touch. She said she wanted ..."

"Objection to hearsay," Tate said.

"Sustained," Judge Desmond said.

"Mr. Caldwell, without telling us what Miss Fallon said, you had a conversation with her after she returned from England?"

"Yes sir."

"As a result of that conversation, did you feel that the friendship was intact?"

"Not like before, but yes. Intact."

"Now, let's go back to August 12, 2003. Was that the first time you'd been to the condo at Highgate where Miss Fallon lived?"

"No. I used to go there a lot, until she changed so much." He broke off as if the memory was painful.

"How would you describe the security at Highgate?"

"Really good, I guess you'd say. It was kind of a pain in the neck sometimes."

"When you say, a pain in the neck, can you explain that?"

"It wasn't too bad for me. I knew the guy who worked at the gate at night and he knew Brooke and I were friends so he wasn't so strict on me. But anybody else who wanted to come in, Brooke had to give permission. It's just that most of us, college students, we're used to coming and going and not having security gates and codes. It could get a little weird."

Eden knew her nephew was talking too much and she had to grip her hands to keep from signaling him. Hardison Smith cleared his throat and stepped forward.

"So," he said. "When you say it was a pain in the neck, you mean the security was tight?"

"Yes sir."

Smith nodded. "Thank you, Mr. Caldwell."

The D.A. took his time going back to his table, making Simon Tate wait for him to cross before moving into the well of the room.

"Mr. Caldwell." Tate sounded impatient. "Were you and Ms. Fallon romantically involved?"

"Objection." Smith stood. "Relevance."

"Your Honor," Tate was strident. "The witness has said that they were close."

"Overruled. Do you need to hear the question read back, Mr. Caldwell?"

"No sir, I got it. We weren't romantically involved."

Eden glanced at Wren, whose controlled expression softened into puzzlement. Eden leaned toward her sister, let their arms touch and hoped Wren would read the movement as sympathy.

"Are you aware that many people believed you were in love?" Tate asked.

"Calls for a conclusion," Smith said.

"Not necessarily," Tate said and the judge overruled the objection.

"People assume things," Sean said. "It didn't matter to us what they thought. Brooke and I were clear."

Tate was quiet a moment. Letting it settle, Eden thought, letting jurors make assumptions. His next question went in a different direction.

"Mr. Caldwell, you're very certain about the time you and Ms. Minton got to Highgate. Are you as certain about where you were and when earlier that day?"

"Can you be more specific?" He crossed his arms over his chest.

"Let's start with where."

"All day?"

"All day." Tate nodded.

"I'd had a problem registering on line for a class I needed, so that morning I went to campus to find my advisor and the professor to get things straightened out."

"And that was at what time?"

"It took probably an hour and a half, maybe two hours. I think I got to campus around 9:30."

Tate nodded, "Go on."

"I was supposed to have lunch with Sydney Minton, so I had to leave campus before I was actually done."

"So you left at 11:30, approximately? And where was Ms. Minton?"

"In the law office where she worked, downtown on Court Street."

"And how long does it take to drive from the university to that office?"

"Fifteen minutes to drive, but I'd left my car at one of the shuttle lots, so I had to catch a bus to get back to it."

"And did you get to the law office on time?"

"I think so, maybe just a few minutes late. Sydney was ready to go, I remember."

"Then where did the two of you go?" Tate lowered his head and glanced at the jury box.

"We ate at the Village Grill and she had to get back to the office at one o'clock."

"Where did you go then?"

"Back to campus to finish registration."

"Wow. I would have thought that a school of Mangum's caliber could fix a class schedule more efficiently."

"Objection." Smith stood.

Tate held up a hand to forestall the judge. "Withdrawn. Please continue, Mr. Caldwell."

"I picked up my schedule—it was fixed by then—and I went to the bookstore to get my textbooks and went to the gym for a workout. I was mostly passing time until I picked Sydney up again. We were going to Brooke's to hang out."

"Did you see anyone you knew while you were mostly passing time?"

"Probably. I know a lot of people on campus."

"Did you see your advisor again? Or the registrar?"

"No. Just the clerk or secretary or whatever who gave me my schedule."

"Do you know that person?"

"No."

"How did you get into Highgate? Given all the security that was such a pain in the neck?"

Eden caught the abrupt change in the direction of the question. Tate wanted the jury to slip into thinking Sean had gone from campus to Highgate. Sean didn't catch it.

"Through the residents' gate. Since Sydney's dad lived there, she knew the code."

"You mentioned having a friend who was a security guard there. Was he working that evening?"

"He was, yeah."

"What is his name?"

"Anthony Huey."

"Did you know him only from your frequent visits to Highgate?"

"No. We went to middle school and high school together."

"On your earlier visits, in the years when you and Ms. Fallon were close, did you go in through the residents' gate, or the visitors' gate?"

"The visitors' gate, if I was driving in by myself."

"Since Anthony Huey knew you, he didn't necessarily check the list. Is that correct?"

"I don't know if he checked it or not."

"Now, on August 12, 2003, once you were through the gate, did you go directly to Ms. Fallon's condo?"

Eden was bothered. Tate had done it again, shifting to blur facts.

"We went to the building and tried to call her, but she didn't answer." His voice got tight.

"What did you do? You and Ms. Minton?"

"We went in. I had the code for the building."

"How did you come to have it?"

"Brooke gave it to me." He put his hands on the arms of his chair and shifted himself.

"Are you and Ms. Minton romantically involved?"

Smith objected and the lawyers went back and forth. Beside Eden, Wren cleared her throat with a small growl.

Finally, by the time Smith's protestations had made the answer to the question clear, Judge Desmond told Sean to answer. "Yes." His voice was clear.

"Were you romantically involved in the summer of 2003, while Brooke was in England?"

"Yes."

"That's all," Tate said.

Eden looked at the jurors. Most of them were straight-faced, but two or three looked confused at the abrupt ending to the cross examination. Tate had left a muddle of facts and implications, just as he had intended to. It was likely at least one juror would already be thinking, the old girlfriend dead, a new girlfriend, no alibi witnesses for hours, he had the codes, or could have. Simon Tate would be glad to pull it together in his closing: reasonable doubt.

Colin glanced at his watch. It was half past eleven. The lunch break would come soon and he had promised to meet Anthony at noon. He nodded a good-bye to Sydney and Marcus and eased himself out of the room.

When he got to the office, he found that Anthony was already there, along with Shayna.

"Here's Mr. Phillips." Jessica sounded relieved. Anthony

jumped up to greet Colin.

"I got here early," he said. "I guess I'm too nervous to be any-place else."

"I understand." Colin shook his hand, then put an arm on the young man's back. "Come in." He moved toward the door to his office.

"I'll watch Shayna," Jessica said.

"Sit down, son." Colin took off his suit coat. Instead of sitting behind his desk, he took the second client's chair beside Anthony's. "You want to hear about court this morning, I'm sure."

"Yes sir. I've been worrying, you know. Did they say my name?"

"Yes," Colin said.

"Damn." Anthony spoke softly. He wasn't looking at Colin.

"Why does that worry you so much?"

Anthony shrugged. "It just feels weird to think people are talking about me and I can't even be there." Then he half turned in the chair. "Mr. Smith wants me to be ready tomorrow even if he doesn't get to me till Thursday."

"My guess is, he'll try to control the timing so that you testify last thing tomorrow afternoon or just before the lunch break on Thursday. He'll want the jury to have a chance to absorb what you tell them."

Anthony shifted again. Colin had never seen him so fidgety or anxious, not even the night Brooke died.

"Anthony, you understand the importance of what you have to say, don't you? You don't have any thoughts of not saying it?"

"You mean, would I run off? No sir. I might like to, but it's like you and Mr. Smith say, all I've got to do is tell the truth." He gave a huff of a laugh that could have been ironic or could have been disbelief at finding himself in this situation.

"Think about it this way." Colin waited to get the young man's gaze again, as if that assured he was listening. "Most of what the prosecution witnesses have to tell is what the jury already knows—that Brooke is dead. The medical examiner will establish that she was pregnant with Dantry's baby and what time she died, but the jury knows that, too, considering all the coverage it got. You're the only person who can say that Dantry was at Highgate that afternoon."

"You're saying it all depends on me." His voice rose. "I could have saved her, that's what you think, isn't it? That's what everybody thinks." He shoved his chair back and stood up, standing so close that Colin couldn't rise, couldn't move.

"Anthony ..."

"But I didn't save her so now I got to be sure this man gets the blame and goes to prison."

"Please sit down, Anthony." Colin's heart pounded in his ears louder than his voice. It took a moment, but Anthony did sit and drop his head.

"I didn't mean to scare you, Mr. Phillips."

"I know that." He paused until they'd both drawn several deep breaths. "I didn't realize that you felt this burden. I should have. I know how you felt about her." As he said that, Anthony began to shake his head.

"Then let me put it this way," Colin went on. "When Hardison Smith and I say just tell the truth, you can take us at face value. That is all we, or anyone, asks of you. You don't have to shade it or shape it. Simply present the jury with the facts as you know them, and you've done your duty. It's out of your hands and off of your conscience."

Anthony looked at him again and this time Colin saw sadness in him, deep sorrow.

"All right," Anthony said.

They went back out into the reception area and found Shayna sitting on Jessica's lap with a cracker in each hand. The baby smiled when she saw her daddy and Anthony picked her up, held her close. She's his only comfort, Colin thought.

"Come here in the morning," Colin said. "We'll go to the courthouse together."

"Thank you," Anthony said. "My mom's taking time off from work so she'll be there, too."

When they were gone, Jessica said, "He's a nervous wreck. Before you got here, I was worried. He said some off-the-wall things. Then I was worried when he was in there with you. I heard him yelling. Should I have done something?"

"No. He needed to let off some steam, that's all." He put his hands in his pants pockets, feeling shakier than his words. The telephone rang and Jessica answered.

"Phillips and Phillips ... I'm sorry, would you repeat that?" She wrote on a notepad and turned it for Colin to read: "Reporter, NY Times. Covering trial. Talk?"

The reporter must be looking for background, he thought—what's the judge like, what sort of prosecutor is Hardison Smith, that sort of thing. He went back to his office and took the call. The reporter introduced himself, explained that he'd gone to the Mangum University School of Journalism and recognized Colin when he saw him in court that morning. Was Colin representing the unnamed eye witness?

"I'm trying to confirm the name I've been given," the reporter said.

"I wouldn't confirm it if I could. Good-bye."

Jessica came in. "You look like you could use some rest." She pointed to the loveseat. "If you want to snooze, go ahead. I'll bring you some lunch."

"You're a gem." He loosened his tie and unbuttoned the top button of his shirt. "I'm thinking this is a younger man's game and I should have stayed retired."

"Oh no you shouldn't have. Where would Anthony be without you? Besides, my favorite days are when you come in." She hesitated. "I was a little bit afraid of you at first, you know."

"And I was a little afraid of you, too." He took off his suit coat and draped it over the chair. "A turkey sandwich would be nice."

The afternoon's witnesses were the police officers who responded to the call and the crime scene techs. Their clinical and matter-of-fact presentations were a clear counterpoint to the morning's emotion, and the jurors looked relieved. Many of them made notes now, whereas when Sydney and Sean were on the stand, they seemed to be too absorbed in the testimony to put words on paper.

These by-the-book, dry witnesses gave Colin time to think back to his fight with Wren. I should have talked to her about Rhetta long ago, he thought. I shouldn't put it off any longer.

The last witness of the day was the medical examiner, and with him the energy in the courtroom changed again. He brought photographs of Brooke to show how she had died, and he explained that the blows to the head had not killed her immediately, but had caused the subdural hematoma that did. The D.A. made sure the jury got the photographs. Some members examined them closely, but the lady in the gray hat barely touched them as she passed them along, eyes closed. The silence was so complete that when someone cleared his throat, Colin jumped.

Then D.A. Smith asked one more question: "If Brooke had received prompt medical attention, could she have lived?"

"If help came fast enough, she could have lived."

Smith nodded. "That's all."

Judge Desmond peered at Simon Tate. "I don't imagine the defense's cross examination will be brief. Then we'll adjourn until tomorrow morning, nine o'clock."

Colin's grandchildren had insisted that he and their parents learn how to send text messages. "Email's way too slow," they told their elders. "Text us."

He had not mastered the skill but he knew Wren embraced it, so after they got home for the evening, he managed to peck out, "Wren, would like to talk to you this evening. Please come to cottage. Dad." He could have walked through the garden to the sunroom with less effort than it had taken to create those words on the tiny screen. He could cancel the text and just call her. But this way, she could respond to the summons at her own pace; it seemed fair. He hit "send."

When she had not come by nine o'clock, he thought she hadn't gotten the message, or was choosing to ignore it. He calmed himself into reading a Ngaio Marsh mystery and listening to the classical music station. When Wren tapped on his door at 9:30, he was surprised.

"Sorry I'm so late," she said. "Caraleigh called and I practically had to read her a transcript. I saw your lights were still on, so here I am." She sat on the settee opposite his chair, kicked off her shoes and curled her legs under her.

"And how's Caraleigh?"

"She's fine. Busy. I think the current young man may be special."

"Wren, I'm sorry we argued today." He held up his hand when she began to respond. "I don't quite know how to approach this but … I have a question. How do you think of your mother?"

"Mother?" Now she was surprised. "Well, she loved us. And we loved her." She shrugged. "I don't know how to answer."

"She and Laurence were about ten when their father had his first heart attack. After that, their mother devoted herself to his care and it was Marie who raised Rhetta and Laurence. It was Marie who showed them how to love." His voice rose. He stopped and took a deep breath.

"I know, Daddy. But then Marie deserted them."

"Marie's daughter died of an overdose and Jabel came to live with her. She had to focus on raising him." *This isn't what I meant to say,* he thought.

"Daddy, why are we talking about this?" She put her feet on the floor as if she would stand up.

"My fault. Avoiding the subject." He reset. "In the courtroom today, you reminded me of how fierce your mother was when she thought someone she loved was threatened. She would do almost anything. She proved that when Laurence was accused. Then he deserted her. She was badly hurt by that. It left us in a hard place."

Now Wren's attention to his words was physical.

He went on. "Laurence left because he knew people here would always believe he got away with murder. Your mother and I, we had to deal with that. Rhetta bore the brunt of it. That's why she gave up so many old friends, parties, bridge, even church work. You girls, the house, the roses—that was her life."

"And you." Her voice was soft, uncertain.

"She was sure I knew the truth about Laurence and wouldn't tell her. That was always between us."

"What truth? He was innocent. She always said so."

"She said so. But she didn't believe it, and nothing I could say would convince her because I keep people's secrets."

"Oh my God." Wren crossed her arms over her chest and bowed her back. "Poor Mama."

Colin felt the sting of tears and pressed his fingers to the bridge of his nose.

"And poor Daddy," she said.

The next morning, Tate started cross-examining the medical examiner. His strategy was to go over minutiae in the reports, to sidetrack as much as he could, to take more than enough time given the small amount of help he could squeeze out; in short, to bore the jury and give them plenty of time to lose the thread of testimony and gloss over the horror.

After lunch, the prosecution called three young women to establish Professor Dantry's history of involvement with students. They each described an arc of special attention, chats after class or around campus, praise for intellectual abilities, seduction, England for summer study, with it all coming to an end after the student graduated.

The defense used innuendo delivered with excessive good manners that crossed into cynicism to make each of the women seem just a little slutty, and then focused on the ease with which Dantry let each of them go, despite his assurances in moments of passion that each was his one and only.

When the third witness was released, Judge Desmond announced the mid-afternoon break.

"He was effective," Marcus said to Eden. He nodded toward Simon Tate who huddled with Dantry and Dantry's wife.

"He's good." Eden nodded.

"Are you worried?"

"Smith will use his closing to remind the jurors of their own sisters or daughters and get their high dudgeon redirected."

"I saw your father leave. I assume he went to see Anthony." They both knew that Colin was anxious about his client. "It's been what, fifteen months since Brooke died? And now it's Anthony's hour. The hour I ran from."

She'd never heard him refer to that part of his past. She reached out and touched his arm.

He looked into her eyes, then blinked and looked away. She let her hand fall.

Anthony and Janelle Huey waited out the time in an unused jury room in the annex. It was a sterile room furnished with chairs and a conference table, a white board on the wall, a coffee maker, and sink.

"How are you managing?" Colin asked them when he went in. "Did you go out for lunch?"

"We did. And we took a walk," Janelle said. "I swear, this is the quietest room I've ever been in. It's a nice change from the pharmacy."

"Soundproofed," Colin agreed. "You can't have people eaves-dropping on juries." He looked to his client who was slumped in a chair, his arms crossed over his chest and his legs stretched under the table. "How about you, Anthony? All right?"

"I can't wait to get out of here," he said. "Are they about ready for me?"

"Just about."

Anthony stood up and grabbed his suit coat off the chair next to him. "Will you fix my tie, Mama?"

He stood still while she tightened and straightened his tie.

"Tug your shirt sleeves down, baby," she said.

"I need to go to the men's room," he said and left.

Colin smiled at her. "It'll all be over for him soon."

"But he's changed, Mr. Phillips." She put her fingers over her mouth and looked at the ceiling.

"I know. It's true, but don't you think he's grown up some in the last year?"

"Maybe. I'm proud of the daddy he's become. But then I think he's put too much on that little girl. She's the only person he wants to be around some days."

Anthony returned, and right behind him, the bailiff who was to escort him to the courtroom.

Colin led Janelle Huey through the maze of narrow back hallways and into the courtroom through the side door in the paneling. He held her elbow as she sat, then seated himself be-side her. A bailiff had made sure that the spaces were available for them on the bench directly behind the D.A. so Anthony could see them as he testified. That meant they sat beside Susan and Avery Fallon. Anthony's name was called and he came in and stood in the well of the room to be sworn in. His voice wavered a bit on "So help me God."

Colin found himself to be nervous. He could not remember being more nervous, even when he had to put a guilty defendant on the stand, and Anthony wasn't charged with anything.

Hardison Smith began questioning Anthony with the same matter-of-fact respect he'd given the law enforcement officers who had testified. He asked how long Anthony had worked for the security company and specifically at Highgate, the nature of his duties, how he had been trained. He elicited the information that Anthony's supervisors gave him excellent reviews.

Both Sean and Sydney had made the security system sound complicated; Anthony explained it more clearly. When asked if there had ever been a break-in or police call to Highgate while he was working, Anthony said no.

Then Smith moved on. "Mr. Huey were you at work the day Ms. Fallon was found dead?"

"Yes sir. I went on at five o'clock that afternoon."

"And did you notice anything unusual as your shift began?"

"I was coming from the employees' parking lot. You have to cross the residents' driveway to get to the security office and I saw a car coming in through the residents' gate."

"Describe the car, please."

"It's a Mercedes Benz SL, silver, and it has a parking sticker for Mangum University."

"To go in through that gate, the driver would have had the code?" Smith asked.

"Yes sir."

"Did residents commonly give visitors the gate code?"

"Actually, no. The Homeowners Association fines people for doing that. It was one of the worst things a resident could do."

"Did you recognize the driver of the silver Mercedes?"

"Yes sir. I'd seen him quite a few times."

"Did you know who this person visited at Highgate?"

"Yes sir. He came to visit Brooke Fallon."

Then, one question and one answer at a time, the jury heard about Brooke hiding from the man who drove that car, about her confession that she'd slept with him and her regrets, her refusal to tell his name, and then how several months later the man and his car began to appear again.

Finally, Smith asked, "Do you see the driver of that car in the courtroom today?"

"Yes sir." Anthony pointed to Joseph Dantry.

Then the D.A. was done and it was Simon Tate's turn. His first question came quickly.

"How many times would you say Professor Dantry came to Highgate?"

"I don't know." He shrugged a little as if to apologize.

Tate asked if Anthony knew the Graysons, the Edmondses, the Stones.

Anthony acknowledged each name and said they live at Highgate.

"Would you be surprised to learn that Professor Dantry was invited to their homes at different times over the last two years?"

"I wouldn't be surprised or not surprised." He sounded a little testy. Colin had told Anthony over and over, don't change your demeanor when you are cross-examined. The jury will like you and they won't want to see you become abrasive or difficult. Now, Colin tried to nod a reminder and hoped Anthony caught it.

"All right," Tate said. "Do you know Sean Caldwell?"

"Yes sir. We went to high school together."

"Did you ever see him at Highgate?"

"Yes sir."

"And who did he visit there?"

"He was friends with Brooke, too."

"To clarify, do you know that he visited Ms. Fallon?"

"Yes, I know that."

"Mr. Caldwell testified here earlier. He described the security at Highgate as a pain in the neck but that he had a friend who worked security there and that his friend made it easier for him. Mr. Huey, did you ever let Mr. Caldwell in without calling Ms. Fallon to make sure he was welcome?"

"No sir." But he hesitated half a beat. Colin glanced at Janelle. She'd caught it, too, and her jaw tensed.

"Never? Not even once?"

Smith rose. "Objection. The question has been answered."

"I'll withdraw that," Tate said. "Mr. Huey, you described Ms. Fallon as being afraid of Professor Dantry, but within a matter of weeks she had given him the gate code and he was visiting regularly. Did I understand that correctly?"

"It wasn't just weeks. It was at least a couple of months."

"Still. Didn't it strike you as strange that a young woman who was afraid ..."

"More ashamed," Anthony interrupted. "She was a good person and she'd done wrong."

"Ashamed?" Tate turned on the word to look at Anthony as if seeing him for the first time. Colin realized this was what he'd worried about—that his client would give away his own feelings for Brooke—and one word was enough to set off a defense attorney's radar.

Tate had to ask, "Are you saying that Ms. Fallon discussed her relationship with my client with you?"

"Objection," Smith said. "Mr. Huey can't speculate about Ms. Fallon's motives or emotions." He was irritated with his witness but scowled at the defense attorney.

"Nor do I ask him to," Tate said. "I'm asking about her actions as he observed them."

The judge shook his head. "The jury will disregard the witness's last comments. The witness will be responsive to questions and not go beyond them."

Tate began to ask a series of questions with yes or no answers, coming quickly enough to blur the order and the meaning. Then, "Did you keep tabs on the comings and goings of all the residents' guests, or just those of attractive young women?"

"Objection," Smith said. "No basis."

"Reword that," the judge said.

"All right. How closely did you keep track of guests, other than my client?"

Anthony sat up straight. "If they came through the visitors' gate, I entered it in the computer and the computer kept track. Somebody who didn't want to be tracked had to come in another way."

Colin covered his mouth to hide a smile.

Tate finished, Smith had a few more questions, and then the prosecution rested. The judge adjourned for the day.

Janelle Huey met her son in the aisle and they hugged tight. Then a bailiff spirited them out of the courtroom by the side door so they could avoid reporters in the hall. As it happened, the Fallons were leaving at the same moment. Susan hugged both the Hueys and Avery shook Anthony's hand. What Colin was left remembering, though, was Anthony's face over his mother's shoulder, eyes closed, mouth neutral, and yet looking ten years older. The sadness he'd shown in the fifteen months since Brooke died had settled into his soul.

Colin found Eden outside the courtroom, looking over the railing. In the lobby below, with the backdrop of marble and brass, Simon Tate addressed reporters and television cameras.

"As you can imagine," Tate said, "Professor Dantry is chomping at the bit to take the stand and tell the only truths that the jury will hear in this case. But the prosecution's case isn't strong and I'm going to spend the evening deciding whether or not to even put on a defense."

"Oh please," Eden said. "Dantry's just the kind of arrogant jackass who can't resist testifying."

"And Tate's arrogant enough to let him," Colin said. "The two smartest people in the room."

The next morning, as soon as court was back in session, Simon Tate began by asking the judge to dismiss charges on the basis that the prosecution had failed to prove them. Colin had done the same many times, and he knew Judge Desmond would turn him down. Once they had gone through that part of the process, Tate revealed to the world the decision he'd made. He called Joseph Charles Dantry to the stand.

Colin caught Eden's eye and she gave him a half-smile.

Judge Desmond sent the jury out and asked the pro forma questions to be sure that Dantry knew he did not have to testify, that if he did not the jury would be instructed not to hold it against him. "You are represented by a very able attorney, sir, and you should take his advice."

"I understand, Your Honor, and I am ready to speak on my own behalf."

As the jury came back in, Colin glanced to his left, where Eden sat, and to his right, where Wren and her family sat. All of them leaned forward just a bit now, caught in the highest drama a courtroom ever saw, the defendant on the stand. On the front row, Susan Fallon tilted her head to lean it against her husband's shoulder. The judge clicked his pen open and closed. Colin knew that Simon Tate's heart was going a hundred and fifty beats a minute.

Dantry wore a dark gray suit, a blue shirt with a white collar, and a blue, gray, and cream striped tie. He had a good head of dark blond hair, well-cut and streaked with silver. He answered questions about his education, his personal life, his years at Mangum, his publications, his teaching awards. He sounded humble, crediting his mentors, his family, his colleagues. His voice rose and fell and conveyed more meaning than his words alone.

That's his secret weapon, Colin thought, and he thinks he can seduce the jury the way he seduced those girls, with his voice.

Then Tate asked, "Is there anything in your professional life you regret?"

"Yes." Dantry drew a deep breath and let it out slowly. "I have had a series of affairs with students. It was wrong. It damaged many lives, including my own, and without the forgiveness of my wife, my family, and my friends, I'm not sure I could go on." His voice broke. He looked at the jury, then at his wife, then down at his hands.

Tate let a moment go by before asking, "Professor, was Brooke Fallon one of those students?"

"Yes."

"How did you meet her?"

"She attended a lecture I gave in the spring of 2002. She sat near the podium and came up to ask a question at the end."

"When did you see her again?"

"Once I was aware of her, I saw her in the hallways of the department's building regularly, sometimes in the library. Our paths seemed to cross naturally."

"Did Ms. Fallon enroll in one of your courses?"

"Yes, in the fall of 2002. She enrolled in what was actually a graduate level seminar. She had to have my permission to do so."

"And how did she do?"

"She was very bright and confident. She more than held her own."

"When did your relationship become sexual?"

"That fall. One evening after class." He shifted in his chair.

"Then she had second thoughts and didn't want to continue. I, of course, honored her wishes." He turned to face the jury as he said it.

"But eventually the relationship resumed?"

"It did. The following February."

"Did you initiate it?"

"No. She came to me." His posture was stiff now and he kept his eyes fixed on Tate.

"You've heard testimony that Ms. Fallon was afraid of you, so afraid that she once hid in the gatehouse rather than see you. How do you explain that?"

"That isn't true. She was not afraid of me." Again, he looked at the jury and extended a hand as if to enlist them in his indignation.

The District Attorney objected on the grounds that Mr. Dantry couldn't know what was in Ms. Fallon's mind and the judge ordered the question and answer stricken.

Tate forged ahead. "While your relationship with her continued, where did you meet her for assignations?"

"I would meet her at the Highgate condo." He ducked his head, then raised it again.

"You heard three young women testify that they had also had sexual relationships with you. I know you are loathe to cause your family and friends more pain, but I must ask, did you hold Ms. Fallon dearer than you had these other young women?"

"I'm ashamed to say it, but I didn't hold any of them dear." He gave the jury a sidelong glance.

He wants them to believe he's sorry, Colin thought. He's trying to get sympathy for being heartless.

"Did you know that Ms. Fallon was pregnant?"

"No, I did not. She told me she took birth control pills."

Colin glanced at the jury and saw crossed arms, shut down faces. They were seeing nothing seductive in the witness now.

Tate moved on. "Let's talk about Highgate, Professor Dantry. You've heard a detailed explanation of the two gates and the security procedures. Which gate did you use?"

"Brooke thought it would be more discreet if I used the residents' gate, and she gave me the code."

"Did you go to Highgate on the day Ms. Fallon died?"

"Yes, I did."

"By prearrangement?"

"No. It was spur of the moment."

"Did you commonly go to the condo when she didn't expect you?"

"No. Never before." He sighed and looked down. "We'd not had time together since we came back from England. In fact, I had not heard from her at all, so I thought I'd take a chance and stop by."

"How long did you stay?"

"I never got out of the car. I called her once I was inside the gate and there was no answer. I waited a few minutes and tried again, and then I left."

Colin had watched many witnesses over many years. He believed he was good at telling when they switched from lying to truth-telling. They relaxed because it was easier. He was seeing Dantry's shoulders drop. He was seeing the lines on Dantry's forehead ease.

"Did you know Anthony Huey by sight at that time?" Tate asked.

"Yes."

"Did you see him as you left, as he described?"

"I saw him, but not as he described."

"Can you tell us where and how you saw Mr. Huey?" Tate faced the jury and so did his witness.

"Building M, the building in which Ms. Fallon lived, is at the back of the Highgate property. As I pulled up to the building to park, I saw Mr. Huey come from behind it."

Colin remembered the night Brooke died, remembered how he and Kenneth had walked behind that very building.

"Have you ever been behind the building yourself?" Tate asked

"I've looked."

"What is back there?"

"A service entrance and a sidewalk used by the groundskeepers."

Colin sat up straight. He remembered the sidewalk Kenneth had taken him to. Dantry's words struck him as truth. Besides the change in the sound of his voice, showing that his throat muscles had loosened, it was not something he needed to lie about.

"Professor, how did you learn of Ms. Fallon's death?"

"On the late news that night."

"How did you react?"

Dantry looked down and closed his eyes. "I thought my heart would stop. I broke down in tears and had to tell my wife everything."

"One last question, Professor. Did you kill Brooke Fallon?"

"I did not."

Then who did? Colin thought and studied the jurors' faces. That's what they're thinking. Suddenly a possible answer rippled through him as if every nerve was under attack.

It was Hardison Smith's turn. He looked at the man without speaking for ten seconds. Then, "Mr. Dantry, perhaps I didn't catch it. At what time did you arrive at Highgate on that unannounced visit?"

"It was five minutes to five when I called Brooke for the first time, and about ten minutes later when I called her for the last time."

"And you heard the medical examiner say that her head injuries occurred at about that time. Do you recall that?"

"Yes, of course."

"So is it coincidental that your spur of the moment drop-in occurred at the crucial time?"

"Objection," Tate said. "Argumentative."

"You can answer." The judge nodded at Dantry.

"I also heard the testimony that the injuries could have occurred as early as 4:30. I wish I had gotten there sooner, before she lost consciousness. I could have saved her." He glared at Smith.

The D.A. paused again. "You said that you did not hold Brooke dear, yet you broke down when you heard she died. Is that correct?"

"Yes."

"Before that, was your wife aware that you were a serial philanderer?"

This brought Tate to his feet and after some back and forth, the question was restated: "Was your wife aware that you had a series of sexual relationships outside of the marriage?"

"Of course not."

"And did you take pains to keep her from becoming aware of that?"

"Of course."

"When you were in your earlier relationships, were you careful to make specific dates with when and where to meet?"

Dantry frowned and pressed his lips together before saying, "Yes."

"Did you ever just drop in on one of the other girls? Just happen to be in the neighborhood and take a chance on catching her at home?"

"No."

"Was that because secrecy was the best protection you had?"

"Yes."

"How would you have felt if one of the other girls had, let's say, died in a car crash?"

Tate objected. "Hypothetical and unanswerable, Your Honor." The objection was sustained.

"When you went home on the day Ms. Fallon died, did you plan to tell your wife what you term 'everything'?"

"No."

"Do you still maintain that Brooke Fallon meant no more to you than any of the other young ladies?"

"That's correct."

"Did any of the other young ladies become pregnant as a result of having a relationship with you?"

"No."

"Did you always rely on the woman to be on birth control pills?"

Tate was quick. "Objection. Not relevant."

"Sustained."

Smith leaned forward. "If Ms. Fallon's pregnancy became public knowledge, would that have damaged your marriage?"

"I'm sure it would have." He shifted in his chair.

"Were your colleagues aware that you had sex with students?"

"I don't know who knew what." Dantry began to sound impatient.

"If such an affair became public knowledge, would it have damaged your career?"

"Objection," Tate said. "Hypothetical."

"Sustained."

"You are a tenured professor, are you not?" Smith asked.

"Yes, I am."

"Are there any conditions under which a tenured professor can lose his job?"

"There are conditions, yes."

"And is moral turpitude one such condition?" Smith looked at the jury.

"Yes."

"And would that include pressuring students into sex?"

That question brought Tate's strongest, most red-faced reaction and, in the end, Dantry had to answer: "I suppose."

Smith nodded and again gazed at the defendant for a few seconds. "No more questions."

Professor Dantry went back to his seat beside his attorney and Tate called another witness. He recalled Anthony Huey.

Colin was shocked, and had a moment of panic. Anthony wasn't ready for this. Everyone in the courtroom turned when the double doors opened and Anthony came in. He looked straight ahead as he walked toward the witness stand. He wore his Highgate uniform as if he had come directly from work.

"Mr. Huey," Tate began, "you testified that you and Sean Caldwell knew each other from high school. Correct?"

"Yes." He was sullen and dull.

"Did you know Ms. Fallon in high school as well?"

"Yes."

"And you were already working at Highgate when she moved in, is that correct?"

"Yes."

"You referred to an occasion when she visited you in the gate house. Do you recall telling us about that?"

"Yes."

"Is that the only time she visited you in the gate house?"

"No."

"How many others?"

"I don't know."

"Three? Ten? Daily? Weekly? Monthly?"

"Objection," Smith said. "He needs to give the witness a chance to answer."

"Sustained. Take it slow, Mr. Tate," Judge Desmond said.

"Did you see Ms. Fallon frequently?"

"Yes. For a while."

"Did the two of you have conversations?"

"Yes."

"What kinds of things did you talk about?"

"School, my little girl, our parents, things like that."

"The things you talk about with a friend?"

"I guess."

"A close friend?"

"Does Mr. Tate have a point to make, or is he just passing the time of day, Your Honor?" Smith crossed his arms.

"Mr. Tate?" the judge asked.

Tate changed direction. "Mr. Huey, you have a detailed knowledge of the property and its layout. Could you explain to the jury what is behind Building M?"

"What?" This question rattled him. "Behind?" For the first time, he looked out into the gallery and seemed to see Colin. Colin nodded and mouthed, okay, you're okay. His own heart rate was elevated.

"That's right. Behind Building M." Tate was on edge.

"All the buildings have a sort of back exit. Stairs in case of fire and you can't use the elevators. So there's that. And there's a shed the gardeners use. It's not part of the building. It's off a little ways." He frowned and shook his head as if he didn't know what else to say.

"Is there access by path or sidewalk?"

"There's a sidewalk that goes around the edge. The grounds guys use it."

"Why were you behind Building M on the afternoon of August 12, 2003?"

"I wasn't. I didn't go back there." He said it quickly, shaking his head.

"Isn't it true that when you saw my client, you were coming from behind the building?"

"No sir. I was crossing the parking lot. I was going to the gatehouse.

"Mr. Huey, you were seen coming from behind the building at the time Ms. Fallon was attacked."

"No sir. That's a lie."

"That's all."

Colin didn't stay to hear what Hardison Smith asked his client. He slipped past Eden and left the room. He waited outside the courtroom to intercept Anthony. It was only ten minutes before the young man came out.

"How could he do that? Why didn't you tell me he could do that?" Anthony pressed the palms of his hands to the sides of his face.

"I'm sorry, Anthony. I didn't expect it. It's not what's usually done."

"Yeah, well." He paced up and down beside the railing. "Who said I was there behind the building?"

"It was Joseph Dantry."

"They're trying to make it look like I hurt Brooke." He banged his fist against the rail.

Colin put a hand on his shoulder. "Look at me, Anthony." He waited until they were eye to eye. "This has all been terrible for you. I see it now. What happens next is up to you."

Anthony looked at him with disbelief in his eyes. "I've got to go."

Colin watched him disappear into the elevator and then emerge in the lobby below, his hands deep in his pockets, his head down.

Colin went back into the courtroom and found a seat on the back row. He felt old and tired. The judge was addressing the jury, explaining the order of lunch, closing arguments, his charge to them, then the beginning of their deliberations.

When they broke for lunch, Colin and his family walked out together.

"Listen," Eden said, "I've got to get back to the office. Dad, if there's some miracle, call me, okay? I can be back in five minutes."

"Let's go home." Kenneth put an arm around Wren's shoulders. "Nothing's going to happen today anyway, right Colin?"

"It's unlikely."

"And you'd have time to call us anyway? Right?"

"I will." Colin nodded.

"Then we're going home. We're going to start getting back to the real world." Kenneth held Wren closer.

"All right," Wren said. She held out a hand to Colin. "Daddy, you'll call me if you need me?"

They were all assuming he would stay. He wanted to say he was done, sick of it, but instead he agreed.

He hardly listened to the closing arguments. In fact, he could hardly hear them above the noise of his own thoughts. Should he have understood sooner? What could he have done if he had? What would he have done?

When he went to bed that night, the trial testimony rolled through his mind on an endless loop. Had the jury seen what he saw? All he could hope for now was an acquittal.

He walked to town the next morning and took a seat in the back row of the courtroom. Once the jury assembled and then withdrew, the judge opened up a laptop and began to work, occasionally talking to his clerk.

Dantry sat beside his wife and read a newspaper. She had a book in her lap, although it seemed to Colin that she spent most of her time looking at the murals on the walls. The supporters who had been there with them on the first day of the trial had long since faded away.

Tate followed the judge's example. On to the next case, Colin expected. Or making notes for an appeal, if it comes to that.

The D.A. was in and out. The Fallons had a line of friends there for hugs and quiet words.

At five o'clock, the judge called it a day.

When Colin left the building, he remembered to turn his cell phone on and saw that Anthony had called three times but had not left a message. When he tried to reach his client, he got voicemail. "Anthony, I'm sorry I missed you. Please call again this evening."

But he did not hear from the young man.

The next morning, at a quarter till noon, the bailiff brought a note from the jury room. Colin knew this part: the rumor of a possible verdict would spread fast. But it came as no surprise to him that this was a false alarm. The jury wanted an early lunch break. The judge told them to be back at work at 1:30.

Colin met Eden at the Grill.

"Do you think it'll be this afternoon?" she asked.

"Probably. The fact that they asked for the break means they want to let the decision settle in just a bit. Then they'll vote one more time, just to be sure, and that'll be it." He pondered whether or not to tell her what he suspected. No, what he knew. But it would mean betraying a client and nothing in his life would let him do that.

"Don't look so glum, Dad. The bastard's going to get what he deserves." She tore a roll into pieces. "If you're sure there'll be a verdict, you need to call Wren."

Colin remembered Tate's opening and his image of a thread stretched thin. It seemed to him that the thread had disintegrated at a million points. If the jury saw it, then yes the bastard would get what he deserved: not guilty.

Forty-five minutes after coming back from lunch, the jury sent out another note and this time it was the real thing. Wren had come into town alone and joined Colin and Eden. People who had any sense of how juries work filled the courtroom.

True to the cliché, the jurors filed in with their poker faces on, looking straight ahead or at their own feet. Colin felt Eden take his hand and he squeezed hers back. She was going to get what she wanted, he was sure of it, and he dreaded it.

"Guilty," the foreperson said when the judge finally asked. "Guilty" each of the twelve said when polled.

Colin absorbed the news and looked at his daughters, first Eden who gave him a satisfied smile and a nod, and then Wren who covered her face with her hands. Ahead of them, the Fallons didn't move.

The judge revoked bail and ordered that Dantry be taken into custody until sentencing in a month. As soon as court adjourned, on-air reporters ran for the doors. Everyone else, including Eden, reached for a cell phone.

"Dad," she said, "I've got a text from Jessica. She wants us back at the office right away."

Colin could tell from her face that something serious had happened. He turned to Wren.

"You two go on," she said. "I think I'll see if I can speak to Susan."

Colin leaned in and kissed her cheek.

The crowd in front of the elevators was deep, so Colin and Eden made their way through the back hallways. They rounded a corner and came face to face with Hardison Smith.

"Colin," he said, "I was coming to find you. Tell Anthony he did a great job. We couldn't have done it without him."

"Yes, I'll tell him." Colin pulled away. Ahead of him, Eden had opened the door to the staircase.

When they finally reached the office, they found Jessica pacing and Shayna Huey sitting on a blanket on the floor, bent over a coloring book with a crayon in her hand.

"Thank God," Jessica said. "Anthony's waiting in your office, Colin. He says he's got to see you."

Colin just nodded and went straight toward the closed door.

Once he had disappeared, Eden grabbed Jessica's arm. "What is going on?"

"Anthony's really, I don't know, freaking out. Some reporter called him at home and asked how he felt, now that there was a verdict. So Anthony brought Shayna and came here. He said he didn't want to be alone."

"When was this?" Eden asked.

"Right after you left at lunchtime."

"But nobody knew for sure if there was a verdict, or what it was," Eden said.

"It seems like somebody did. Or made a good guess," Jessica said. "Anyway, we were watching it on TV together. When they said 'guilty' I cheered but when I looked at Anthony, it was like looking at a ghost. He was all gray and slumped over. Then he picked up Shayna and squeezed her so hard. He was crying and that's when I texted you."

Eden looked toward the closed door to her father's office. "Do you think Dad's safe?"

Jessica knelt down beside the busy little girl. "I can't see Anthony hurting anybody. Can you?"

Colin found Anthony pacing.

"I know the truth now, Anthony," he said. "You tried to tell me but I just didn't get it. I am sorrier than I've ever been for anything."

Anthony stopped moving. Colin heard him breathing. Then, "Not your fault, Mr. Phillips. You tried." Anthony said. "I don't know where to go or what to do now."

"Take all the time you need. Will you sit down and tell me about it?"

Anthony collapsed into the client's chair. Rather than sit across the desk from him, Colin pulled his own chair around.

"When Brooke got home from England, she told me about her baby and I said let's get married. We could raise our kids together. I'd take care of her."

"That was a wonderful offer."

"She said she'd have to think about it. I gave her a few days and then—that day—I went by to see her before my shift started and she said she'd decided to get an abortion."

"And you argued?"

"Yeah, and I shoved her and she fell. She banged her head on the floor and then I don't really remember. I think I got down and took her by the shoulders and maybe I banged her down again. I guess I must've. But then she screamed at me to get away from her. She was up. She was crying. I told her I'd always love her and I left."

"And that's when you and Dantry saw each other."

Anthony talked on. "That night when I found out she was dead, if you hadn't been there, I would have told the police what happened. But by daylight, all I could think about was my baby girl and my mama and it was like you were sent to save me. Even if I didn't deserve it."

Even though none of this came as a surprise now, the muscles in Colin's throat and chest would not let air in or out. Heart attack? He thought. No, just a heart broken. Then he forced a gasp so he could speak again.

"Anthony, we'll get through it." He gasped again. His thoughts ran ahead of his voice. Involuntary manslaughter, first offense, people who would line up in support of Anthony.

"I got to go." Anthony got up, tipping his chair over. He didn't wait for Colin to answer. Colin let him go. He felt sure that this young man, of all people, would do the right thing. He would give him time to calm down and then talk to him about a confession, about a plea and possible sentences. Talk to him about the future, beyond all of this.

When he collected himself, he left his office and found the reception area crowded. Wren was there now, and Clyde Raeburn. Jessica held Shayna, who was crying and reaching toward the front door. Wren patted the child's leg and cooed at her. Eden and Clyde whispered to each other.

Eden saw him. "It was Anthony? Anthony killed Brooke?"

He didn't answer, still unable to betray his client. "Where is he?"

"He ran out," Jessica said. "He said his baby's better off without him."

"When did you know?" Eden asked.

That he could answer. "Much later than I should have. When I heard Dantry testify and not lie." He tried to think through what it meant, that Anthony had left his child behind.

"What are you going to do?" Eden asked.

"I'm concerned about his state of mind. For that, I can call the police. And his mother."

"Eden will do that. You come with me, my friend." Clyde took his arm and led him back into his office. "You have a bottle in that desk drawer? Let's have a snort."

Colin stared at him, then reached into the desk for a bottle and two glasses. Clyde poured.

"That Tate," Clyde said, "he had me at first. He started off strong but he didn't get it done. Hell, when we were young and pretty like him, we'd have gotten Dantry off."

"Well, I'm not young." Colin left his glass sitting on the desk. "But I'm going to get him off."

"They'll take your license."

Clyde knew exactly what he meant and that felt good to be understood. He picked up the glass and lifted it to salute his friend. "They can have it."

Some twenty years earlier, the highway south of town had been widened and straightened. The bridge over the Black Haw

River had been replaced. A section of the old road and the old bridge still existed, if a person knew where to turn. They were popular with joggers and walkers. There was a barrier to keep cars out.

At mid-day on a weekday, the area was often deserted but this particular day, two young women were walking and pushing strollers. They called 911 at 3:30 to say a car had driven around the barrier, sped by them, stopped on the bridge, and someone had jumped into the shallow rocky river fifty feet below.

Anthony's funeral was on Saturday. The next afternoon, Colin called Janelle Huey and asked if he could see her. He spent an hour at her house, telling her what he knew and what he felt he had to do. She assured him that she understood, it was the right thing to do, and then asked him to please go away.

Tomorrow's November 22, Colin thought as he drove home. He always noted the date of President Kennedy's assassination, and it always took him back to the Thanksgiving in 1963—less than a week after the assassination—when Laurence and Sheila were with the family. He remembered the comfort they had taken in being together.

Is this what it's like? He asked himself. You get old and everything reminds you of some long gone solace?

He parked in his usual spot beside the house. Kenneth had gradually added space as one at a time the children and their friends had acquired cars. That afternoon, only Wren's aging minivan was there. He'd intended to go right to the cottage, to make notes for himself so as to present the district attorney with an orderly sequence of events. But he thought of Wren in the house alone and he went to the sunroom door instead.

Wren sat at the work table in the kitchen, gazing out at the hard-pruned rose garden, with a stack of cookbooks in front of her.

"You're the soul of your mother," he said. "How many times did I come home and find her sitting just so?" He lowered himself into the chair beside her, at the end of the table.

Her smile was tentative. "And how many times did Eden and I come clomping down the back stairs and ruin your moments together?"

"When do the twins get home for the holiday?"

"Sometime Wednesday. Caraleigh, too. It'll be like old times."

"That'll be nice." He heard his voice fade.

"It's been so hard for you, Daddy. I'm really sorry." She covered his hand with both of hers. "I want this to be a special holiday."

"Tomorrow, I'm going to do the worst thing a lawyer can do. I'm going to betray a client."

"Daddy." She said it as if the word was squeezed out of her.

He blinked back tears. When his vision cleared, he saw she was once again gazing out the windows.

"Eden and I have been talking," she said. "I told her what you said about Mama thinking Uncle Laurence killed Sheila."

And then in Rhetta's voice, "She suggested that I invite Marcus and Sydney and Marie to dinner."

"Did she? And what did you say?"

"I said I couldn't believe they would come. Maybe Sydney, but Marcus and Marie? She said it's worth a try. I got the feeling she'd already put out some feelers. You know how she is."

He knew this was just the sort of thing his younger daughter took for her sister's attitude of superiority. To his surprise, Wren laughed a real laugh and talked on.

"So I said, 'Okay Miss Smarty, you'll just have to ask them what they like to drink.'"

ACKNOWLEDGEMENTS

I have been encouraged in my writing by my Gaskin family, my Esthimer family, and by the good friends I cherish.

I was made to work hard and then harder by teachers Barbara Lorie, Max Steele, Louis Ruben, and Joyce Allen.

I have learned from the talented writers I've shared space with; in recent years, Joyce Allen, Paula Blackwell, Kim Church, Laura Herbst, Ruth Moose, Nancy Peacock, and Pat Walker. We've played Comma Pong and Prologue, Prologue, Who's Got the Prologue, and formed bonds of community.

One last word to Pat: you may have won this round of Comma Pong but I will never say die!

Thanks, too, to editor and book designer Kelly Prelipp Lojk.